"A melding of the psychological and the high-adventure story, [a] gripping, emotion-evoking narrative."
—BOOKLIST (starred review)

Earthseed

THE SEED TRILOGY

Pamela Sargent

Praise for the Seed Trilogy by Pamela Sargent

Earthseed

An American Library Association Best Book
for Young Adults Selection
A *Booklist* Young Adult Reviewer's Choice Selection ·
A New York Public Library Books for the Teen Age Selection

"A melding of the psychological and the high-adventure story, this gripping, emotion-evoking narrative is the first young adult novel by the author of *Watchstar* and other adult science fiction."
—*Booklist* (starred review)

"The story is thought-provoking and full of odd surprises."
—*School Library Journal*

"This fascinating novel is very reminiscent of the better Heinlein juveniles (particularly *Tunnel in the Sky*). . . . A very impressive novel . . . should not be overlooked." —*SF Chronicle*

"Pamela Sargent's *Earthseed* demonstrates again what a resourceful, intelligent, and humane talent she possesses. Zoheret is a reluctant, self-doubting heroine whose reluctance and self-doubt endear her to us and give her ultimate victory over adversity a strong spiritual dimension. Indeed, *Earthseed* reminds me a little of a far-future, interstellar version of Golding's *Lord of the Flies*, with the telling exception that it concludes on a note of hope rather than of bitter irony."
—Michael Bishop, *The Atlanta Journal-Constitution*

Farseed

A New York Public Library Books for the Teen Age Selection

"The interpersonal dynamics, plus the challenges of adapting to another world, give this long-awaited second book in the Seed Trilogy strong appeal." —*Booklist*

"Well-told, moving, and thoroughly gripping SF."

—Faren Miller, *Locus*

"Readers will enjoy the tension and interplay throughout this survival story with a science fiction twist."

—*School Library Journal*

"This thoughtful planetary adventure is extremely well done. Sargent is a significant figure in modern science fiction, and this novel is a fine example of her work."

—*Voice of Youth Advocates* (starred review)

Seed Seeker

"With prose as spare as the unadorned clothes and tools of her characters, Sargent digs down to the raw emotional roots below the contentment of a materially satisfied life."

—*Publishers Weekly*

"A graceful coming-of-age story set on a colony world . . . an engaging story."

—Annalee Newitz, *io9*

"*Seed Seeker* has plenty of charms, even if most of them are so subtle that you don't realize how well-crafted the story is until after the book ends. It's a quiet tale, one that builds to a climax with whispers rather than screams." —Adrienne Martini, *Locus*

"The Seed Trilogy presents a much more complex coming-of-age story than that contained within any of its individual volumes. Hidden behind three stories of political strife and warring colonists is sweeping, thought-provoking science fiction about how technology holds the capacity to make gods out of men, and children out of gods . . . the story of how the fruits of human science might one day stumble—with an adolescent awkwardness and with clumsy charm—toward adulthood, too."

—Phoebe North, *Strange Horizons*

Earthseed

The Seed Trilogy by Pamela Sargent

Earthseed
Farseed
Seed Seeker

Earthseed

Pamela Sargent

TOR
TEEN

A Tom Doherty Associates Book
New York

EARTHSEED

Originally published by Harper & Row, Publishers, Inc., in the United States and published simultaneously by Fitzhenry & Whiteside Limited in Canada

A Tor® Teen Book
Published by Tom Doherty Associates, LLC
175 Fifth Avenue
New York, NY 10010

www.tor-forge.com

Tor® Teen is a registered trademark of Tom Doherty Associates, LLC.

ISBN 978-0-7653-3215-8

First Tor Teen Trade Paperback Edition: February 2012

Printed in the United States of America

0 9 8 7 6 5 4 3 2 1

For Kristin

Part One

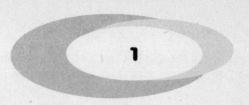

Zoheret rolled slowly down the corridor, flexing her knees as she skated. The wide, brightly lit hall curved ahead of her; the lights above flickered past as she speeded up, careful not to skate too rapidly. The gleaming white wall to her right became a blur of bright colors as she passed a mural. Several of her friends had painted the picture; Zoheret's own face, topped by thick, black hair, peered out from among the green leaves of a bush. Other faces nestled among trees and flowers. She frowned. Someone had blackened her painted white teeth, and the mural was marred by a long, red streak.

She could go on and skate toward Ship's center, or turn and roll toward the corridor's end, meeting the tubeway that could whisk her through Ship or up to another level. Beyond the corridors were empty caverns and rocky passageways enclosed by a thick layer of rock; outside the rock and its shielding was the black space through which Ship rushed, distant stars distorted by its speed. Zoheret had seen what was beyond only through Ship's screens or in its observatory.

Her earliest memory was of Ship's voice soothing her, though she could not recall why she had needed consolation. Ship had always been there, around her, watching and tending her.

She slowed down when she saw a boy limping through the corridor. "Anoki," she called out. He turned and she skated up to his side. "Where are you going?"

"The library."

"I'll go with you. Feeling better?"

"I'm all right."

"You look better." She skated ahead, then waited for him to catch up. Hearing the sound of other approaching skaters, she moved quickly toward the wall and peered down the corridor. Anoki was still in the middle of the hall; he began to limp toward her. Two skaters, now visible, sped around the curve, knees bent, heads down. Zoheret recognized Manuel and Ho. The skates were supposed to speed their progress through Ship, but some had made skating a game.

"Slow down!" she shouted at them. The two boys lifted their heads. Manuel frowned, and swerved slightly; Ho seemed to speed up. He was heading straight for Anoki. Anoki stumbled to one side and Ho brushed him with an arm as he passed, knocking the other boy down.

"Don't go so fast," Zoheret said as they passed her.

Manuel grinned, showing even white teeth. "Sorry," he said, whipping by. He and Ho disappeared around the curve ahead; she heard them laugh.

She hurried to Anoki. As he climbed to his feet, he waved

her hand away. "I'm all right." His straight black hair was hanging over his eyes; he brushed it back.

"They know they shouldn't skate so fast."

"I'm all right. It doesn't matter." Anoki's brown eyes were without expression; his mouth twisted into his familiar bitter smile. They moved down the corridor, Zoheret rolling slowly so that Anoki could keep up with her. "They can't be expected to look out for me. Almost anyone else could have gotten out of the way."

"You're doing much better," she said. "You don't need crutches anymore, and—"

"Yes, I'm doing better. I'm still not well."

"But you can do a lot more now."

"Don't tell me what I can do. You wouldn't know anything about it. You're healthy. Ship helped me, but it could have been more careful at the beginning."

"Ship can make mistakes, too."

"I know. It's easy for you to say, Zoheret. You're not one of the mistakes."

She had no answer to that.

"You and Lillka were the only ones who came to see me when I was healing," Anoki went on. "And Willem."

"That isn't true. Almost everybody did."

"Once or twice. And I'll bet it was only because Ship told them to."

They approached the library. The door slid open and they entered the large room. Zoheret would not admit it to Anoki, but she understood why he had not had many visitors while he had been in the infirmary. He often seemed bored or contemptuous. His disability also frightened others, reminding them of their own vulnerability; Zoheret had felt that fear herself. It could have happened to any of them. It might have happened to her.

Screens and chairs were clustered around the room; booths lined the walls. The library's microcircuits held millions of books; Ship could provide a printed copy, a slide of the book to be read with a reader, or could show an illustrated book on one of the screens. A cube as high as the ceiling and almost as wide as the room jutted out from the far wall. Inside the cube, holograms from Earth, the world they had never seen, could be shown.

Lillka was curled up in one chair, a reader on her lap. She looked up from the flat rectangle as Zoheret and Anoki came near, then went back to her reading. Lillka lived in the library; she would have spent all her time there if Ship had let her. She had grown shortsighted from all her reading, and Ship's surgical lasers had already made adjustments in her eyes.

"What are you reading?" Anoki asked her.

"Just a story."

"You shouldn't read for so long. Have Ship tell you a story, or show you one."

"It isn't the same."

Zoheret skated toward the cube. "Ship?"

"Zoheret. Hello." Ship's voice was an alto. "You did not eat your lunch yet." The voice dipped, and became a tenor. "You should."

"I'm not hungry."

"You won't get extra food at supper," the tenor voice warned her.

"I know. Show me my parents again."

"Certainly." Ship was speaking in its alto once more. A woman appeared inside the cube; she had long, dark-brown hair and olive skin. The image was so real that Zoheret felt as though she were looking through a window. Behind the woman, Zoheret saw a barren, brown landscape and, on the horizon, the glitter of tall, shiny spires. The woman disappeared, and a black-haired man took her place. His bearded face smiled at her uneasily as he sat in his laboratory, his fingers around a microscope. The image changed. On one side of the cube, the woman stood before a small group of people, while on the other the man, now clothed in a long, white robe, sat in a garden; a hooded falcon clutched a perch near him. The images were still, frozen in time. Zoheret wondered how long the two had been dead.

The woman's name was Geula Aaron; the man was Hussein Taraki. It was from their genetic material that Ship had made Zoheret. Ship had told her that the two had worked on the Project together, but it did not know whether the two had known each other well. It had also told Zoheret that Geula had been a chemical engineer and that Hussein had been a medical researcher and poet.

Zoheret stared at the images, searching the faces. She had asked about them at first only out of curiosity. She had wanted to know something about the people who had built Ship, who had wanted to send something of themselves into space, to another world. Ship had explained enough to her for her to know that they were dead, that they had been dead long before Zoheret had been born. Ship had been traveling through space for over a century.

Zoheret had not thought much about her parents until recently. She was fifteen years old, as Ship reckoned time; on the day she had turned fifteen, she had found herself gazing at the images and asking herself if it had bothered them, knowing that a child of theirs whom they would never see, would never know, would be traveling to another world. It was silly to think of it that way, she knew; she had not been alive then, and they would have had to worry about someone who did not exist.

"You look like her," Anoki said as he came to her side. "But you have his nose."

"I know. My nose is too big."

"It is kind of beaky. It looks all right on you, though. It wouldn't on somebody else."

Zoheret smiled, knowing that this was as close as Anoki would come to a compliment. "Do you want to see your parents?"

"No." He said it quickly. "I've seen them before. What's the point? They would have been disappointed if they had known how I turned out." He frowned. "Maybe it was on purpose. Maybe I was supposed to be like this."

"You can't believe that."

"Why not? Maybe it's part of the Project, seeing whether someone like me, or like Willem, can survive."

"But Ship—"

"There's a lot Ship doesn't know. I'll bet there's a lot Ship hasn't told, either."

"I convey everything I can," Ship said in its alto. "And I know quite a lot—more than you do, I might add. Do you wish to continue viewing, Zoheret?"

"No." The images faded. Ship always showed the same holograms; Geula standing in a desert outside a city or with her friends, Hussein in his laboratory or garden. They never spoke; she had never heard their voices. They could have left a message, she thought. They could have recorded something for me to hear.

"Do you want to see something else?" Ship asked.

Zoheret shook her head.

"I must say," Ship went on, "that I do think you look at those holos much too often. They would not have wanted that, I'm certain. To know that some part of themselves will live on elsewhere was their desire. They would have wanted you not to look back, but to look forward. You must become yourself."

"I *am* myself. What else could I be?"

"That isn't what I meant. I meant that all of you here are a new human society, unhobbled by the past. The weight of history will not hold you back. You will be starting a history of your own, and in times to come, your descendants will tell legends and myths about you. You will live as human beings were meant to live. You will have a glorious destiny." Ship's voice rose a bit as it spoke.

Zoheret felt irritated. She had heard these comments of Ship's before. When she had been small, they had thrilled her, provoking formless daydreams of adventure in which she was the central figure, battling alien creatures or commanding her friends. She now knew that the glorious destiny Ship spoke of was going to be hard work.

She skated back to Lillka and sat at her side. Anoki gripped the arms of a chair, slowly lowering himself. "I'll bet you know as much as Ship does about Earth," Zoheret said to the other girl.

"Not quite as much. A lot, though. Don't forget, Ship never saw Earth. It only has what was programmed into it."

It was true. Ship's mind had been assembled on the asteroid that had become Ship's body. All of them had been born and raised on Ship, but Ship had been traveling through space for years before that, alone, moving at close to the speed of light while time slowed for Ship and centuries passed on Earth. Ship was moving toward a planetary system with a habitable world. When it reached that world, it would be time for all of the young people to leave Ship and to settle there.

Zoheret had longed for that time. No longer would Ship constantly watch them and tell them what to do; they would decide things for themselves. Now, as that time drew closer, she worried.

"It's funny," Lillka continued. "Ship knows so much. But things are missing. You don't notice that at first, but if you read enough, you begin to see it."

"What, for instance?" Zoheret asked. Ship had taught them much about Earth, beginning with its geological history and ending with the Project, with a lot in between. They had been given reading assignments and holo viewings; they had listened to Earth's music and seen Earth's art. Sometimes Ship simply told them stories. The point of it all was simple; all of Earth's history had led to the Project designed to fulfill the destiny of their species—to settle on other worlds and create new and varied cultures. Zoheret had wondered why, if they were to build their own society, they had to know so much about Earth's. "What's missing?" she went on.

Lillka shrugged. "The wars."

"Ship told us about those."

"Not really. It told us when they happened and how many people died and how they were fought and how they ended. It even told us the causes. Everybody thought that wars were horrible, but they kept having them. And then they stopped, because their weapons became too powerful and there was too much to lose. That doesn't make sense. It seems to me they would only stop if they didn't have any weapons."

"You're wrong," Zoheret said. "They stopped because they could have killed everyone, and no one would have won. That sounds like a good reason to me."

"War would have been suicide," Ship said. Its soft but resonant voice filled the room. "There is nothing worth sacrificing one's entire species."

Lillka shook her head. "But they still had the weapons.

Why did they keep them if they weren't going to use them? I'd get rid of them."

"I wouldn't," Anoki muttered. "Engineers learned a lot building weapons that they could use for other things. You might not like it, but it's true."

"The weapons are totems," Ship said. "Humankind keeps them as reminders of its past savagery, so that no one forgets. The weapons are guardians, forever holding the powerful in check, as a king on a chessboard is limited by the position of the opponent's pieces. If someone held a gun to your head, you would do as he told you. The weapons are held to the head of all the world, and the world behaves. No one has an advantage; no one can win. By now, knowing that they will fight with them no more, they have most likely dismantled the weapons." Ship shifted into its tenor voice. "You, Lillka, should pay more attention to your lessons and my exposition."

"What if they didn't dismantle them?" A flush spread over Lillka's pale, broad face.

"I don't know why you're so upset about it," Anoki said. "Ship's probably right. Anyway, it has nothing to do with us."

"But it does." Lillka's gray eyes gazed past Zoheret. "What if the people working on the Project thought there was going to be another war? Maybe they sent Ship out because they wanted some people to survive. Maybe we're the only human beings left."

"They didn't program anything about another war," Ship said loudly. "They were past that point. There were no ideological, economic, or social reasons for a war. It would have been suicide. They were well aware of that, and loved their lives too much to risk it."

"Maybe they fooled themselves," Lillka argued. "Maybe they thought they could survive one. I don't know. You tell us about Earth and how wonderful it is with its science and its art. But a lot of the science was used in wars, and a lot of the art depicts war. And they never gave up their war games and their little battles. It's as if people were made to fight." She glanced from Zoheret to Anoki. "Don't you see? It's as if it's an instinct. We have the same instincts. It means we're like them. It means we'll be just as violent."

"My, my," Ship said. "You're confusing possibility with necessity, Lillka. Because human beings have fought in the past doesn't mean they'll do so in the future."

"They might."

"Of course they might. And so might you. But it is not inevitable. The people of Earth, it's true, are a species that tends to seek danger and challenges, that has thrived on struggle and adversity. But the universe itself provides enough of those things. People came to realize that they could channel their aggressive instincts into other activities. There were the planets near Earth to explore, and enough danger in that to challenge anyone. The Project itself involved danger. People died building me. Nature often allows a person only one mistake. You'll find enough to keep you occupied on your new home, believe me. You won't have time for pointless and costly battles."

Lillka leaned back in her chair. "Maybe." She pulled at a strand of her short blond hair.

"Every quality," Ship murmured, "can be either a good or an evil thing. It depends on how it is directed. You are conscious, thinking beings, and you have a choice. You have a rich heritage, as well as the chance to begin anew. Concentrating only on the bad will give you a distorted picture, and will cripple you in the end."

Anoki started. "I'm already crippled," he said bitterly.

"I was speaking figuratively. And you can walk around

without your crutches now. Besides, you have compensated, Anoki. You have strong arms and shoulders."

"Great. I'm so glad. You could have been more careful when I was born."

"You were expelled from your womb too soon—you know that. Your limbs were damaged. But it's not a genetic defect. You won't pass it on." Ship's alto voice was soothing.

"So you fixed me, and you could have done more if I'd wanted to take a chance on new limbs. But you can't do a thing for Willem."

Ship was silent.

"Maybe," Anoki said, "you just should have let us die."

"Oh, no," Ship said softly. "I couldn't have done that. It was my purpose to care for you and to raise you. That was what I had to do."

"You don't want to die, not really," Zoheret said.

"How would you know?" Anoki pushed himself out of the chair with his arms and stood up. "Anyway, it doesn't matter. Ship watches us all the time. It'll look out for me whether I want to die or not." He limped from the library; the door opened and slid shut behind him.

"I'd better go after him," Lillka said wearily.

"Don't worry," Ship said. "I think he needs to be alone for a bit. He'll feel better later on. It's normal for him to be depressed or impatient during his convalescence. That's what my records tell me."

Zoheret sighed. Ship never seemed to realize that others might want to be truly alone for a while, without Ship's constant surveillance. They could escape it only in the caves and passageways just outside the corridors. Ship had watched them all their lives; even when it withdrew, not speaking, it watched. Its consciousness seemed to be everywhere. That had comforted her when she was small, knowing that she was guarded and watched—at least it had comforted her as long as she had done nothing wrong.

She had personified Ship then. She still recalled the childish concept she had once held. She had imagined Ship as a person, as a nebulous and insubstantial body dwelling in the circuits, traveling along them as it watched over the children. When Ship had spoken in its alto, she had seen, in her mind, a pretty woman with a strong but gentle face and flowing silvery hair. When it used its tenor, she had imagined a kindly man with the same silvery hair and face. Even now the old images would return, unbidden, but she knew that Ship was not human. She remembered how, when she was little and still living in the nursery, Ship would hold her with its metal attachments and press her gently against its wall when she needed affection. It had seemed very human then. She wondered who had changed more—she or Ship.

Lillka was staring at her reader. "I don't care what Ship says. The more I try to find out, the more questions I have. Remember when we looked at the holos of my parents?"

Zoheret nodded. Lillka's parents had been broad-faced, stocky people with laughing faces and cold gray eyes. They had, according to Ship, made a pledge to each other called marriage, which meant that they had promised to live with each other for a certain period until it was time either to make a new pledge or to separate. "I remember. What about them?"

"Ship told me they had both been trained as astronomers. It said they had worked in an observatory on Earth's natural satellite. Then it said they had spent many years on Earth living in an agricultural commune until the Project."

"They lived outside an old city called Odessa," Ship said, "near a large body of water called the Black Sea."

"I'm not talking to you, I'm talking to Zoheret. Will you keep quiet?"

"Certainly. I was only trying to be specific."

"Why does that bother you?" Zoheret asked.

"Think about it. They were on this satellite, the Moon. Ship told us that astronomers couldn't work as well on Earth because its atmosphere interfered with observations—the telescopes couldn't see the stars as well. But they went back to Earth, and then they became farmers. Don't you wonder why?"

"Maybe they just wanted to do something different."

"Maybe. But something about it bothers me. They worked on the Project. Ship says they were responsible for much of the work that decided its destination. But for a long time they didn't do any astronomy at all."

"I still don't see what's so strange."

"I've looked at their faces," Lillka replied. "I've watched them walk around. They look angry sometimes, even when they laugh. They look as though there's something they hate."

"I think you're imagining it."

"I thought I was. Now I'm not so sure."

Zoheret got up. "I think I'll go to the Hollow. Want to come?"

Lillka shook her head. "I want to read some more. Maybe I'll be in the gym later."

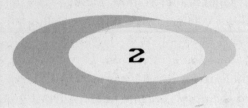

2

Zoheret skated down the curved corridor until she came to its end, near Ship's center. She took off her skates and slipped on the moccasins she had tied to her belt, then opened a panel in the wall, putting the skates inside. There were several other pairs on the shelf.

The wide door slid open, showing her the Hollow. Ship said, "You should not go in there alone."

"I won't go far. I'll stay near the entrance."

"You should exercise some caution. I can watch, and issue warnings, but there's little I can do here."

"I know."

"The natural realm has its beauty—it is the true home of humankind. But it also—"

"—has its dangers," Zoheret finished, having heard these words before. She walked through the entrance and stood under a slender tree. "Be careful," Ship's voice said from the tree. She leaned against the trunk, staring at the Hollow.

She was standing on a small grassy hill. Below it, she saw the tall trees of a forest. The Hollow was greater in size than any other part of Ship; it would take at least two days to cross it on foot. The land stretched out before her, appearing to be flat, but the distant horizon was higher than it would have been on flat ground, and overhead, just beyond wispy clouds, she could see ribbons of water and the leafy green tops of trees made tiny by the distance. The Hollow was like the inside of a sphere, an enclosed world. A diffuse yellow light permeated the area. A finch chirped nearby; Zoheret glimpsed a nest in the tree's limbs.

She took a deep breath, smelling the odors of grass and leaves and flowers, and noticed that she was not alone on the hill. A few paces below her, a boy sat, his back to her, his arm resting on a pack. She took another breath. The air of the corridors always seemed stale and sterile after she returned from the Hollow.

Ship had first brought all of them here several years ago, allowing them to remain for short periods of time as long as they stayed near the entrances. They had been prepared for the experience, since they had all spent some time wired up while Ship reproduced in their minds the images and sensations of a natural environment. But those experiences had been like dreams compared to the Hollow itself. The dangers she had encountered while wired—the bear, the deep waters of the lake, the dark woods where one could easily get lost—had been insubstantial. Here, they were all too real. She remembered Etienne, who had wandered off alone to the lake, and who would have drowned if Ship's voice had not guided the others to the lake in time.

Home, she thought. Earth lived in the Hollow, and

humankind had always called Earth home. It was what hu-man beings were made for; Ship had told them that. The world they were moving toward was like Earth; it would be another home. They would become part of that world and would grow to love it as their ancestors had loved Earth.

Ship was always talking of it. "Don't you ever wonder," Lillka had said, "why Ship's always harping on it? Nature, our destiny, being in harmony with our world." Lillka, of course, preferred the library to the Hollow.

Zoheret walked down the hill. "Gowon," she shouted to the boy, wondering why he was there alone. He looked up and smiled. He wore beige pants and a brown shirt almost as dark as his skin. "What are you doing?"

"Nothing." He gestured at the pack. "Manuel and Ho went into the woods—they dumped this here and told me to watch it for them."

"Well, you don't have to. They could have left it in the corridor."

Gowon shook his head. "When those guys tell you to do something, you do it." He glanced up at the tree. "Ship can't hear us if we keep our voices low."

"Ship'll shut down some of its sensors if you ask it to."

"I know, but I don't like to ask. Ship starts to think you're hiding something."

"Are you?" Zoheret asked. "Hiding something, I mean. You must be if you don't want Ship to hear."

"I'm not. I just don't want to talk to it now." Gowon ran a hand over his stiff black hair. "I'll tell you what Manuel and Ho think."

"Manuel and Ho." Zoheret sat down. "Those two are just looking for trouble. You shouldn't bother with them."

"I suppose I should bother with Anoki and Willem instead."

"Don't make fun of Anoki."

"I'm not. I don't care about his limp—it's his attitude I can't take. He's so gloomy. Willem's the only kid who's dumb enough to put up with it." Gowon let his mouth hang open and widened his brown eyes, then flapped his arms.

Zoheret tried not to laugh. "Stop it." She pushed against his shoulder.

"That's how he looks. Does Ship actually think somebody like Willem is going to stay alive when we get where we're going?"

"He will if we help him."

"He's retarded, Zoheret. He's never going to get better."

"It could have happened to you. You could have been born like Willem. Would you want people laughing at you?"

Gowon shrugged. He stretched out his legs and pointed his toes. "Poor Willem." He said it as though he did not care. "Manuel likes you."

"What?"

"He likes you. I can tell. He thinks you have a nice face."

"Don't be stupid." Zoheret suddenly felt flustered. She looked down at the ground so that Gowon could not see her eyes. "Anyway, I don't like him." She was blushing; she could feel her cheeks growing warm. "Anyway, he's with Bonnie."

"They don't get along so much now. He got what he wanted from her. Bonnie had a big argument with Ship about it. Ship told her she should have more respect for herself and consider her actions, but she just laughed and said she'd do what she wanted."

"I don't want to hear about it," Zoheret said, waiting for him to tell more.

"I think it's kind of strange for Ship to tell us we should restrain ourselves when nothing's going to happen." He gestured at the tiny white line on his lower right arm; each of them had such a mark where Ship had inserted a tiny contraceptive implant. "We can't have kids now anyway. And when we leave Ship, we'll have to have kids to survive. So we might as well learn how to enjoy what we have to do to get them. That's what I think."

She laughed. "You never did it."

"How do you know? Anyway, it doesn't mean I wouldn't."

Zoheret drew up her legs and wrapped her arms around them. Sometimes it was hard being friends with boys now; it had been easier when she was younger. She often felt uneasy and awkward around them. She would be talking to one, and then, without warning, would feel flustered and embarrassed, unable to be herself. At least Anoki, whatever his faults, didn't make her feel like this.

"Ship says we have to learn restraint," she said slowly, "because we'll need a stable society, and we won't have one if we don't have some sort of code of behavior." Even as she spoke, she hated the prissy sound of her words. "Ship doesn't tell us what to do, it just says we have to think about what it means, and be sure we know what we want, and not just go on our feelings."

"Oh, sure." Gowon tilted his head. "You learned your lessons. Ship ought to give you a big prize. Maybe I won't tell you what Manuel and Ho said."

"About what?"

"About Ship." He leaned toward her. "You'll find out soon enough anyway. They think Ship ought to shut down its sensors here in the Hollow. I mean all its sensors, not just its ears once in a while."

"But why?" She brushed back a lock of hair. "So they can get into more trouble?"

"No, so that we can get along on our own. When we get to the new world, we're not going to have Ship to save us if something happens."

"It'll be in orbit."

"But it won't be able to help us directly. Manuel thinks we should have more practice in taking care of ourselves. Ship's going to want us to spend more time in the Hollow anyway— we're supposed to live in it soon. Why shouldn't it shut down and see how we do without it?"

Zoheret rested her chin on her knees. It might be Manuel's idea, but it made sense. Maybe Ship would agree with Manuel; if it did, it would shut down its sensors and keep its promise. Ship always kept its promises. She thought of being without its constant watching eyes, and her excitement was tinged with fear.

"When are they going to ask it?" she said.

"Soon. I don't really know."

"Want to skate back with me? I'm going over to the gym."

Gowon looked around uneasily. "I'd better stay here. Those two will get mad if they can't find me."

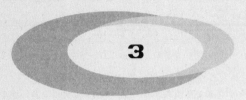

3

There was one room Zoheret had never seen; neither had anyone else. It stood at the end of the corridor on the last level. The room was a storage area, according to Ship; it contained biological materials that had to be stored at low temperatures, which was why no one could go there.

The room had two large, sealed doors. As she untied her skates, Zoheret glanced toward the end of the corridor at those doors. Ship carried part of Earth not only in the Hollow, but also behind those doors—seeds and animal embryos and a computer that would analyze their new home's life forms and determine which plants and animals could thrive there, and which would be needed.

Lillka, surprisingly, was in the gym. She sat in a rower, pulling at the oars with grim determination. Her stocky body was strong, but Ship often had to urge her to go to the gym.

Exercise was not something that Lillka enjoyed, but a duty; she did what she had to do and no more.

Zoheret waved at her friend as she walked toward the mats; for once, they had the gym to themselves. A doorway at the far end of the gym led to the swimming pool; she could hear the echoes of splashes and shouts. As she bent and stretched, she thought of Lillka's comments about the storage area.

"They wanted to make the world we're going to like Earth," Lillka had said. "But it'll have its own life forms, its own ecology. Either we'll end up destroying it, or we won't fit in." Zoheret had dismissed the doubts; surely Ship and the people working on the Project had known about possible difficulties and had allowed for them. Ship's probes would explore the world thoroughly before they went down to it to live.

She sat down, stretched out her legs, grabbed her ankles, and touched her head to her knees. Her knees were bony. She thought of Bonnie, with her curving calves and high, round breasts; that was all Manuel really cared about. Lillka was panting as she rowed. Lillka asked too many questions and thought she could answer them by thinking and reading. Well, she couldn't. Some of them could be answered only by experience, and others would never be answered. That was the way things were, and there was nothing to be done about it.

Lillka abandoned the rower and sprawled on a nearby mat while Zoheret lay on her back and lifted her legs. "Competition's coming up," Lillka said.

"I know."

"Ship hasn't even had us draw for teams yet. I hope we're on the same one. Not that it matters. Who cares who wins those things? I don't." Lillka sighed. "I hope it's problem-solving or games this time, and not swimming or something like that."

"Ship hasn't said. I get the feeling"—Zoheret paused as she lifted her legs one last time—"that it's planning something different."

"I think so, too."

Zoheret sat up, waiting for Ship to interject a comment, but it remained silent.

"I don't know why Ship makes us have a competition anyway," Lillka continued. "Everybody gets all worked up about it as if it matters who wins, and some kids get nasty about it, and then when it's all over, Ship tries to make it seem as though we all gained something and gives us that stuff about teamwork and building your character. Building your character!" Lillka sniffed. "I'm going back to the library. Maybe the competition'll be questions and answers. I could beat anybody on that."

Zoheret retreated to her room after supper. She had never cared for the noise and disorder of the dining hall, and ate as many meals in her room as Ship would allow. Fortunately, her room, which she shared with Lillka and a girl named Kagami, was empty.

Ignoring the vases and drawings with which Kagami had littered her part of the room, Zoheret slid her desk top out of the wall and set up her reading screen. She sat down, determined to master her anatomy lesson. As she stared at the diagrams of muscles, her mind drifted.

I'm not very good at studying, she thought. She could learn what others learned, but it seemed to take her longer than some. That might be only because she found it difficult to concentrate. She tried to force her attention back to the diagrams. Lillka could study something and learn it quickly and have questions about it and come up with implications that would never have occurred to Zoheret.

She was still staring at the diagrams when Ship spoke. "Manuel has asked me to tell all of you that he will have a proposal to offer during your meeting in the dining hall. He and several others wish to discuss your relationship with me during your forthcoming sojourn in the Hollow. If you cannot attend in person, please turn on your screens at that time. If you cannot participate in the meeting at all, give me your excuse, and I'll provide a recording for you later."

Zoheret frowned. It might be interesting to see Manuel actually offer a proposal, since he usually spent his time at meetings addressing humorous remarks at the speaker or fooling around with his friends in the back of the room. But she already knew what he was going to say.

"I'll watch it here," she said to Ship.

"No, you won't. You'll go to the hall. You don't have an excuse."

"I do. I have to study. I need every minute."

"You'll have plenty of time until then. You would learn more if you applied yourself and spent your time more efficiently."

"I know what they're going to talk about," Zoheret said angrily. "They're going to say you should shut down your sensors in the Hollow while we're living there." Ship was silent. "Aren't you mad?"

"Why should I be mad? I see no reason for not raising the issue."

"But you always worry about what might happen to us there. You're always saying to be careful."

"I feel it's wise to scan the area. But I cannot coddle you forever. I don't worry, and I don't get mad. It is unconstructive to do so." Ship paused. "You are all older now. Things will change."

"Then you think Manuel's right."

"I haven't drawn a conclusion. I must hear his arguments first. You had better study, Zoheret. You'll want to be on time for the meeting."

On one side of the dining hall's doorway, the round, pretty face of Kameko Sato, captured in a holographic portrait, stared sightlessly into the corridor; on the other side, the angular, thin face of Halim al-Haq seemed to glower. Images of the two were almost everywhere—in classrooms, Ship's laboratories, the nursery where the children had been raised. Zoheret had grown up under their gaze, had heard Ship's stories of the mother and father of the Project. Zoheret had, like the others, become oblivious of the images. Now she glanced at them and felt a sharp resentment. Two people, who had died long ago, still ruled; their dream controlled everyone inside Ship and even Ship itself.

As she entered the dining hall, Zoheret searched the room for Lillka. The blond girl was sitting in one corner on a table, legs folded; the chairs and spaces around her were taken.

Someone bumped against her. Zoheret turned around quickly and saw Gowon. She followed him to the nearest table and sat on its edge; Gowon sat next to her, but not too close. She did not like people to get too near her in a crowd; in this, she was like all the others. They all shied away from too much bodily contact, unlike the people of Earth she had seen on the holo during lessons on Earth's customs. But the people of Earth had had mothers and fathers to hold them and care for them when they were little. Zoheret and her companions had been held and fed only by Ship's mechanical limbs.

Some of the others were growing restless. "Let's go," one boy sitting on the floor shouted. This comment drew a few catcalls and whistles, and then one group began to clap.

Anoki and Willem were sitting on chairs near one wall. Anoki scowled at the clappers; Willem grinned and began to clap. One girl turned around, stared at Willem, then motioned to a friend. The two girls watched Willem; their lips curled. Willem continued to slap his hands together, his shaggy brown hair swaying as he bobbed his head to the rhythm. His mouth was open; saliva glistened on his lower lip. Anoki touched Willem's elbow; the two girls turned away.

Manuel suddenly climbed onto a table near the front of the room and held up his arms. The clapping became a smattering, then stopped. Someone hooted; Manuel turned toward the hooter. He looked proud, and a little cruel; his regular features seemed sharper in the lighted room. He wore no shirt; his olive skin gleamed. Ho stood on the floor, behind Manuel; Bonnie was next to him. Bonnie raised a hand and smoothed back her long, brown hair; she gazed possessively at Manuel with her large green eyes. Zoheret looked away, then glanced apprehensively at Gowon, but he was watching Manuel.

Manuel waited until the room was still, then spoke. "We'll all be going to the Hollow soon to live. That's what I want to talk to you about."

"So what else is new?" someone shouted from one corner. A few people giggled; the giggling stopped when Manuel glared at that corner.

"We have to learn how to live by ourselves," Manuel went on. "So I think Ship should shut down its sensors while we're there. We're getting too dependent on Ship. We always expect it to be there, and it keeps us from thinking for ourselves."

Zoheret heard the hum of murmurs; then Lillka waved a hand. Manuel nodded in her direction.

"Won't that be dangerous?" Lillka asked. "We're not used

to living there—we've only been there for short periods. We might need Ship."

"I've thought of that," Manuel replied smoothly. "Ship wouldn't have to shut down until we're settled and it's sure we can handle things. And we wouldn't ask it to shut down unless most of us are agreed. Well, that's all I have to say. We ought to start thinking about it."

Zoheret looked down. If anyone else had proposed the idea, she might have agreed easily. But Manuel had said it. He was always in trouble even with Ship watching; what would he do without Ship's vigilance?

A boy named Tonio had just asked a question she had missed. She forced herself to concentrate. Manuel shrugged. "Even that isn't a problem," he answered. "If we do need Ship's help, we can always send someone back to the corridors. It isn't as though Ship won't be there for an emergency. But I think we can work things out for ourselves."

Some of those near Zoheret were getting restless; they fidgeted and began to whisper. She glared at them, irritated. Manuel was asking them to consider an important decision, and they wanted to leave and go back to what they had been doing. They would all do what Manuel wanted in the end. They would go along with him either because they did not care one way or the other or because they were afraid of him. She was no different. She would sit and remain silent until the meeting was over.

"What does Ship think?" a red-haired girl named Rina shouted.

"Why don't you ask it?" a boy shouted back.

"What do you think?" Rina said to the ceiling.

"I have formed no opinion," the alto voice replied. "I trust that all of you will consider Manuel's suggestion and discuss it among yourselves and with me. Then I shall tell you what I think."

Zoheret felt relieved. If Ship has any doubts, she thought, it won't let us go into the Hollow alone.

"I've said all I have to say," Manuel said. "We can talk about it again after Competition." Zoheret heard grumbling behind her. Someone whispered Manuel's name, but she could not make out the rest of the remark.

"If no one else wishes to speak," Ship said, "I have something to say now. As you know, Competition is coming up, and I'm sure you're all anxious to hear about the sort of contest I have planned. As it happens, it will be an entirely new sort of game, and will tie in with Manuel's suggestion."

Manuel sat down on his table; Bonnie and Ho perched on either end. "It's a very simple game," Ship murmured. "You'll draw for teams, as always. Each team will enter the Hollow and cross it; the object will be to reach the door farthest from that entrance on the other side, which means you'll leave from the door down this corridor and go to the one outside the nursery and observatory. One member of each team will draw to see which team goes first, second, and so forth. The team that crosses the Hollow in the shortest amount of time wins, and each member of the team must reach the door before I record that time. That's all you have to do."

"What are the rules?" Gowon shouted.

"There are no rules. You may take any path across the Hollow you wish. You may divide your team into smaller groups if you think that will make you move more quickly, but I'll not note your time until every member of the team is at its destination. You may even circle the Hollow to avoid danger, but you're hardly likely to win that way, since it will take longer than cutting straight across. I should point out one thing. I'll shut down all my sensors there while you're crossing, so I won't be monitoring you, and you'll get no help from me. You'll be on your own. I urge you to be careful, since if a team loses a member, that team will be disqualified. I'll tell you what you'll be allowed to take before Competition begins. Any questions?"

No one spoke.

"We'll draw for teams tomorrow. I'm sure you'll all do your best."

"I move we adjourn this meeting," Ho shouted. There was a chorus of assent, and then a thundering of feet as people moved toward the doors. Gowon mumbled a goodbye and disappeared. Zoheret remained seated, waiting for the crowd to thin out.

"Zoheret."

She looked up, startled to see Manuel standing in front of her. She gazed at his curly black hair, afraid to look at his eyes. Her neck felt stiff.

"You didn't say anything. Do you think I have a good idea?"

"I agree with Ship," she said loftily. "I have no opinion at this time."

"Oh, come on. You must have some opinion." He tilted his head and smiled, as if amused. "I think Ship agrees with me, whether it admits it or not. I think that's why it's having this kind of Competition."

"You might have a good idea," she said. "It depends."

"Depends on what?"

Bonnie had walked over and now stood at Manuel's side. She nodded coldly at Zoheret.

"It just depends," Zoheret muttered. "I have to go." She got off the table and moved toward the door, thinking of things she could have said to Manuel; she always thought of such remarks too late.

Zoheret and Kagami were in their darkened room, lying on their beds, when Lillka entered. She tiptoed across the room quietly, then bumped against something. "Ow."

"We're still awake," Kagami said.

"Can't you keep your stuff in the same place so I know where it is?"

"You wouldn't have the problem if you didn't stay in the library all night."

"I wasn't in the library." Lillka's shoes slapped the floor; her sheets rustled. "I was talking to Roxana and Brendan. They're not too happy about this Competition."

"That's what they say now," Kagami said. "Wait until it starts. They'll get all worked up about it, just like they always do."

"No rules. We always had rules before. They don't like it."

"What difference does it make?" Zoheret said. "There isn't any way to cheat. Everyone has to cross the Hollow, that's all. That shouldn't be too hard."

"But Ship was always watching before."

"Go to sleep," Kagami said. "The drawing's tomorrow. Maybe we'll all be on the same team."

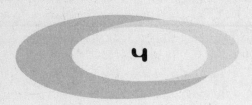

4

Zoheret's team crowded together in front of the entrance to the Hollow. Each team was designated by a color; her team was Blue. They had finished their planning yesterday and had gone to bed early, but Zoheret had not slept well.

She loosened the short blue scarf around her neck. Lillka was not on the Blue team; Kagami had drawn Red. Each had kept her team's plans to herself. As the members of her team jostled one another, Zoheret hung back, leaning against the wall. Manuel was on her team. The others were all deferring to him, allowing him to lead. It had been that way ever since they had drawn for teams and had found themselves grouped with Manuel. He was determined to win; he had made that very clear. Ho was on the Brown team; his friendship with Manuel had been replaced by rivalry.

The Brown team had drawn the right to go through the Hollow first, followed by Red. Zoheret and the Blue were third. They had studied maps of the Hollow and planned their route; they could bring no maps with them and had to rely on memory. Their knapsacks each contained a poncho, some dried food, and a canteen filled with water. They also had matches and one stun gun each. Zoheret worried about the guns. They were not lethal weapons, and Ship had said that they would need them to protect themselves; at the same time, it had warned them to use their wits and not to rely too much on the guns. She was a good shot and had always done well at target practice, but Ship had never allowed them to carry the weapons before. It was testing them, she was sure.

Annie came to her side. "I'm nervous," the short, blond girl said. "Aren't you?"

"Sure."

"I think—"

"You may enter the Hollow," Ship said. The group went forward; Zoheret heard someone giggle. She was the last to go through the entrance, just behind Annie; the doors slid shut behind her.

Manuel led the way. They moved over the grassy slope and toward the trees below. There were twenty people on the team. Annie marched beside Zoheret on short, stubby legs; her head came to Zoheret's shoulder. They passed Jennifer, who walked with a slight lurch; Jennifer, like Anoki, was one of Ship's accidents.

Zoheret slowed down. "Are we going too fast?"

Jennifer shook her head; her chestnut curls bobbed. "I can keep up." She spoke in her peculiar, slurred, halting speech, as if every word were an effort; her arms flapped against her sides.

When they reached the trees, Manuel stopped and removed a piece of paper from his shirt pocket. The others crowded around him as he unfolded it. "I've got our route marked," Manuel said. "We should be able to get to the lake by tonight—we can refill our canteens there. But we'll have to keep moving. No stopping to rest, except for lunch."

Annie said, "You have a map."

"I made some notes. I sketched a route."

"Ship said we couldn't bring maps."

"Oh, shut up," Jorge muttered; his chubby face was petulant.

"You cheated," Annie said. "We'll be disqualified."

Manuel grinned. "Ship said no maps. It didn't say no notes, and it didn't say we couldn't bring sketches. I know, because I asked. If the other teams were too stupid to ask, that's their problem."

"It's not a sketch," Annie replied. "It's a map. You copied everything. I know it didn't want us to do that."

"Ship's not going to know," Manuel said slowly, "because no one's going to tell it. I'll get rid of it before we come out. And if you say anything, I might get mad. You understand."

Manuel turned and they followed him into the woods. "It doesn't matter," Zoheret whispered to Annie as they walked, stirring the dead twigs and pine needles with their feet. "We all studied the maps so much we practically have them memorized anyway, so that map of Manuel's won't make any difference."

"He copied everything. I wish I knew how he pocketed it without Ship finding out." Annie scowled. "Don't worry. I know enough to keep my mouth shut."

It was cooler under the trees; the air was still. Zoheret wondered what the trees were hiding, and wished the team had skirted the forest, but that would have taken too long.

Manuel was speaking to Dmitri; the muscular boy shook back his long, brown hair and moved ahead of Manuel. Zoheret resented the way Manuel had taken command of the team. No one had stood up to him, or questioned his authority. Ahead of her, Gervais churned through the underbrush on skinny legs. Zoheret would have trusted Gervais to lead, but the intense, solemn boy had contented himself with making suggestions. Maybe he had been wise. Manuel had listened to him, and Gervais had avoided the sort of confrontation that would have had the team taking sides.

Manuel might be disliked, but he would help them win, and that was more important. He knew the Hollow as well as anyone, except possibly Ho, because the two had always been sneaking off to the Hollow, even against Ship's wishes. She walked more quickly, not wanting to be left behind.

*T*he team stood on a hill, looking down. A clearing lay before them. They had made it this far seeing no more than squirrels, a few birds, and a deer that had disappeared quickly among the trees. But now their way was blocked. A bear and her cub were in the clearing.

They were downwind of the animals, and the creatures had not noticed them yet. Manuel whispered to Dmitri.

"No," Gervais said in a low voice, moving closer to Manuel. "It's too dangerous."

"We've got stun guns," Manuel said. "I think we should shoot. We'd have plenty of time to get across before they revive."

"No," Zoheret said. She forced herself to look directly at Manuel. "It's too dangerous. That's a mother with her cub. She'll attack if she feels it's threatened. We might miss."

"Not if enough of us shoot."

"But you could hurt them." One or two shots, she knew,

would stun the animals into unconsciousness, but several shots might damage their central nervous systems. Enough shots, even with stun guns, could kill. She was suddenly afraid of the weapon at her waist. "Why risk it when we can go around the clearing?"

"We'll lose time," Dmitri said.

"We'll lose more time if we stand here arguing about it." Zoheret looked at the others, hoping for support.

"She's right," Annie said. "Let's go around the clearing."

"Do you know how much time we'll lose?" Manuel said angrily.

"I don't care."

The larger bear looked up, sniffing the air. Manuel moved quickly, racing a few paces down the hill, then raised his gun. He fired.

The bear roared as the beam of light shot past her. She lumbered toward them, moving faster than Zoheret had thought she could. Two more beams struck her in the chest and she fell at the foot of the hill. Dmitri hit the cub.

The two animals were still. The team scampered down the hill and ran across the clearing. Jennifer stumbled as she ran; Manuel ran swiftly, head high in triumph. When they reached the trees on the other side, Zoheret rested for a moment, leaning against a trunk. The knapsack on her back felt heavy.

"Come on," Manuel said. He was standing next to her. "We should be far away when they wake up."

"You shouldn't have done that."

"I had no choice. It worked, didn't it?" He turned away.

After lunch, they kept up a steady pace until the light permeating the Hollow began to grow dimmer. The hills around them now bore only a few trees and bushes; if nothing went wrong, they would reach the lake, and more forest, before dark.

They had, Zoheret thought, been lucky so far. The trip had been uneventful, except for the bears. Ship had always kept its word; it had said it would shut down its sensors. But she still felt as though it were watching, making sure that they came through the Hollow safely.

She rejected that notion. She was being childish, thinking that Ship was looking out for them, that it cared. Ship didn't care. Ship was a mind core. She had thought of it as human, but it wasn't. Ship had as many feelings as the library computer catalogue. Ship had held the children and sung to them and told them stories and comforted them because that was what it had been programmed to do. Ship was going to take them and dump them on a strange planet and orbit that world while they lived and struggled and died on the planet's surface. Someday, their descendants would be able to journey to Ship again; they might even build ships of their own. It all seemed wasteful and pointless. They had been thrown into the sea of space as if they were the spawn of fish, to live, breed, and die.

A few members of the team were singing softly, marching in time to the song. They marched as if they were devices set in motion by a hidden hand.

It was dark when they came to the lake; a rippling black surface lay before them. Annie and Gervais began to gather wood for a fire, taking care not to get too far away from the rest of the group. The sandy shore was strewn with rocks; the air blowing in from the lake was damp and cool.

When the fire was finally ablaze, they all huddled around the flames, warming their hands and eating their meager meal. The trees bordering the shore were silent sentries. Zoheret devoured her dried meat and fruit and finished her food still hungry.

Manuel studied his map by the firelight for a few moments, then put it away. "We have to get moving at first light, or earlier. We still have to circle the lake and get up to where we can cross the river—we can crawl across that old tree that fell there. After that, we should make good time and get to the goal before dark. I think we have a good chance of winning."

Zoheret ached all over and was certain her muscles would be stiff by first light. Jennifer had twisted her ankle, but seemed to be all right now; they'd had no other injuries.

Annie moved closer to Zoheret. "I was mad at him," she said softly, "but he did get us this far. I was sure we wouldn't make it to the lake by now."

"We'll take turns on watch," Manuel said. Someone groaned. "We have to be careful. I'll take the first turn with Jorge. Who wants the second?" A few voices volunteered. Manuel handed out the assignments, giving Zoheret and Gervais the last watch. "Yours is the most important," he said to her. "As soon as it's even a little lighter, we have to get up and start. We can eat while we walk—we shouldn't run into any obstacles along the shore."

A few people were already bedding down, making beds of their ponchos and pillows of their knapsacks. Others were relieving themselves in the darkness just beyond the fire's light. Zoheret got up and found a spot near a tree.

She looked around, then squatted, grateful for the dark. She finished quickly and crept back toward the lake. Robert was banking the fire; the glow made his red hair gold.

A dark shape suddenly loomed in front of her; she backed away. "Zoheret." It was Manuel's voice. "Sit with me for a while."

"You're supposed to be on watch."

"Jorge can take care of things. Besides, you can watch with me."

"I have the last watch."

"You have all night to sleep. You won't have to get up and then try to sleep again. I did you a favor."

"I'm tired." She sat down anyway. A breeze whistled through the trees above them, then died. They were several paces from the group, hidden in the shadows on the edge of the shore.

"Admit it," Manuel said. "We're doing well. If we'd listened to you, we wouldn't have come this far."

"All right. I admit it."

"We were lucky with our team. We didn't get stuck with any real losers except for Jennifer. Poor Ho. He got stuck with Willem and Anoki. That'll slow him down."

"Willem's strong."

"But he's dumb. And Anoki—"

"Anoki's stronger than you think."

"He's a cripple. Oh, I forgot—you're his friend. Maybe you're more than his friend."

"I'm not," she said fiercely, and was suddenly ashamed of denying it so vehemently. "He's just my friend, like Lillka. Sometimes he tutors me, that's all."

"I believe you." Manuel moved closer and put his arm around her.

She froze, unable to move, and felt his breath on her face. He began to stroke her shoulder. "Take your hands off me."

"If you don't want my arm there, then take it away."

She shoved his arm. He grabbed her waist with the other, forcing her on her back. His hand groped at her shirt. "You like me. You try to act like you don't, but you do." His lips found her cheek.

She raised her arms and pushed against him as hard as she could. He rolled over; she heard him chuckle. She had wanted him to hold her; she had wanted to respond. She got to her feet, trembling.

He said, "Another time."

She walked back to the fire and lay down on her poncho. She was angry and embarrassed, but with those feelings came another that she could not name. I hate you, she thought as she remembered the feel of his arm. The spot where his lips had touched her cheek still tickled.

Someone was shaking her shoulder. Zoheret slapped the hand away and opened her eyes.

"It's Gervais," a voice said. "Come on, it's our turn."

Her muscles ached as she sat up. Her legs were stiff and sore. She rubbed her neck and groaned. "I feel awful."

"So do I. You'll feel better after you move around."

Her head hurt and one of her feet was asleep. She got up and stamped on it, waiting for her eyes to adjust to the darkness, then picked up her poncho and put it on. The light, cottony fabric did not make her feel much warmer.

She followed Gervais to the edge of the sand. "This is stupid," she muttered to him. "We can't see a thing. If there was any danger, we wouldn't know until it was too late anyway." She shivered.

"I think it's already getting lighter," Gervais said.

"No, it's not." She squinted, at last able to make out the shoreline. "There's no point in leaving until we can see where we're going. The others probably need more sleep anyway. Robert grinds his teeth, did you know that? He woke up about five people."

"I don't want Manuel getting mad at us."

"He won't. And so what if he does?"

Gervais sighed. "I was on a team with him once, a couple of Competitions ago. It was questions and answers."

"I remember. I was terrible at it—lucky for me we had Lillka on our team."

"Well, I missed a question, right at the end."

"I remember. You lost then. I was sure you would win."

"We got second place. Manuel was mad. He jumped me later, in one of the caverns outside the corridors, and slapped me around. He told me I'd found out what would happen if I ever messed up again. He knew Ship didn't have any sensors there."

"You should have told Ship."

"What am I going to do, go running to Ship with everything? And what's it going to do—throw him off? I didn't want him coming after me again."

The land around the lake was oddly quiet; even the chirping of the birds seemed subdued. She peered at the nearby trees, then turned back to Gervais. She could barely see his pointed face. A few drops of water fell on her nose, and she pulled up her hood. "It's starting to rain."

"They'll have to wake up now."

Jorge made sure the fire was out. The group huddled together in their ponchos, hoods over their heads; the rain had become a steady drizzle.

"It isn't fair," Dmitri said. "I'll bet the teams ahead of us didn't get rain. This'll really slow us down."

"It won't if we start now," Manuel responded.

"No rules," Jorge muttered to Dmitri as they began to make their way along the shoreline. "Of course, we forgot to ask Ship if it had any rules for itself." Zoheret, just behind the two boys, slowed down and let Gervais and Annie pass her. She did not want to get too close to Manuel, who was just ahead of Jorge and Dmitri.

The wet rocks were mossy and slippery; mud caked her boots. The mist, silvery in the faint light, was so dense that the wooded hills on the lake's other side had vanished; the water seemed to stretch out before them infinitely. The damp air had seeped inside her, making her bones ache.

She nibbled at some cheese while she walked, forcing herself to swallow it. Her stomach was tight, her body tense. The thought of Manuel made her throat close on the last bit of cheese; she coughed and swallowed. He had taken her will from her, making her feel as though she could no longer control her own thoughts and actions. Her cheeks burned.

Manuel was keeping up a quick pace. Zoheret paused, and looked behind her. Jennifer had become a shadow in the mist, her body swaying and lurching even more than usual as she struggled to keep up.

They continued along the shore until the mist lifted and the rain stopped; a small island near the distant shore could now be seen. They paused to put away their ponchos, then hurried on. The air was sticky. Zoheret wiped her face with one arm, feeling sweaty and dirty.

When they stopped to fill their canteens, she heard Dmitri ask if they had time for a swim; Manuel shook his head. He gazed at Zoheret for a moment as she filled her canteen; his brown eyes seemed to be reading her mind. She looked away, still feeling his gaze.

At last they turned from the shore and scrambled up a hill, hurrying along a clear space under the pine trees. Zoheret slowed, letting others move ahead of her. She noticed that Jennifer had fallen even farther behind; she was at least twenty paces away. Zoheret waited for her to catch up.

Then she saw the bobcat. The large, tawny beast was in the air, claws out, arcing toward Jennifer as Zoheret pulled out her gun. She flicked the switch releasing the safety, sighted along her arm, aimed, and fired, knowing she had only one chance. A beam shot out of the barrel. Jennifer leaped toward a tree, striking the trunk with her shoulder as the cat fell at her feet.

Robert and Serena ran toward Zoheret; soon everyone was gathered around her. "What happened?" Serena shouted.

"A cat," Zoheret managed to say, gesturing at the still form with her gun. "It must have a cub nearby, or it wouldn't—"

"It almost got me," Jennifer said. "Zoheret shot it."

Someone grabbed Zoheret's elbow. She looked into Manuel's eyes. "Good work." He smiled. Her anger was gone; she took a breath. His fingers squeezed her arm gently, then released her. "Are you all right?" he asked Jennifer.

She nodded. "I'm fine—just whacked my shoulder."

"Are you sure?"

"It's just a bruise."

"Then let's get out of here before it wakes up." He began to walk up the path, turned, and stared at Zoheret as if wanting her to walk with him, then went on.

The others followed. Zoheret walked at the end of the line, with Jennifer. The girl was walking with a pronounced limp now; her lips were pressed so tightly together that they were white. Her pretty face was drawn. "There's a ravine up here," Robert shouted from up the hill.

Zoheret took Jennifer's arm when they came to the ravine. "Can you jump across?" she asked the other girl. The ravine was deep, but not too wide. She did not remember seeing it on a map, but then Ship had not shown them every detail. Zoheret frowned. The bottom of the ravine, about six meters below her, was filled with pine needles, dead tree branches, and heaps of dead leaves; a piece of red fabric rested on the leaves.

Jennifer pointed with one trembling hand at the fabric. "A scarf," she said. "The Red team came this way."

"Can you jump?" Zoheret asked again.

Jennifer nodded. Zoheret leaped across first, then turned, holding out her hand. Jennifer jumped toward her, moaning as she landed on her feet. She began to slide. Zoheret caught her and pulled her forward.

"Are you sure you weren't hurt?"

"It's my ankle," Jennifer replied, "the one I twisted yesterday. It's been hurting ever since we started out this morning."

"What's wrong?"

"It isn't broken. I don't even think it's sprained. But I pulled something, and it's getting worse. It might be a ligament—I don't know."

"Then we'd better stop and see."

"No." Jennifer spat out the word. "No. The others'll get mad." Her tongue stumbled over the words. "They didn't want me on the team anyway. Don't say anything, please."

"But if you're hurt, we'll have to carry you. We could rig up a stretcher somehow."

"I can walk." Jennifer sputtered as she slurred her words.

"Take my arm."

"No."

"Jen. Take it."

She took Zoheret's arm. They walked together, managing to keep the others in sight. They walked as quickly as they could; Zoheret could tell from the pressure of Jennifer's arm that the other girl was trying not to lean too hard against her.

"Oh, no!" someone shouted up ahead. Manuel and those with him had reached the river. "What do we do now?" another voice said. As they drew nearer, Jennifer released Zoheret's arm and limped more quickly.

Manuel was pacing back and forth. Dmitri was staring down the steep bank. The gorge through which the river ran was almost twenty meters deep, and the tree that should have connected the two sides of the gorge was gone. Zoheret walked to the edge and looked down. The tree had fallen and now lay half in the river, half on land.

"It didn't get there by itself," Manuel said. "Someone pushed it there. And I know who did it. Ho. I'll bet it was his idea."

"The Red team might have done it," Zoheret said, but she doubted that. They could climb down the bank on this side, which sloped enough for footing, but she was sure they could not get up the other side, which was muddy and slippery and much too steep. Manuel had pulled out his map again and was frowning at it. He did not seem to know what to do.

Jorge peered over his shoulder. "We could climb down, cross, and head upriver on the other side until we find a spot we can climb."

Manuel shook the map, then crumpled it in his fist. "It'll take too long. We'd have to go up practically to the bend."

"How about heading back down toward the lake?" Annie asked.

"Swampland," Manuel reminded her. He was right; they had hoped to avoid the hazardous terrain bordering the lake by crossing up here. "It's too risky—there's quicksand there." He smoothed out the map, folded it, and put it away. "It doesn't matter what we do now. We've already lost the Competition. I was counting on crossing here. We'll lose too much time no matter what we do." But he was looking around, as if trying to find another way. "If only we had some rope."

"We have our ponchos," Gervais said. He took off his

knapsack and removed the garment from it. "Give me yours. We can get down this side and cross the river below. If we tie our ponchos together, we should be able to climb up the other side using them."

"There's only one thing wrong with that," Manuel responded. "Someone's going to have to climb the other side without them and then tie them to something."

Gervais's eyes narrowed. "You could do it, couldn't you?" He paused. "Unless you think someone else would be better at it."

The others were watching Manuel. He pressed his lips together. "I can do it," he said at last. "Let's see if we can knot these things tight enough first." He handed Gervais his own poncho. Gervais fumbled with the light fabric and finally tied a knot. Then he and Manuel tested it, pulling hard at each end. "Let's hope it doesn't rip," Manuel muttered.

They began their descent. It was slow work; the slope was steep, though not nearly as steep as the opposite bank. Zoheret went down ahead of Jennifer, lest the other girl should slip. She wanted to mention Jennifer's injury to Manuel, but knew that Jennifer would be angry if she did. She moved carefully, finding handholds and footing among rocks and tree roots. Her knapsack pulled at her shoulders. Above her, Jennifer clung precariously; her hands were shaking. Zoheret knew the other girl's arms were weak. Jennifer's head shook from side to side. As she reached the bottom, Zoheret helped her down.

They stood on flat rocks, staring at the river; they were coated with mud. Gervais peered at the flowing water. "There's a strong undertow. We'd better use the ponchos to cross. Make sure the knots are tight."

Zoheret tied her poncho to Jennifer's, then handed one end to Annie. When all the ponchos had been tied together,

Manuel waded into the water, clinging to one end of the chain. When the water was up to his chest, he began to kick with his feet, pulling the makeshift rope after himself. Eddies swirled around him; he drifted downriver. He kicked some more, fighting the current. Gervais followed him while Dmitri and Jorge held the other end of the garments. Manuel struggled out on the other side and ran back along the bank, tightening the chain.

Everyone crossed while the chain was held at both ends. Zoheret felt the undertow of the river as she crossed; it wetted her clothes and made her knapsack seem even heavier. The sound of the river pounded against her ears. Dmitri and Jorge waited until everyone was across, then followed; the others pulled them through the river quickly.

Manuel tied one end of the string of ponchos to his belt, then looked up, studying the muddy, rocky precipice before him. He reached up and tried a piece of rock jutting out from the cliff, then began to climb.

He clung to the surface like an insect, reaching up cautiously with his hands, digging in with his feet. He had left his knapsack below. Zoheret could see his muscles straining under his wet shirt; his hands were muddy claws. She held her breath for a moment, remembering the routes they had considered and rejected; she wished that they had taken the other way around the lake. She no longer cared about winning.

It's what you do when things are hard that counts. Ship had told them that often enough. Humankind is made for difficult tasks; without them, you will grow weak. Ship would not have wanted them to take the easy way. Ship's words were little comfort to her now.

Unable to watch Manuel climb, she glanced at the large dead tree, part of which lay at their side. Manuel was right; Ho would have thought of pushing it there. He had guessed their plans; he knew Manuel too well and might have known the route he would choose. Maybe he hadn't guessed; maybe he had known what the Blue team was planning. She was suddenly sure of it. Ho would have known how to get someone to talk, would know how to force the information from someone.

She looked at Gervais. His upturned face was tense as he watched Manuel. He had talked. Ho would have known he was vulnerable; he would have known about Manuel's revenge on Gervais. And Gervais had been ready with a plan, as if knowing that Ho would get his team to dispose of the tree. She tried to work up some anger at the boy, but failed, wondering what she would have done if Ho had tried to pry the information from her.

Manuel slipped. Zoheret darted to one side as a shower of mud and pebbles fell toward her. Manuel's hands grabbed at a rock and his legs dangled until he found footing. He was almost to the top of the precipice now. Ho, she realized, must have lost some time in moving the tree, so her own team might still have a chance.

Manuel reached the top and hoisted himself over it. Soon he was standing, waving his arms. The others cheered.

Climbing up the cliff, even with the makeshift rope, was not easy. Zoheret, feet flat against the rock face, pulled herself along, not looking down. She hoped that the knots would hold and quickly decided not to think of that.

When they were all at the top, they pulled the ponchos and Manuel's knapsack up after themselves. Then they untied the frayed ponchos and put them away. Jennifer lay on her back until they were ready to leave; she was very pale.

They hurried through the trees and were soon out on the plain. The grassy land rippled. The air was clear; far overhead, on the other side of the Hollow, thin silvery streams wound among clumps of green.

They jogged across the plain; the grass slapped their thighs. They slowed, but kept to a stride. Jennifer was limping badly now, but was somehow keeping up. She had picked up a long stick in the woods and was using it as a cane.

"When do we stop for lunch?" Robert shouted.

"We don't," Manuel shouted back. He stood aside and let the others pass him. "If you want to eat, eat while you're walking." Annie moaned and a few others grumbled, but they kept on. Victory was again possible; no one would argue.

Manuel came to Zoheret's side and walked with her. His face was dirty; dark curls clung to his forehead. "Maybe we'll win after all," Zoheret said, not knowing what else to say.

"If we do, we'll celebrate," he said. "You'll come to the party with me, won't you?"

"I'll see if we win first."

Jennifer, just behind Manuel, gazed at Zoheret with raised eyebrows. The boy turned and saw her. "You hurt yourself."

Jennifer nodded.

"You're doing all right, Jen. I didn't think you would. I guess I'm glad you're on our team after all."

Jennifer beamed; her cheeks grew pink.

Zoheret thought of what Gervais had told her. It did not matter. Manuel was older now; he had probably changed. If they won, it would be mostly because of him. She realized that she wanted the others to see her with Manuel, to know how he felt about her.

In the distance, a small herd of horses grazed. They passed a few sheep, which bleated as they went by. Zoheret was sure that wolves were not far away, but doubted they would attack such a large group of people.

"Even if we lose," Manuel murmured, drawing closer to

her, "you can come to the winners' party with me, can't you?"

"Bonnie might want you to go with her." She said it lightly.

Manuel scowled. "I didn't make her any promises."

"That isn't what I've heard."

"I'm not interested in her anymore. And what do you care about it anyway?" He laughed and poked her gently in the side. "Don't tell me you're jealous."

"I'm not."

"You are."

"You're always with her. It's natural to wonder."

"She'll find somebody else. Ho can have her. It doesn't matter to her where she gets it."

Zoheret looked down. He said it as if Bonnie were something he could use and throw away. The pleasant spell had been broken.

They walked silently for a while. Manuel shot her one last look and then darted ahead.

It was still light when they reached forested land; they were not far from their goal now. Zoheret would sleep in her own room that night. Manuel had been trying to make her look foolish; she felt as though he was using her in some game of his own. Perhaps it was Bonnie who had grown tired of him.

She could hear voices. Annie turned and shouted, "There's someone up there." They hurried forward to a small clearing; Zoheret pushed past Dmitri for a view.

The Red team was in the clearing. Most of them still wore their red scarves around their necks, but their clothes were shredded and torn. Four members of the Red team were lying on makeshift stretchers made of tree limbs, ponchos, and torn pieces of clothing. Kagami, lying stiff and still, was one of the injured.

Zoheret ran to her friend's side. Kagami opened her almond-shaped eyes; she tried to smile, then bit her lower lip. Zoheret knelt and took her hand. "What happened?"

Kagami shook her head. Gowon hurried over. "I'll tell you what happened." He looked around at the others. "The Brown team boobytrapped us, at a ravine on the path leading up to the river. They'd covered part of it with leaves and twigs, and we didn't see it until it was too late. Maybe Ho was hoping you'd fall into it." Gowon made fists of his hands.

"We weren't going to take that route," Kagami said weakly.

"We were going to take the long way around the lake," Gowon continued, "but we'd lost too much time getting there, so we decided to head up to the river instead. We were going pretty fast when we came to the ravine. Brendan broke a leg. Kagami has a couple of fractured ribs. I think Federico's hurt bad—he's dizzy, and he passed out a couple of times. Karl has a sprain and his leg's swollen." He paused. "It took us time to make stretchers. Then we made a splint for Brendan and bound up Kagami's ribs. When we got to the river, we saw that the tree was down and we couldn't cross, so we had to go all the way around. That's why we only got this far. When I catch up with Ho—"

"Why did his team let him do this?" Annie asked.

"You ought to know. Anyone who didn't want to help was probably too scared to stand up to him."

Zoheret stroked Kagami's hand. Anoki and Willem had been with Ho. She looked up at Gowon. "Why didn't you send someone for help?"

"We were going to. But they wouldn't let us." He waved a hand at the injured. "They made us promise to finish the

Competition, even if we can't win now. Kagami said we had to show we could do it. We've been taking turns with the stretchers."

Zoheret gazed at her injured roommate, then at Manuel, who was fidgeting. She turned back to Gowon. "Come on. We'll help you carry them."

"Wait a minute," Manuel said. "We can still win, you know. They can get there by themselves, and we can tell Ship to get a cart ready to take them to the infirmary."

Something snapped inside Zoheret. "You go ahead and do that," she shouted. "But I'm going to help them. We don't have our time recorded until we're all through, so you just go ahead, because you'll have to wait for me anyway."

"I'll help, too," Annie said. A few others murmured in agreement.

"I'll help, too," Gervais said. He faced Manuel. "If we all help, we can move them more quickly. If winning means leaving them behind, I don't want to win."

Manuel gave in. Zoheret helped Gervais lift Kagami's stretcher; Robert and Jorge held its sides. She rested the poles against her shoulders. Manuel stepped back into the shade of the trees, took the map from his pocket, and tore it into little pieces, scattering the white flakes.

They reached their goal by dark. Gowon and another boy had gone on ahead; a medicart with four cots was waiting at the door. The young people put the four stretchers on the cots; Jennifer climbed in after them. The cart rolled down the corridor.

Zoheret glanced at Manuel. He looked away quickly. "Remember," Ship said, "no talking to other teams about your journey until Competition is over. You will only give them an advantage if you impart your experience. The Black team is already in the Hollow; the Yellow team will leave tomorrow, and the Green and Violet teams are scheduled to follow. I trust that you have all learned something."

Few seemed to be listening; most were already wandering toward the tubeways that would take them to their rooms.

5

Zoheret, with her room to herself, had slept restlessly. She had assumed that she would fall asleep right away after washing up, but the silence of the room and the ache in her muscles had kept her awake and given her too much time to think.

She remembered walking with Manuel across the plain. He had smiled at her then, delicate lips curving over white teeth. He had never shared the awkwardness of other boys, had never seemed insecure. He had turned away from her in the corridor as his shoulders seemed to shrug her away.

She ate breakfast in her room and then went to the infirmary. Kagami was sitting up when Zoheret entered the room, her back supported by the raised bed. A long white curtain separated her part of the room from the beds near her. Federico, his head bandaged, was sleeping.

"How are you?" Zoheret asked as she came to Kagami's side.

"All right. It still hurts a little when I breathe too deeply. Ship gave me more injections this morning—the bones will regenerate and heal quickly now. Karl's lucky—he got to go back to his room because he only has a sprain. So did Jen."

"Where's Brendan?"

"In the treatment room. He'll be all right." Kagami lowered her voice. "Federico has a skull fracture. He'll heal, but he could have problems later on. Head injuries sometimes have long-term effects—he might have headaches for a while."

"Is that what Ship said?" Zoheret pulled a chair to the bedside and sat down.

"Ship doesn't have to say it. I know. I'll have lots of time to learn about medicine while I'm here."

"I brought you something." Zoheret held out a small box.

"My charcoal pencils." Kagami smiled. "Ship'll get me paper." The smile faded. "Have you seen Ho anywhere?"

Zoheret shook her head.

"He'd better hide if he knows what's good for him. I heard Gowon and a couple of other kids are looking for him. You know what Ship said? It said it was proud of us, proud that we finished the Competition. Thanks for helping—I know it slowed you down."

"It doesn't matter." Zoheret saw that Anoki had entered the infirmary. She was surprised, knowing how much he disliked the place after his own long stay. He glanced at Federico, then came over to Kagami's bed.

Kagami stared at him impassively; her mouth tightened. Anoki bowed his head. "I'm sorry about what happened."

"You were on Ho's team," the injured girl said slowly.

"I know. I tried to talk him out of it. But a lot of the others went along with him, and all I could do was just refuse to help. He said no one would really get hurt."

"You should have known that wasn't true."

"There wasn't anything I could do about it. I told Ship—it didn't say anything." His black hair hung over his brow, hiding his eyes. "Willem sure cooperated. He didn't know any better, it was all a game to him. He'd do what Ho said, and Ho was telling him what a fine fellow he was and laughing at him at the same time. It made me sick."

"You might lose anyway," Zoheret said. "Your team must have used up a lot of time doing all that stuff."

Anoki shook his head. "Not really. We never stopped to rest, or to eat, and we didn't sleep long. He had us marching along in the dark while he and some others blasted away at anything that moved. Manuel was the one he really wanted to beat—somehow he knew which route Blue would take. He didn't know Red was going to go that way, too."

Kagami sighed, holding her ribs as she did so. "Those two. When they fight about something, they're crazy. I just hope one of them gives up before they start dragging the rest of us into their fights."

Zoheret said, "I thought they were friends. At least I always thought they were before." She wanted to say that Manuel wasn't like Ho, but she did not know that; it was only something that she wanted to believe.

"They were never real friends." Kagami adjusted her pillow. "Sometimes I think they hang around together because each one is afraid to let the other out of his sight. They're always daring each other into things. I used to run into Ho a lot in the library when we were younger."

Zoheret raised her eyebrows. "You never told me that," she said. Anoki lowered himself into a chair.

"It isn't what you think. We'd talk about our parents. We

were both kind of interested in the history of their part of Earth, so we'd study it and talk about it. Ship was helping us learn some Japanese—that was my parents' language." Kagami folded her hands. "Ho's parents were from the southeast part of the Asian continent—that great big land mass. Their country and Japan were part of a group called the New Co-prosperity Association."

"Ship told us about that in history lessons," Anoki said.

"I know. But what it didn't go into very much was how much some of the members hated the Japanese. Japan really ran the Association, it seems. After a while, Ho said he didn't care about studying Japanese, and I didn't see him much anymore. It was like he took it personally."

Anoki lifted his head. "I can understand his feelings. Look at my ancestors—they were practically wiped out before the resource crisis began. That was the only thing that saved them—everyone else in North America was too busy fighting to worry about Indians, and by the time they formed new nations, we had a nation of our own."

"Nations," Zoheret said, exasperated. "That was Earth. Who cares about it now? It makes me wonder how they ever agreed on the Project. Sometimes I wish Ship hadn't told us anything about it. What good is knowing all that going to do us?"

"You might be right," Kagami said. "Anyway, Ho used to talk about Manuel sometimes. He was always competing with him—who was stronger, who was smarter, who was better at everything."

"Who was meaner, who was more stupid," Anoki muttered. "They're probably tied on those things."

Kagami yawned and then moaned a little, holding her side. "You're tired," Zoheret said. Kagami nodded. "We'll come back later."

They stopped at the door to Anoki's room. As Zoheret entered, a small black cat leaped onto Anoki's bed. The boy sat down and scratched it behind the ears. The cat began to purr.

Anoki's side of the room was a workshop. Bits of equipment—wires, circuits, boards, and tools—lay on a wooden table and hung from shelves on the wall. Two models of gliders dangled from the ceiling. Zoheret sniffed; the room, as usual, smelled a little of ammonia.

She sat down while Anoki crooned to the cat. "I don't know what to do with Mimsy when we start living in the Hollow," the boy said.

"She'll be all right there. Roxana'll bring her cat, and Serena's probably going to take that big dog of hers."

"Mimsy hates that dog." The cat jumped off the bed and scratched in the box under it. "How'd your team do?"

"Better than Red," she said accusingly. "We got across the river, no thanks to you."

"You're in a wonderful mood." Anoki bit his lip, as if trying to make a decision. He suddenly reached for her. She sat still, then pulled her head away abruptly as his lips brushed hers.

She jumped up. "What's the matter with you? What did you do that for?"

"Why do you think?"

"I don't know." Embarrassed, she looked away from him.

"I thought you had some feelings for me."

"I do."

"Then why'd you pull away?"

She raised her eyes. His coppery face was stony; his high cheekbones and strong chin made him look harsh. "Listen, Anoki. I like you. You're my friend."

"I see. Your friend, and that's all." His eyes were cold. "You never even noticed. You couldn't see how I felt. You pity me. I'm not supposed to be like other boys."

"That isn't what I meant. It's just . . ." She gestured helplessly with her hands. "I like you. It isn't that. It's just that I always got along with you because I knew you wouldn't act the way some of the other boys do sometimes. You know. We could always be the way we were when we were little kids."

"All right, Zoheret. I'm sorry. It won't happen again, I promise. I don't want you to feel uncomfortable or anything. I made a mistake, that's all."

"Anoki," she began, but there was little to say. "I'll see you at supper. All right?"

"Sure."

She left him sitting with his cat.

The Competition was over.

Everyone had gathered in the dining room to hear the results. The injured young people sat in the front. Federico still wore a crown of bandages; Brendan sat in a wheelchair, his leg enclosed in a cast. A few other people had sustained injuries, mostly sprains and bruises. Zoheret sat next to Kagami, with Lillka on her other side.

The teams were beginning to gather in groups. Lillka got up and went to join her team, the Black; Zoheret went to hers, shying away as she brushed against bodies. Almost everyone wore a scarf with a team's color. Manuel glanced at Zoheret as she sat on the edge of a table, then turned away.

The room grew quiet. Even before she looked, Zoheret knew that Ho had entered the room. He stood in the doorway for a moment, fingers touching his brown scarf, then went to his team. Someone hissed. Ho smiled slightly. She wondered where he had been hiding.

"I know," Ship began in its alto voice, "that you are all anxious to hear the results of the Competition." The room was still. "I'll start with last place. That goes to the Red team, with sixty-one hours and forty-one minutes." Zoheret heard sighs and groans from the front of the room; that had been expected. "But I want to add that the Red team deserves a commendation for finishing the course against great odds. You should be proud." There were a few desultory cheers.

"Sixth place goes to the Green team, who made it in forty-nine hours and three minutes. The Green team was cautious, as I discovered in talking with its members, but they deserve credit for coming through without a single major or minor injury." The Greens groaned and grumbled.

"Fifth place goes to the Violet team, with a time of forty hours and fifty minutes." Zoheret stared at Manuel's back. He was leaning forward, his muscles straining under his thin shirt. If they won, perhaps he would stop being angry with her.

Lillka's team, the Black, won fourth place; the Yellow took third. Zoheret held her breath. Dmitri and Jorge were eyeing Ho.

"Second place goes to the Blue team," Ship said. The room erupted with cries and a chorus of boos so loud that their time was inaudible. Ship was commending their ingenuity; Manuel shook his head. Ho jumped up on a table and waved his arms, bringing on more hisses.

"The Brown team has won," Ship said over an ebb in the protest. Voices drowned out their time as well.

"Hey!" Dmitri shouted above the noise. He raised his eyes to the ceiling. "You know what happened. You know what the Brown team did to win. They should be disqualified." There was a chorus of agreement.

"The Competition is over," Ship said. "Your party will be

held here tomorrow, as always, and you will have the day to yourselves. Have a good time."

Several young people had already left the room. Willem, who had been standing just behind Ho, grinned and put his hand on Ho's shoulder. Ho shook the hand away, glaring contemptuously at the other boy.

Zoheret waited. Perhaps Manuel would ask her to come to the party with him after all. He stood up, then turned and caught her eye. She tried to smile. He was walking toward her, pushing past others. As he came up to her, he said, "We could have won if we hadn't stopped to help Red."

"No—they were too far ahead."

"It might have been close. We might have had a chance."

"Second place isn't so bad."

"It isn't winning." He gazed past her. Then he turned, muttering something to Jorge. The two boys walked toward Ho.

Ho, surrounded by a small group of people, was accepting congratulations. Anyone who held a grudge, Zoheret knew, was unlikely to take it up with Ho while he was with friends. She saw that Bonnie was with him. Bonnie pulled nervously at her yellow scarf as Manuel and Jorge made their way to the victor. She took Ho's arm. Manuel watched her without expression as he extended his hand to the other boy.

"I'm not going to that party." Zoheret turned toward the voice and saw Lillka.

"I probably won't, either," Zoheret replied.

"It's disgusting how that team won. I can't believe Ship just let it go."

"Ship's stuck. It said no rules."

"I know one thing. You can't trust Ho. He'll do anything."

"I think we knew that already."

Lillka walked toward the door.

Zoheret looked around for Manuel, still hoping, but could not find him. The room was almost empty. She walked into the hall and stared for a moment at Halim al-Haq's portrait; his eyes seemed to follow her.

She felt closed in; the corridor suddenly seemed too small, too constricting. She hurried down the hall toward the Hollow, and then spotted Jennifer; the other girl was moving slowly, head bobbing. Zoheret caught up with her. "Where are you going?"

"The Hollow."

"I'm going there, too. Want company?"

"I don't care," Jennifer sputtered.

"Are you sure you can walk that far?"

"My ankle's all right now."

They continued in silence. The corridor was still; the voices of the others receded. Jennifer's head, as usual, trembled slightly; her face was stony.

They came to the Hollow; the door slid open. It was dark; Zoheret squinted as her eyes adjusted to the dim light. "Be careful," Ship murmured.

Jennifer sat down. Zoheret stretched out on her back. A bird chirped above and was answered by the howl of a distant wolf.

"We lost," Jennifer said softly, "because of me."

Zoheret rolled over and rested on one elbow. "You did fine. Even Manuel said so." His name caught in her throat. "We might have won if we hadn't helped Red, but I doubt it. You kept up."

"It isn't that. We lost because I told Ho our route."

Zoheret sat up. So it hadn't been Gervais after all. "I thought someone told him, but I never guessed it was you."

"Not so loud. Ship might hear." Jennifer mumbled something else that Zoheret could not make out, then said, "He scared me. He said he could really hurt me and not leave marks."

"It's not your fault."

"I was in one of the tunnels just outside the corridors. I used to go there when I was little, just to be alone—I had my own secret place under a tarp, by some girders. Ho must have followed me. He started slapping me around. He didn't even do that much, but I knew he would, so I told him. I shouldn't have gone where Ship doesn't have sensors, and it wouldn't have happened."

"It doesn't matter."

"He knew I couldn't fight back. And now he knows I'm afraid of him. He said it didn't matter, no one would know I told him. He couldn't even tell his team. But I knew." Jennifer was slurring her words more than usual, and Zoheret had to concentrate to understand them. "Don't tell the others. Manuel didn't want me on the team, and he was right."

"I won't tell. I promise."

"I know you won't. You don't go around talking. That's why I told you. I had to tell somebody."

"You should have told Ship. It would have disqualified him."

"Sure. And Ho really would have fixed me then."

"Don't blame yourself, Jen. Ho's just—"

"Ship said his team won. That's like saying everything he did is all right."

Ship does think it's all right, Zoheret thought. That's what it wants us to learn, that we have to survive and that means doing whatever we have to do. No rules, no fair play. You look out for yourself, and if somebody gets in the way, too bad. Ship should have been clearer about that during all the years it had taught them.

"Jen, we'd better go back."

"Go ahead."

"I won't leave without you." Zoheret got up and waited. At last the other girl stood. "Just forget it. A lot of people would have done the same thing you did." Not me, she thought. I wouldn't have given in.

Jennifer did not respond.

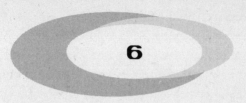

6

Zoheret studied herself in the mirror and brushed back a lock of straight black hair, then smoothed her pink shirt and pulled at her white pants. She had spent part of the day in her room, glancing at the screen, imagining that Manuel would call. She had gone swimming later, hoping she would see him in the gym, and had raced back to her room afterward, thinking he might have left a message. He had not. Then she had called his room. No one had answered; she left no message.

As she walked toward the door, she felt a twinge of guilt about attending the party; Lillka had looked dismayed when she had heard Zoheret was going after all. Well, it was easy for Lillka not to attend; she would rather read in the library no matter what was going on.

She paused in the doorway, adjusting her shirt again. Ship said, "You look fine."

"What would you know about it?" she said harshly. "If I take a shower and comb my hair, I look fine to you."

"Vanity, vanity," Ship chided.

The corridor was empty; she would be one of the late arrivals. She could have asked Anoki to go with her. But she no longer felt at ease with Anoki; she wouldn't have known how to act. She clenched her teeth. Perhaps Anoki, who was proud, would have turned her down. She wished Ho had asked her; that would have gotten to Manuel. She saw herself entering the party while clasping Ho's hand. She sucked in her breath. It would have been worth it, just to see Manuel's reaction; it wouldn't matter what anyone else thought. She was lost in that fantasy until she came to the dining hall.

She shook back her hair and entered. The large room was brightly lit; the walls sang with music as feet pounded the floor. The tables had been pushed to one side and were piled high with various foods and beverages. A circle of young people danced while others stood near the tables, eating.

Zoheret walked toward Kagami, who was wearing yellow. "You look a lot better."

"I am. Can't dance, though—I still hurt a little. Ship told us we could come." She waved at Brendan, who was hobbling past the dancers on his crutches. "Federico said he didn't want to, so I promised I'd bring back some food for him. You can come with me if you want."

"Sure."

"Some other kids said they'd come. Federico's still mad at the Brown team."

"Aren't you?"

Kagami frowned. "I guess I am. But I'm not going to let it ruin my fun. Ho'll get his; the time will come." She rolled the words around in her mouth, as if tasting them. "I saw Lillka earlier. She says you're acting funny. Is something wrong?"

"No."

"There's Lars." Kagami went toward the boy. Zoheret made her way to the tables and picked up an egg roll. Ho and Bonnie were in one corner, holding hands while they tapped their feet to the music. Manuel was with the circle of dancers, swinging one leg as he hopped on the other. Zoheret lowered her eyelids and peered at him through her lashes while forcing herself to swallow her food.

Another piece of music came on, an Arab ballad punctuated by wails. The circle of dancers broke up. Manuel was standing with a red-haired girl named Deanna. He draped an arm around her waist, pulling her closer to him. They walked toward the far end of the tables; he released her, took a plate, and loaded it with food, then offered an orange to Deanna, who blushed and seemed bewildered.

"Hey, Zoheret." Dmitri was next to her, munching on a piece of cake. "This party's dead."

"It hasn't got going yet."

"I've got something in the lab I've been working on. Want to see?"

"Not particularly."

"Oh, come on." He reached for a large bottle of fruit juice, tucking it under one muscular arm. "It's something special. Aren't you curious?"

"Why would I want to go to the lab now?" She glanced at Manuel and Deanna. He was picking food from the plate and feeding it to the girl with his fingers. Zoheret pressed her lips together. "All right. I'll go."

They left the party together. Zoheret hoped that Manuel had seen them but did not look back to find out.

The laboratory was just down the corridor. As they entered,

she saw an apparatus of copper tubing and funnels; beakers filled with a clear, colorless liquid lined the table in front of the blackboard and screen. Dmitri put down the fruit juice and picked up one of the beakers, pulled out the stopper, and poured the liquid into a glass.

"I've been working on this all day." He handed her the glass. "Go on, try it."

She stared at the waterlike substance. "What is it?"

"Drink it and find out."

She sipped and swallowed. The tasteless liquid burned her tongue and throat, making her gag. "Ugh." Her stomach felt warm.

"It's alcohol. I made it myself, from grain."

"I can't believe Ship let you."

"You are long past the point where I can tell you what to do," Ship said. "You'll soon be looking out for yourselves. Dmitri wanted to build his still, and I suppose that it's a potentially useful skill."

Dmitri added some fruit juice to the liquid. "This'll make it go down easier." Zoheret took another cautious sip while Dmitri mixed a glass for himself. "We can have our own party here."

She was beginning to feel a little happier. She emptied the glass and set it down, almost knocking it over. Dmitri refilled it, then raised his glass. "To us. To our team."

"I would advise some moderation," Ship said. "That alcohol is strong."

Zoheret laughed. "To Ship," she said, and drank.

Zoheret lay in bed, pretending to be asleep. Lillka's sheets rustled; her feet slapped against the floor. The door to the bathroom whispered open, then closed.

She opened her eyes, squinting; there was a sharp pain

around her temples and eyes, and she was thirsty. She had been thirsty during the night, barely making it to the bathroom, where she had gulped two glasses of water before vomiting. Now she felt paralyzed, unable to move. She wanted more water, but the bathroom was too far away.

Dmitri might have distilled something poisonous; maybe he hadn't known so much about making liquor as he had pretended. Ship wouldn't have let him do that, she told herself, trying to believe it. Jorge, Serena, and Tonio had joined her and Dmitri in the laboratory, bringing food from the party. She had laughed heartily at something Tonio had said, and vaguely remembered helping Dmitri to his room; her memories were faded images, separated by blank spaces. She winced and closed her eyes.

Lillka came out of the bathroom. Zoheret wanted to ask her to get a glass of water, but then she would have had to explain why. Lillka was humming; her voice came closer. Zoheret pulled her sheet over her face as the room grew lighter.

She moaned. "Tell Ship to dim the lights." A shadow fell across her eyes and then a hand pulled the sheet from her face.

"Zoheret?"

"Don't. I'm tired."

"You must have had fun." Lillka said it as though she disapproved. "I went to the infirmary last night. Kagami was wondering where you were." The room darkened. "Are you sure you're all right?"

"I'm fine. I was in the lab with Dmitri."

"I heard about him and his still. I can't believe you were so stupid."

"Leave me alone." She pulled up her sheet.

Zoheret dozed uneasily for a while. When she woke up

again, Lillka was gone. She sat up, feeling better, though her neck ached and her head still throbbed.

She drank water and took a shower, rubbing her temples as the hot water soothed her head, and was suddenly very hungry. She hurried out of the bathroom. "Ship? May I have some breakfast here?"

"You mean lunch," Ship said. "Yes, you may, but I trust you'll be well enough to have supper in the dining room. I also expect you to join your friends in the laboratory this day. You have a lot of cleaning up to do." Zoheret groaned. A panel near her screen slid open, offering eggs, toast, and milk. She sat down and began to eat. "I hope that you have been chastened by your experience."

"Dmitri must have done something wrong with his still."

"He did not. I saw what he did. If you'd been content with the beer I provided for the party, you wouldn't be ill now. If you'd had one drink, or used moderation, as I advised, you wouldn't have suffered. But I suppose you had to learn it for yourself. Human beings are so unreasonable sometimes. I warned you. You should have listened."

Zoheret pushed the plate and glass away; the tray slid into the wall and the panel closed. She felt depressed. They'd had their last party in this part of Ship, and she'd had a rotten time.

She said, "I'm not ready."

"Not ready for what?"

"To live in the Hollow." She went to her bed and threw herself across it, hiding her face.

"You'd better be ready," Ship said harshly, "because that's where you're going soon. It's the next part of the program."

Zoheret lifted her head. "You'll look out for us, won't you?"

"I shall shut down my sensors once you're settled. I've thought about it, and I think most of you will agree that it's best if I do. If you need my aid, you can always go to the doorway nearest your settlement and request it."

"How can you do that after what happened?"

"What did happen?" Ship was speaking in its alto, but its voice was a bit higher than usual. "Are you talking about the Competition? I thought you all did quite well. There were no deaths and the injured are healing. Every team finished the course. I'm proud of you."

"Ho cheated."

"He did not. He broke no rules. You may not like what he did, but it worked—he won. Life involves trading one thing for another, Zoheret—setting priorities. You have to decide whether or not your goal justifies the means used to achieve it. Ho and his team decided that winning this Competition meant a lot to them. Your team decided that other things, such as helping injured friends, meant more. If you feel you did the right thing, then you should feel satisfied." Ship paused. "Come to the screen. I would like to show you something."

Zoheret reluctantly rose and sat at her screen. She was gazing into black space; pinpricks of light fled from her. Again she marveled at the blackness, the ocean of night; Ship was only a tiny speck in its vastness. Ahead, she saw one star larger than the rest. Five metallic creatures with spidery legs and wide, shiny wings flew out, moving toward the distant star.

"I have sent out my probes," Ship said. "They will study your new home while you prepare for your new life in the Hollow. There is so much to learn, so much to see. One could journey through space forever without encompassing all its wonders."

"Ship?" she said, suddenly afraid, but Ship did not respond.

Part Two

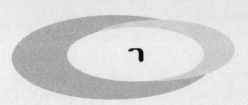

Zoheret closed the last bottle of fruit and handed it to Serena, who put it on the shelf. The large kitchen, even with the screened windows opened, had become hot and oppressive, filled with the heat of wood stoves. She leaned against the long table, wiped her hands on her apron, then wiped her brow with one arm. She looked up at the colorful rows of bottled fruit and canned vegetables and longed for Ship's food dispensers, which Ship had allowed them to use only until they had put up their houses and planted their fields.

There had been protests. Why did they have to give up the dispensers when they would have them to use after they reached their destination? Ship had lectured to them about too much dependence on technology they might not be able to reproduce for generations, and the dangers to those who were too separated from their world. They had dined on a dull diet of venison, chicken, eggs, and edible plants while waiting to harvest what they had grown. But now the storehouse was filling up with food, and Zoheret's pants were growing tighter around her waist.

It was work, feeding themselves: They worked to eat and did not have much time for other pursuits. Most of the things Ship had taught them seemed useless here. Lillka had said that all of human history could be summed up by saying that people worked hard so that they could find ways to keep from having to work.

"You can go, if you want," Gowon said to her and Serena. "I'll clean the pots."

Serena narrowed her eyes; her thin lips tightened, forming lines at either end of her mouth. She tucked a stray curl of short brown hair behind one small ear. "For what? What's the price?"

Gowon thought for a bit. "If you sweep my floor later and mop it."

Serena frowned. "It probably hasn't been mopped since we planted the corn." She glanced at Zoheret.

"All right," Zoheret said quickly, anxious to leave the stuffy kitchen. Serena nodded. "It's a deal, as long as we can do it tomorrow."

"Agreed."

Serena tore off her apron and fled. Zoheret left more slowly, ambling out through the storeroom with its shelves of lanterns and bags of grain and flour. A large, heavy door to her left led to the cooler. It had been fourteen days' work to put the cooler together, and Anoki often had to tinker with the small generator that powered it.

She went through the doorway and stood on the porch. They still had no dining hall; people lined up for food and ate in the clearing together or took the food to their shacks. In front of the storehouse, Robert and Miriam were butchering a dead deer. Lillka, sitting by the long, rectangular stone grill, was dickering with Ho. They sat facing each other, legs folded; Ho had brought three wicker baskets filled with fresh fish. Two people were with him, a small, pink-faced girl named Dora and a big-boned, bronze-skinned boy named Vittorio.

Lillka stabbed the air with one finger, obviously hoping to finish the bargaining so that the fish could go into the cooler. Brendan sat with her, wearing a wide-brimmed hat to protect his freckled skin from the light. Lillka turned, consulted with Brendan, then muttered a few words to Ho, who shook his head. Zoheret came down the steps and walked around the group. Lillka would make a good trade for the fish, and the others, realizing that, were happy to let her handle the bargaining.

Ho and a small group had been living by the lake for some time now, having moved there thirty days after they had entered the Hollow. Occasionally they traveled up the river in their boats and fished near the settlement, trading their catch for a few supplies. Zoheret knew that they could have caught their own fish, but it was easier to let Ho do it. When he had first offered to trade with them, Lillka had agreed readily; it was hard to tell if she traded because she wanted the fish or because it was a way to buy Ho off. Ho's group had to spend only a day fishing to acquire supplies worth several days' work; Zoheret sometimes resented that. But she supposed that it was better than having to put up with him here.

They had built their settlement along a bend in the river that ran into the lake. Their fields bordered the plain she had crossed during Competition; ditches dug from the river irrigated the fields. The storehouse was at the end of a wide space that had become their common meeting ground; the grass that had once grown there was being worn away, and now grew only in patches. Two rows of plain wood shacks with screened windows and sloping tile roofs stood on either side of a dirt road that led from the storehouse and meeting ground; gardens were between each shack and its neighbor. Zoheret walked toward her own house, which she shared with Lillka, Kagami, and Annie; it stood at the end of one row, overlooking the river.

The yard between Zoheret's home and the house next to it bloomed with colorful blossoms. Kagami and Bonnie, who lived next door, tended the flowers and grew herbs as well. Zoheret had thought that the two were only making extra work for themselves and had wondered why they didn't grow something more practical. But the herbs added flavor to their food, and enough people wanted the flowers to be willing to trade with the girls for them. Bonnie herself always wore at least one flower in her hair, and others followed the fashion. Zoheret would not see Bonnie until Ho and his friends were gone; the other girl always seemed to find a task which would keep her away from anyplace Ho was likely to be. She had not left the settlement with Ho and had never told anyone why she had not.

Zoheret thought of Manuel. She had not seen him in a long time, though she had once caught a glimpse of him on one of the fishing boats. He rarely came to the settlement with Ho. She looked out at the river. The three boats she had seen out there earlier were gone, having tied up farther downriver to wait for Ho.

She could think about Manuel calmly now, as long as she did not see him. Whenever Ho came here, she would feel both a twinge of disappointment and one of relief whenever Manuel was absent. Their last days in the corridor seemed far away, the problems that had occupied her then unimportant.

Dmitri was standing at the edge of her vegetable garden, staring out at the river. His wavy, dark-brown hair was redder in the daylight. His once-pale skin had become tawny; he could go shirtless now without worrying about burns. Ship did not seem to regulate its light properly; many of them had acquired pink, peeling skin during their first days in the Hollow, and a few fair-skinned people had been sick with fever and pain from the burns.

Dmitri turned and saw her; he motioned to her with one arm. She lingered by her door, then went to his side. He put his arm around her shoulders and pulled her closer.

Here, the river's banks sloped gently. The river narrowed at the bend, then flowed on. Its currents were not as strong here, and it was possible to bathe or swim as long as one kept near the shore.

Zoheret leaned against Dmitri for a moment, then yawned. "I was going to take a nap."

"I guess I tire you out too much at night." He sounded proud of it.

"It isn't that. I've been in the storehouse kitchen all day."

"I thought we could go for a walk. I'm supposed to check the fences around the fields."

"Do you mind if I don't go along?"

He shook his head. "I'll see you later anyway, won't I?"

"Sure," she said wearily, yawning again. He released her and marched off to begin his rounds.

She went inside. The house had only one story, which they had divided into three rooms. The largest room, in the front of the house, was used by all four girls; it was bare except for a makeshift table and five large cushions she and Annie had sewn. A dark, narrow passageway led to the two bedrooms, separating them. Their latrine was at the end of the passage; Anoki had worked on all the latrines, devising, with the help of diagrams from Ship's library and some of their building supplies, a toilet which did not require water and which collected their waste for use as fertilizer in the fields. The drawback was that the latrine stank.

Zoheret entered her room, which was hot and still, and stretched out on her cot, lying on her side. Across the room, Lillka's shelf held a few piles of clothing, a small box filled with books on microdot, and a reader. Lillka had not had much time for reading, having become preoccupied with organizing the settlement.

Lillka had surprised her. She seemed to know what work people would be best at, and tried to give everyone a combination of necessary chores and work that was more enjoyable, though they were free to trade jobs among themselves. Anoki, unable to do a lot of heavy work, did carpentry and tended the robots that had tilled the fields and now weeded them. Brendan hunted and cooked; Annie helped with the sewing; Bonnie supervised the crops. Zoheret, along with Dmitri and several others, was primarily a strong body to be assigned to work where needed.

Occasionally she found herself resenting her old friend, whose air of authority had made her more distant. But Lillka suggested, she did not command; she consulted but did not order. She had no enemies and, because she had read a lot, others assumed she had special knowledge. She was good at settling disputes, did her share of the physical labor, and thus avoided bad feeling. She complained about not having more time to herself, but that complaint contradicted her self-satisfaction. When the settlement had voted to call her leader, she had tried to refuse, but had been forced to accept; she was the leader anyway.

Lillka was lucky. She had found something she excelled at, which put her a step ahead of Zoheret.

She rolled over onto her stomach. She missed Ship, missed talking to it and just knowing it was there. She longed for her room, her comfortable bed, even for the lessons she had disliked studying before. The sound of distant voices reached her through her window. Someone laughed, and she heard a splash and then a shriek. She buried her face in her arms.

The candle flame flickered, lighting the low table next to Dmitri's cot, bathing his face in a soft, golden glow. Zoheret stretched an arm across Dmitri's bare chest and reached for the bottle next to the candle. She sipped and put the bottle down.

Dmitri stirred and opened his eyes. "I only have one big bottle left," he said. "Lillka thinks I've been getting out of too many chores by trading liquor to people, but I've been making up for that, so maybe she'll change her mind. She wants to limit the supply anyway, so we don't get too used to it."

Zoheret lay on her back. The cot was narrow; her shoulder was pressing against the wall. "Nobody drinks much anyway. It only takes getting sick once to learn."

"Yeah. But people can get used to drinking more. You did. You don't even want juice with it. You can really put it away."

"No, I don't."

"You do, Zoheret." He reached for her hand and held it. "Almost every time you stay with me, you do. Am I so bad that you have to have something else help you along?"

"It isn't that." It did make it easier for her. She could forget that she did not have the strong, dizzying feeling for Dmitri that she had once had for Manuel.

She had begun to spend time with Dmitri after the night of the party. Soon everyone had been treating them as a couple. It had been better than being alone and had made her transition to life in the Hollow simpler. She had also felt some satisfaction in thinking that Manuel might have noticed, before realizing that he was probably indifferent to her actions.

She did not love Dmitri and was sure that he did not love her. They had managed at last to overcome their aversion to close physical contact, though she often had to remind herself not to shy away from him, and Dmitri sometimes seemed nervous when he touched her. She liked him, but her warmer feeling for him had faded; he told her that he needed her, whatever that meant. That was what it came down to—need and habit. For a few moments, at least, she could lose herself while making love to him.

It isn't supposed to be like this, she thought. She had even learned to enjoy the lovemaking, which at first she had endured only for the sake of his companionship; love hadn't even been necessary. Often she felt more caring of Dmitri when they were in a group than when they were alone. They smiled at each other, or held hands gingerly, because that was what others expected. She wished that she had waited, wondering if Dmitri would still have been her friend if she had.

She swallowed and trembled slightly, then took a breath and closed her eyes as tightly as she could.

"You're not going to cry, are you?"

"No," she managed to say.

"I can't stand it when you cry."

"I don't cry much."

"You didn't used to. You'd get mad instead. I liked that more."

You made me weaker, she wanted to say. She lay very still, letting him hold her until she was in control of herself.

"I get impatient, waiting for night," he went on, "and then

I have to work hard so I don't have time to think about it. Remember when we were down by the river, and you kept thinking someone was going to see us?"

"Is that all it is for you?" she said harshly as she sat up, almost pushing him off the cot. "You can do that with anybody. Why me?"

He folded his arms under his head. "What's the matter with you?"

"You just need a girl. Anyone would do."

"What are you talking about? I'm here, aren't I? What do you want, anyway?"

"I don't know."

"Well, if you don't know, how do you expect me to?"

She supposed that if Dmitri got mad enough, he might not want to see her anymore. Why should that disturb her so much? She had been by herself before, and she had been happy enough then. She hadn't had to pretend or conceal part of herself. She had not been as dependent.

"It's nothing," she said at last. "It's just a mood. I'm fine." That was becoming a habit, too, keeping her thoughts to herself when she was sure Dmitri would not understand. "I have to go."

"You can stay. Sleep in Tonio's bed—he's going to be gone all night anyway."

"No, I really have to go. Serena and I have to clean Gowon's floor tomorrow, and I'll have to get up very early if I'm going to have time to do it." She swung her legs over him and stood up. "Good night, Dmitri."

"Good night." He yawned. She kissed him on the forehead and left the shack, almost tripping over a pair of boots in the doorway.

As she pulled on her shoes, she noticed that it was even

darker than usual. There was a pattern to the Hollow's nights; for fourteen days, they would grow progressively lighter, until it was possible to find one's way about in the silvery glow. During the following fourteen days, the light would fade, until it was dark again. Lillka had been keeping track of time with the night cycle, and the custom was spreading; others now spoke of "light to light" and "light to dark." They had been living in the Hollow for almost eight cycles.

Zoheret, waiting for her eyes to adjust, welcomed the darkness. The settlement, and everything in it, had vanished behind a dark curtain; she would create it anew as she wanted it to be. The few lanterns lighting the way between the rows of shacks shone through the curtain, then dispelled it; to her left, the large square storehouse seemed to loom, blacker than the night. She decided to borrow a lantern.

Anoki had built the storehouse's steps. Why hadn't she turned to him when she had had the chance? At least she had known he cared, and she would not have had to hide her thoughts from him; in time, her feelings might have grown. Was it that he was too familiar, that she had always placed him in the category of friend and former childhood play-mate? Or was it his physical shortcomings? He had guessed that reason even when she had denied it, shaming her.

As she climbed the steps, she heard a thump inside the storehouse, then a scrape. She hurried to the doorway, wondering who else was up so late. "Who's there?" she said softly. "Come on, don't try to scare me." She walked inside, trying to recall which shelf the lanterns were on. The room was completely dark.

Fingers clutched her wrists, pulling her forward. She opened her mouth and a hand slapped over her lips, cutting off her cry. She kicked, hitting a leg. Something hard struck the side of her head, and bright specks of light danced before her eyes; then she was thrown against a wall. She was stunned, unable to move. Someone tied her hands behind her; a piece of cloth was stuffed into her mouth and secured with a scarf.

She lay very still, wondering distantly what would happen to her. Her head was beginning to throb. Very slowly, she turned her head so that she was facing the door.

"She's out," a voice whispered.

"Are you sure?"

"Yeah."

"Let's go."

A pocket light shone for a moment, just long enough for her to see a head of curly dark hair on a figure bending over a sack of flour. Two other people ran out of the storehouse with baskets. The light went out; footsteps padded across the floor, receding.

She waited, trying to come to her senses, then sat up. The room spun. She worked at her bonds furiously, at last tearing them from her wrists; they hadn't tied her very well. Untying the scarf, she spat out the piece of cloth.

She rose and stumbled dizzily to the door, then hurried toward the bell on the porch and rang it, pulling the cord again and again. Lights swam through the darkness toward her until a crowd had gathered and the area before her was illuminated. Dmitri ran toward her, bounding up the steps to her side.

"Are you all right?"

She tried to nod; her head hurt. Lillka hurried to the porch. "What happened?"

"Thieves," Zoheret answered. "They were stealing from the storehouse. They hit me and tied me up."

"Who was it?" somebody below shouted.

"I only saw one of them clearly." She closed her eyes for a

moment before saying the name. "Manuel. Manuel was one of them."

Lillka had called for a meeting at midday. After lunch, everyone gathered in front of the storehouse. Zoheret, still eating the bread and goat's cheese she had carried from the kitchen, sat with her back against the stone grill, listening to indistinct but angry muttering.

She had heard plenty of wild talk earlier while finishing her chores. While she and Serena had been mopping Gowon's floor, he and his housemates had been working in their garden, talking of reprisals. They outnumbered Ho's group, didn't they? Why not go and take what was theirs and teach the thieves a lesson in the process? They had grown impatient with Lillka, who had asked everyone to wait until the issue had been discussed and who had dissuaded one group from going after the raiders immediately. Gowon had questioned Lillka's authority, and one of his friends had said that it was time for someone stronger to be in charge. Serena, overhearing the conversation as she mopped, had nodded, her elfin face turning grim. Zoheret did not know if Ho had been with the thieves, but she found it hard to believe that he hadn't planned the raid.

Lillka, along with Kagami and Brendan, came out the storehouse's door. She raised a hand for silence while her two companions stood to one side. Dmitri, arriving late, wound his way past those who were seated and sat down next to Zoheret. He had cared for her during the night, putting cold cloths on her bump and insisting that she stay in Tonio's bed.

"We know what was taken," Lillka said, speaking clearly so that everyone could hear. "We've lost a bag of flour, three dead chickens, five bottles of fruit, six bottles of tomatoes, and some dried meat. In other words, we didn't lose that much, and shouldn't have shortages. They might have taken more if Zoheret hadn't surprised them."

Tonio jumped to his feet, Gowon at his side. "Are you just going to let them keep it?" Tonio shouted.

Lillka raised both hands. "I didn't say that. I know we have to do something. We can post a guard in front of the store-house and by the fields, but we have to let the other group know that they can't do this and get away with it."

"But they've gotten away with it," Tonio said, shaking back his long, dark-brown hair. "We should have gone after them last night."

"In the dark? When they might have set a trap for anyone who followed? When they were probably halfway back to the lake in their boats? We don't even know if the whole group is responsible—maybe a few did this on their own."

"You don't believe that," Gowon said.

"I don't know what to believe."

"Well, what are we going to do about it?" Serena called out. Her dog, a setter, sat up and barked.

Lillka held out her hands. "I think the only thing we can do is send a group to talk to them." The suggestion brought groans. "We can ask them to return what they took, and warn them that we're posting guards. They won't get away with it again."

"And what if they do try again?" Tonio asked.

Lillka seemed at a loss. "We can round them up," Serena said. "We could force them to work for us, and tie them up the rest of the time. They'd be sorry." Several people clapped and whistled their approval.

"All right, all right," Lillka shouted back, trying to regain control of the meeting. "We'll send out a delegation tomor-row, make our request, and give them a warning. If they re-fuse to cooperate, we can take action—they know there are more of us. But don't get into a battle with them. We'll try to figure out who we can spare for the trip. Right now, just try to get as much work done as you can today."

The meeting broke up with murmurs of discontent. Dmitri patted Zoheret's shoulder and left. She waited until the crowd had thinned out, then went to Lillka.

Brendan was speaking to her; Lillka shook her head violently. The blond girl's face had broken out in red blotches; she glared at Zoheret as she approached. "Don't you have work to do?"

Zoheret nodded. "I'll get it done." Kagami passed her on the steps and hurried away. "I want to go with the delegation."

Lillka said, "We'll see."

"I have a right to go. I caught them, and they could have hurt me badly. You can get along without me for a little while."

"Ask Brendan. Maybe he should decide." Brendan gazed at Zoheret with his pale blue eyes and shrugged; his freckled jaw tightened. "It's my fault in a way," Lillka went on. "Someone else can be the leader after this. I'm tired of trying."

"What are you talking about?"

"It happened once before," Lillka said in a low voice. "Brendan knows. I didn't tell anyone else. The last time Ho was here to trade, I checked our supplies the day after, and we were short some flour and vegetables. At first, I thought I'd made a mistake, so I got a lot more organized with my record keeping. I thought someone here might have taken the stuff and forgotten to mention it, so I asked around, but nothing turned up. Then I told Brendan."

"I thought Ho might have taken it." The boy took off his hat and scratched at his sandy hair. "But I wasn't sure, and it was too late to do much about it by then."

"It's my fault," Lillka said. "I should have had the storehouse guarded after that, but I kept thinking it wouldn't happen again, that maybe Ho just needed a few extra things that one time. And I was afraid of getting everyone worked up about it if I told them."

"Why did they do it?" Brendan asked. "It doesn't make any sense. They could have borrowed from us and paid us back with more fish later. They must have known we'd find out eventually."

"Maybe not." Lillka shook her head. "They got away with it once. If Zoheret hadn't been there, we would have had another mystery, that's all. Why trade or borrow when you can get something for nothing?"

"We'll go and talk to them," Zoheret said. "They're not going to lose their whole trade in fish for a few vegetables and some flour. It'd be stupid."

Lillka sighed. "I hope you're right."

8

*T*onio held up an arm. "Wait."

The lake was still and glassy. The midday light above was hazy; fingers of water lapped at the shore. On a rise several paces from the lake's edge, five log cabins sat on cleared land. A wide ditch formed a semicircle around the cabins, as though someone had begun to dig a moat, then abandoned it. A stone fireplace in front of the cabins held charred, blackened pieces of wood.

"Do you think they're hiding?" Zoheret whispered.

"They might be. They might be waiting to see how many of us there are. They could have set a trap."

Bonnie edged closer to Tonio. "Their boats aren't here. Either they're gone, or they took the boats away and sneaked back. We should send in just a few people while the others wait here."

Tonio glanced at Bonnie with narrowed eyes. "We can figure out what to do without your advice." Bonnie stepped back. Her green eyes were hidden by the shade under the trees, and Zoheret could not read her face. Tonio had been needling the girl since early morning.

"Five of us will go in," Tonio went on. "The rest of you wait." The others huddled closer in order to hear him. "If anyone comes out and looks threatening, fire." He slapped the stun gun at his waist. "There's only twenty of them, so that shouldn't be hard."

Zoheret wanted to object, but Tonio was already pointing to those who would accompany him. He grabbed Bonnie by the arm. "You, too. You can go in first. You were their friend—and a real good friend from what I heard."

Bonnie stared back at him impassively, then shook his hand away. She had cut her long, flowing locks before coming to live in the Hollow, and her light-brown hair now curled around her ears and over her forehead; she wore a crown of daisies. She left the shelter of the trees, marching forward as though she had nothing to fear. Tonio followed, leading Helena, Muhammad, and Julius. The blond Helena towered over the two dark-haired boys; she took long strides while Muhammad and Julius scampered. The three, always anxious to get out of extra work, had willingly volunteered for the trip.

Zoheret waited with the others. Robert seemed nervous; he pulled at his red hair and chewed on his lower lip. Federico's tanned, chiseled features were grim. He had been complaining of headaches ever since his injury; she wondered if he had one now. Serena and Cho Lin had their hands at their waists, near their guns.

Tonio picked up a stick and stirred the ashes in the fireplace while the others searched the cabins, disappearing inside for a few moments and then emerging, shaking their heads. Helena walked around the settlement, peering at the trees beyond the clearing. The land around the rise was barren, the brush cleared away.

"Hello," Tonio shouted. "Come on out. If you give back what you took, or trade for it, we can come to an agreement." Bonnie came toward him; he pushed her away. "Come out."

He waited, then signaled to Zoheret. She came out with the others, keeping her hand on her gun. "I don't think they're anywhere around here," Bonnie said.

"There's nothing in the cabins except cots," Muhammad muttered as he approached. His scowl made his round cheeks chubbier than usual. "They could be anywhere. Maybe they knew we were coming."

Tonio's wide mouth became a thin, pale line; his cheeks grew red. "The fireplace is cold," he said. "They might be on the other side of the Hollow for all we know." He glanced overhead at the distant land beyond the thickening clouds. "They got to the storehouse, and then they got away. Maybe they had help. Maybe one of us helped them all along." He faced Bonnie.

She backed away. He raised an arm and struck her, knocking the circlet of daisies from her hair. Bonnie raised her hands; Helena slapped them down. Tonio hit her again, then punched her in the abdomen; Bonnie doubled over as Helena kicked her with one long, muscular leg.

"Leave her alone," Zoheret cried, moving in front of the girl. She looked up at Helena's hazel eyes; the taller girl glared back, her full lips pursed.

"I always wondered why she stayed with us," Helena said. "Now I know. I'll bet she's stolen plenty for them, a little here, a little there—who would notice?"

"It isn't true," Bonnie moaned.

"Prove it," Muhammad shouted.

"Ask Lillka," Zoheret said. "She keeps records. She'd know if one jar were missing. Bonnie hasn't done anything. And if she had, I'd know—I live right next to her house."

"So what?" Helena responded. Zoheret put an arm around Bonnie, who was shaking. "Maybe you're in it together. You were the one who said you saw the thieves. But they didn't really hurt you, and you didn't sound the alarm until they got away. So how do we know it wasn't some kind of plan?"

"You're crazy," Zoheret said. "If I'd been helping them, I wouldn't have sounded the alarm at all. And I wouldn't have said who they were." She looked from one angry face to another. Deprived of a confrontation with Ho's group, she realized, they would take out their anger on someone else.

"Why aren't they here?" Tonio asked her.

"They're probably out hunting or fishing. And if they thought we might show up, they'd take everything with them."

Tonio spun around and ran toward the nearest cabin, picking up a large stick before he walked inside. The others waited.

Zoheret drew Bonnie away from the group. "Are you all right?" Bonnie nodded; her green eyes glistened. "I know you didn't help them."

"Are you so sure?"

"Of course." Zoheret fought off her doubts.

Tonio came out of the cabin; he threw back his head and crowed. Smoke curled from the side window, becoming a pale cloud and then a streamer.

Federico cheered. He ran toward another cabin, pulling out a pack of matches. "Light the cots," Tonio shouted. "They're stuffed with dry grass." Others raced toward the remaining cabins. The space behind the doorway of the nearest cabin flickered and then glowed.

"What are you doing?" Zoheret shouted. "Do you want to burn down the forest, too?" She hurried toward Tonio. "This isn't why we came here."

Tonio grinned. "They're going to pay for what they took, one way or another. And the wind's blowing toward the lake. The fire won't get out of the clearing."

Zoheret stared past him at the cabins. As flames licked at one doorway, the group cheered. Helena and Cho Lin danced; Helena kicked up her legs while Cho Lin's long black braid slapped her back. Muhammad and Federico linked arms and beat the ground with their feet. Zoheret watched the burning buildings, glancing toward the trees beyond the clearing while hoping the wind would not change direction. The air was thick with the smell of burning wood.

The flames were beginning to die. Zoheret stood at the edge of the clearing with Bonnie. The wind blew toward the lake in gusts. Whitecaps had formed on the dark-gray water; thick slate-colored clouds had formed overhead. The rest of the group sat by the fireplace, giggling as one cabin, a charred cube of wood, collapsed.

The wildness had almost infected her. The light of the fire had flickered over the faces of the dancing young people until it seemed that they too were aflame. Now the fire was burning out. Tonio thrust a stick into the fireplace, stirring the ashes aimlessly.

The rain came quickly. Thunder slapped Zoheret's ears; the rain fell in sheets, driving them all under the trees. As Tonio raced by, he pushed Bonnie out of the way.

Zoheret grabbed his arm. "What are you going to tell Lillka?"

"What we did. Ho and his crowd won't steal anything again." Water dripped from his long brown hair. "Do you really think Ho would have bargained with us?"

"We could have left him a message."

"I thought that's what we just did." He looked at Bonnie. "Your friends'll be sorry."

The others hurried up the hillside, disappearing in the darkness under the trees. Tonio ran after them. Bonnie huddled against a trunk, her head down. Zoheret said, "We have to go back."

"I won't go."

"You can't stay here."

"Why can't I?" Bonnie raised her head; her hair, darkened by the rain, was plastered against her brow and neck. "They don't want me back there."

. "Bonnie, please."

"You go. I won't move. I'm not going back."

"Then I'm staying. I won't leave you here alone."

Bonnie looked at her wildly, then began to cry. Zoheret took a step toward her, wanting to console the girl. Bonnie's shoulders shook; her face was wet with tears and rain. "It isn't true. I didn't help Ho and I didn't help the thieves."

"I believe you. Will you come back with me?"

Bonnie nodded. They climbed the hill. The rain fell more slowly, trickling down Zoheret's neck.

"I tried to talk Ho out of leaving the settlement," Bonnie said. "I told him it would divide us, that we should stick together. I was right. Look what happened."

"So you decided not to go with him because of that?"

"No." Bonnie pushed a low tree branch out of the way and waited until Zoheret had passed. "I didn't want to be with him anymore." She walked at Zoheret's side. "When he left,

I was glad, even though I thought he was making a mistake. And Manuel left with him. It meant I could start over. I was wrong about that, too."

"You left Manuel for Ho, didn't you?" Zoheret tried not to sound too curious.

"Is that the story? I've heard others, like that they were both sharing me. I didn't leave anybody. Manuel was getting tired of me, and I started seeing Ho, and then Manuel wanted to see me again, so I did, and then he didn't seem to care. He wanted to keep me around while he did what he wanted. So I went back to Ho, because that was the only way I could get back at Manuel. Stupid, isn't it?"

"No."

"It is. Ho got tired of me, too, and I didn't like him that much anyway. So it was all for nothing. I thought I cared about Manuel, but I guess I really didn't. I slept with him just to get it over with."

They circled a bush. "I guess Ho got bored, too," Bonnie went on. "Well, it doesn't matter now."

"Bonnie—" Zoheret started to say.

"I'm glad they burned the cabins."

It had been dark for some time before Zoheret and Bonnie reached the settlement. Lillka and Brendan sat on the storehouse porch; two lanterns hung above the doorway. Two glowing eyes peered out from the shadows by the steps; Dmitri, sitting on one step, reached toward the eyes. Mimsy slunk up the steps, followed by three kittens; she had mated with Roxana's tawny tom and had set up housekeeping under the porch.

Dmitri lifted his head as the two girls came into the light. "I'm hungry," Bonnie said. Brendan got to his feet and went inside.

"Tonio told us what happened," Lillka said. "What took you two so long?"

Bonnie lifted her head. "I didn't want to catch up with them. I didn't want to come back at all. They think I helped Ho. Zoheret talked me into coming back."

"They didn't say anything about that."

"Why should they? It doesn't matter. Zoheret told them not to burn the cabins, but they didn't listen to her."

Brendan came outside and down the steps, handing each girl some cold roast meat wrapped in bread. Bonnie tore at her food while Zoheret nibbled.

"I'm tired," Bonnie said when she was finished. "I'm going to bed." She turned away and walked through the clearing to the road, disappearing into the shadows.

Zoheret sat down next to Dmitri. "I hope you weren't worrying."

"I wasn't." He held her hand for a moment, then let go. Lillka and Brendan came down the steps and sat on the one below them.

The rain had cleansed the air; the night was cool. "I don't know what to do now," Lillka said without turning around. "I don't want to be the leader. Someone else can run things now."

Zoheret said, "I think we ought to talk to Ship."

Lillka turned her head. "No. We have to stick it out."

"Don't talk about sticking it out when you're ready to give up."

Lillka looked away. "I haven't done a good job."

"That isn't the reason. It's because things are getting harder. It was easier before. If you give up, I'll go talk to Ship."

"You can't."

"Try to stop me. And if you resign and call another meeting, I'll ask everyone to vote you in again."

"I'm not so sure they'd make me leader now."

"Lillka, you've got to stay on. Don't you understand? If you try to get out of it now, you'll just be telling everyone that we're losing control. Do you know how discouraging that'll be? And all the disagreements will come out as soon as we try to pick another leader."

"She's right," Brendan muttered.

"If you don't stay on," Zoheret said, "I'll go to Ship. But if you do, I won't, because then I'll know we can settle things. You can give it up later when we've worked things out, if you want, but it isn't fair to resign and hand the mess to someone else." She paused. "You wanted it. I saw the look on your face when you got approval. So you'd better keep the job."

"All right." Lillka sounded defeated.

"I don't know what the problem is," Dmitri said. "Ho's group will know better than to come here now. We don't need his fish—we can learn how to catch them ourselves. They got a good lesson. Maybe Tonio did the right thing."

"We have to live with them, though," Brendan said. "Here, and where we're going. Sooner or later, we have to settle this."

"Just wait." Dmitri got up. "They'll need something from us eventually, and then they'll have to come here, and we can talk." He went down the steps and turned to face them. "And if they don't, too bad. The Hollow's big, and a planet's bigger." He gestured at Lillka. "We'll do all right. I'll talk to Tonio." He left them.

"Are you coming to bed?" Zoheret asked Lillka.

"We can't. We have to guard the storehouse now, remember? It's our turn. Roxana and Lars are patrolling the fields with Serena's dog." She sighed. "I wish we had more dogs. We could use them now."

"Breed Red with that female retriever of Jorge's."

"I think she's already pregnant. But we'd have to train the puppies—Red doesn't know what danger is. He thinks everyone's his friend. I'm scared. This isn't the end of it, Zoheret. I'm afraid something else will happen."

9

Zoheret lay on her cot, a cloth over her brow. Her fever was down and her skin felt damp and clammy. She remembered vomiting during the night until there was nothing left inside her; now her head and abdomen ached.

She heard footsteps at the door. Someone crossed to her side and removed the cloth. Kagami looked down at her. "Are you feeling better?"

"I think so. I stopped retching."

"Do you need another cold cloth?"

"No."

Kagami handed Zoheret a small bottle. "Here, drink some of this. You ought to be able to keep it down by now." Zoheret lifted her head and swallowed; the liquid was thick and sweet.

"That feels better." She handed the bottle back to Kagami. "Did you figure out what I have?"

"It wasn't hard. It's an intestinal virus." Kagami had a small medicanalyser in her room, on which she could run simple tests. "I think it got into some of our food. Bonnie's really sick. Anoki's over it already. Dmitri had a bellyache and then it went away."

"You mean everyone's got it?"

"No, only about thirty people. I've been asking them what they ate yesterday, and then I'll talk to a few who aren't sick, and maybe I can track it down." Kagami sat down on Lillka's cot. "I'll bring you some soup tonight. By tomorrow, you should be well." Kagami sighed. "I think we're going to have to be more careful with how we store our food." She rose.

"Don't go yet."

"I have to make my rounds. I'm leaving this medicine with you. There's a bottle of water under your bed—try not to drink too much of it, though." Kagami left the room.

Zoheret was now sure she was getting better, if only because her worries no longer seemed distant. She thought about the sullen faces she had seen during the past few days and the whispers that were muted when she drew too near the whisperers. Tonio's revenge had made quite an impression; to her surprise, a lot of people had approved of it. There were those who were saying that Tonio should be the leader because he could act. She had overheard enough to know that, and wondered if Lillka knew.

Someone was limping through the front room toward her door. "Who's there?"

"You're awake." It was Anoki's voice. He entered the room. "Feeling better?"

"Yes."

"Good. Kagami said you were really sick."

"I was."

"I got over it fast." He leaned over her for a moment, then retreated. Lillka's cot creaked. "I have the robots clearing another area between the field and the plain for planting."

"Really?"

"Yeah. They break down sometimes. They're just hanging together. I wish I had more components. I have to do a lot of tinkering."

"Well."

An awkward silence fell. She tried to think of something to say. She had missed his company; she could never be as easy with Dmitri as she had once been with Anoki, and the thought brought her pain. "How's Willem?" she said at last.

"He's fine. If I tell him what to do, he's all right. He knows he's needed here, that there are jobs he can do. You should see how happy he looks when he gets something right, and here it doesn't matter if he can't read or doesn't know certain things. But it's hard for him when he sees other boys with girls."

"It is?"

"He's getting older. He has feelings, too, even if he isn't sure what they are. But there's not much of a chance for him." Anoki paused, as though he knew he had wandered too close to dangerous ground. "I'd better go."

"Thanks for coming to see me."

He walked toward the door. "You visited me when I was sick. I don't forget." He was telling her that he was repaying a debt, nothing more.

Dmitri came to see her that evening. Zoheret had finished her soup and was still hungry, but Kagami had told her not to eat more until morning.

Anxious to leave her room, she walked down to the riverbank with Dmitri. A few people splashed about in the water
near the shore, their nude bodies gleaming in the reddish
light. Helena's breasts seemed larger without clothes; Gervais was sprouting body hair. Lillka and Brendan sat near a
large, flat rock, speaking with Tonio. Dmitri waved a hand in
their direction and said, "Lillka got smart."

"She always was."

"Not about some things." They sat down on the soft grass.
"I talked to Tonio, and then I talked to her, and now she'll ask
him about things—consult with him, she called it. All Tonio
really wants is to feel somebody's listening to him, and now
maybe some people will stop talking about how he should be
leader." He smiled, obviously proud of himself.

"I hope so."

"Lillka didn't like the idea, but I talked her into it. Now if
she has any problems, Tonio'll get some of the blame, too.
Brendan agreed with me. Lillka needs someone to nudge her,
anyway." He stretched out on his back. "Everything's going
to be fine."

She felt that way, too, but that might be only because she
was well. Lying down next to him, she said, "I think I'm happy."

"You are or you aren't. You don't think you are."

"I am, then."

"I wish you could stay with me tonight, but I have to get
plenty of sleep. Tomorrow night's my turn in the fields. And
you need to rest." He said that as if it were an afterthought.

They were silent as the swimmers ran past them; droplets
of water sprinkled her face. She said, "I'll come to see you
when you're on patrol."

"I have the last watch, with Helena and Jorge."

"I'll get up early, then."

"I hope one of them takes Red. Serena doesn't discipline

that dog. He slobbers all over me, and he barks. Well, at least he'd warn us of anything."

"Dmitri—" She stopped, suddenly afraid to dispel the serenity she felt with words. "It's nothing."

Zoheret opened her eyes. Had she overslept? She struggled to remember why she had told herself to wake early. Dmitri—she was to join him on his watch. The freedom of sleep was lost to the bonds of consciousness. She rubbed her temples, regretting the promise. She could go back to sleep and tell him she had forgotten. He would not mind. She sat up and stretched. If she had felt more for Dmitri, love might have excused a broken promise or a disappointment, but she had only reliability and steadiness to offer him.

She tiptoed from the room into the narrow corridor. Lillka, behind her, snorted in her sleep. She crept from the shack and stood outside for a moment, listening to the birds. As she walked toward the fields, she noticed a bright light near the ground and frowned in puzzlement. The light danced, flickering, then flared.

She lifted her hands. "Fire! There's fire in the fields!" She kept shouting until others had come to their doors. "Sound the alarm!" Voices echoed her cry until she heard the ringing of the storehouse bell. Lillka appeared, ordering those nearby to fetch buckets.

Zoheret ran toward the field. The corn was burning; the flames crackled. "Dmitri!" She passed Anoki's three robots, which stood helplessly in a row, metal limbs at their sides, silent sentries on rollers. "Dmitri!" The smoke made her eyes water. A tall, dark form rose before her and grabbed her arms. She recognized Helena in the red light.

"What happened?" Helena asked.

"You tell me. You were supposed to be on watch."

"Something hit me on the head and knocked me out." The tall girl leaned against Zoheret, holding her shoulder.

"Where's Dmitri?"

"I don't know."

Zoheret left her and ran on, imagining Dmitri among the flames. I'm sorry, she thought, not knowing what she was sorry for. I'm sorry, I'm sorry. She jumped over a ditch and almost fell. The flames were close; the smoke made it hard to breathe. She coughed, and spat on the ground, and saw the dog.

Serena's setter lay in front of her. "Red?" she whispered. "Red? Come on, boy." Then she saw the gash, and the blood; the dog's neck had been slit.

"Dmitri!" She lifted her head. Two feet protruded from among the burning cornstalks. She ran toward them, reached down, and pulled Dmitri from the flames. Helena appeared, reached for his arms, and helped her carry him away from the fire toward the river.

A bucket brigade had formed at the edge of the settlement to fight the fire. Buckets traveled from hand to hand in a line from the main ditch; other young people beat the flames with blankets. The robots, directed by Anoki, rolled around the fire's periphery, sucking up dirt and spewing it over the flames.

Helena let go of Dmitri as Zoheret lowered his legs. "I'm going for Jorge," the blond girl shouted. Zoheret knelt at Dmitri's side, feeling for injuries. The boy, apparently unburned except for singed hair and clothing, still breathed.

"Dmitri, Dmitri." She splashed dirty water from the ditch onto his face and he moaned, eyes closed. She felt his head and found no bumps. A stun gun, she thought; he would be out for a while. She thought of Red. They could have used a gun on the dog; they didn't have to kill him. They. They. She knew what had happened. They were out there somewhere, running away, waiting for their vengeance to light the Hollow.

She thought of the plain. It would burn, the fire would spread. She started up, and then remembered. Anoki had cleared more land, and that might save the plain. Make it rain, she wanted to scream at Ship, make it rain now. She coughed, peering through the smoke. Brendan passed her and threw her a blanket.

She went toward the field, beating the flames with the blanket, driving the fire. The cornstalks were black. She looked toward the plain. A line of people advanced from the cleared land toward the burning crops; some swung blankets, others wielded shovels. A wide circle had formed around the field, containing the fire and saving the settlement, but the field would be lost.

The fire had burned itself out by morning, leaving the field black. Jorge had been carried out, stunned but otherwise unharmed. People sat alongside the ditches and by the river, tired by the battle.

Dmitri had revived; his head rested on Zoheret's lap. She trembled, thinking of what might have happened. The plain might have burned; they might have wakened with their shacks burning over their heads. They might not have awakened at all.

Lillka stood near her, gazing at the field, assessing the damage. "What are we going to do?" Zoheret asked.

"I think we'll get by. We still have our gardens. We'll have short rations for a while, though. We'd better start learning how to fish."

"I didn't mean that."

"You want us to go after them," Lillka said fiercely. "Then it'll start all over again, won't it? What do you want, a war?"

Dmitri said, "Isn't that what we have now?"

Zoheret shook her head. "That isn't what I meant. I think we have to talk to Ship now." She waited for the other girl to object, but Lillka was silent.

Serena was still crying. She paced the edge of a ditch, turning violently from Tonio whenever he stretched out a comforting arm. Her voice keened as she mourned her dog.

Zoheret lifted Dmitri's head gently, then stood up. "Where're you going?" he asked.

"To get some food. There's nothing left to do here."

"Bring me something."

She stood up and walked toward the settlement, feeling too tired for anger. As she passed the shacks and approached the clearing, Bonnie emerged from the storehouse. Her head was bare of flowers; she wore a stun gun at her waist and a small pack on her back. Zoheret ducked behind a shack. Bonnie hurried down the steps and ran around the side of the storehouse.

Zoheret ran after her, passing the chicken coop and pig-pen behind the storehouse before she caught sight of the girl again. Bonnie was on the plain, moving rapidly through the tall grass. Zoheret wondered if she should go back to the storehouse, ring the bell, and assemble a group to go after Bonnie. She recalled Tonio's suspicions, and then remembered that Bonnie had confided in her. She was sure that the girl had not lied.

She ran after her, trying to keep up; the grass slowed her movement. Bonnie turned and saw her, but kept on walking. "Bonnie. Stop." The girl turned her head. "If you don't, I'll get the others, and they'll come after you."

Bonnie halted. Zoheret swished through the grass and came to her side. "Where are you going?"

"Away." Bonnie started walking again.

"Why?" Zoheret trailed after her.

"Why do you think? I handed Tonio a bucket and he almost hit me with it. He said he'd deal with me later." She turned her head and glared at Zoheret. "You suspect me, too. Admit it."

"Do you think I would be out here alone if I did?"

"I won't go back."

"Don't you know this'll just make it look as though Tonio's right?"

"I don't care. He'll believe it no matter what I do."

"Don't you know a lot of people won't believe him? Lillka would stand up for you."

"No, she wouldn't, Zoheret. You think she would because she's your roommate. But she's not a good leader, not when things are going wrong." Bonnie turned and stared at the now-distant settlement. "She can't make the hard decisions."

"Where are you going?"

"Back to the corridors. I'll be safe there."

"Ship won't let you stay."

"I won't go back to the settlement."

Zoheret struggled to control her exasperation. "Bonnie, listen. I already told Lillka I wanted to talk to Ship. We have to tell it what's going on. But I have to go back and tell her where I'm going. If you wait—"

"I'm not waiting."

"Then I'm sticking with you."

"They'll worry about you."

"Let them."

"You're going to follow me whether I want you to or not." Bonnie handed Zoheret her stun gun. "You'd better take this. I'm a bad shot anyway."

10

It was night when they reached the entrance. Bonnie seemed weak from her recent illness, and both girls were tired from fighting the fire.

The door slid open, revealing the corridor. "Bonnie?" Ship's voice said softly. "Zoheret? Why are you here?" The door closed behind them.

"Everything's going wrong," Zoheret burst out. "We weren't prepared."

"Let me find you a place to rest."

"You're not listening to me." She glared at the nearest lens.

"You're tired. I want to hear your complaints, but I think we can discuss them more profitably when you've had some rest. You may find things aren't as bad as you think."

Zoheret glanced at Bonnie. This was not the sort of welcome she had expected from Ship; she had been prepared for a scolding, or perhaps Ship's sympathy. It didn't seem very concerned.

"Let's go to the tubeway," Bonnie said.

"I'm afraid," Ship answered, "that I'm repairing the tubeway here."

"Get us a cart, then. We want to go to our old rooms."

For a moment, Zoheret thought that Ship had not heard the request. The corridor was silent, so silent that Zoheret, used to the noises of the settlement, the chatter of others, the hoots and twitters of the night and the rustlings of trees in the woods, tensed, as if expecting danger.

"I shall offer you a room here," Ship said at last. "There's the observatory. Or you may stay in your old nursery playroom—there are beds there, where you used to nap, and a bathroom."

"The nursery, then," Bonnie said.

"There really is no point in traveling elsewhere when you're tired. I'll serve you supper there. You may have anything you like."

Zoheret, who had longed for the familiarity of her old room, was about to object when she saw Bonnie sway slightly and lean against a wall.

The nursery was just down the hall; Zoheret guided Bonnie to the door. It slid open; child-sized chairs and tables stood in the center of the room, and there were several beds against the far wall. The room seemed barren, with no sign that children had ever played there. Their drawings were missing, their toys absent, their childhood seemingly erased. Zoheret approached one table and saw the Z she had carved there; one corner of the table was chipped. She sank into one of the small chairs, her knees rising toward her chin, and rubbed the Z with one finger.

"Rest," Ship said. "Tomorrow we'll talk. Please—" Zoheret

and Bonnie exchanged a glance; Ship's voice had risen slightly on the last word. "Please don't worry," Ship went on in its alto. "Everything will work itself out. The Project will succeed, and you'll return to the Hollow."

This reassurance was more disturbing than silence would have been. Was Ship afraid? Zoheret wondered if their return to the corridors had made Ship believe that the Project was in danger.

They gorged themselves on the foods they had missed—pastries, spicy meats on rice, candies, exotic vegetables. Ship even provided a small bottle of wine. They slept on the small beds, bodies curled so that their feet did not hang over the edges.

When they awoke and sat up, the room grew light. Bonnie stretched and stood up. "How about breakfast?" She seemed more cheerful after sleeping. "And then I need a bath—a real bath."

They ate a light meal, then bathed, splashing each other with the water as they washed. The hot water soothed Zoheret's muscles; she leaned her head against the side of the wide, sunken pool and wished she could wash her worries away with the dirt. Ship had been silent ever since supper the night before.

After drying their hair, they returned to the playroom and found fresh clothing on a shelf under the food slots. Zoheret pulled on the larger set of clothes, noticing that the brown pants were a little loose around her hips while the matching shirt was too tight in the shoulders. Bonnie dressed in the pale green clothes, then sat down.

"Shall we talk?" Ship asked.

Zoheret started at the voice. "May we go back to our old rooms first? I wanted to bring a few things back with me."

"I'm sure you can do without them. If there's anything you really need, I'll be happy to provide it."

"Why can't we go there?" Bonnie asked.

"Why return to your old haunts? That part of your life is over now."

Bonnie narrowed her eyes. "You don't want us there. Why? What's wrong?"

"Nothing is wrong." Ship's voice dropped to a tenor. "I simply think you should stay here and discuss the problem that brought you into this part of me before you go back to the Hollow. There's no need to dawdle in your old rooms."

"We'll walk, then." Bonnie got up and went to the door. It remained closed. She hit the smooth white surface with her hand. "Open the door."

"I'm afraid I cannot do that."

Zoheret lifted her hand to her mouth. Had Ship gone mad? If it had, they were lost; there was no escape.

"Open the door!" Bonnie cried, kicking it.

"After we talk."

"What's the matter? Why won't you open it?"

"I've done my best to carry out this Project. But you are placing it in jeopardy." Ship's words chilled Zoheret. She went to Bonnie and stood at her side. "I've done my best." Zoheret had never heard that tone before; it was the sound of despair. "I should tell you that you—" Ship paused. "No. Explain your problem to me. We can talk and you may then return to the Hollow, where you belong. Believe me, that would be best. You shouldn't be here now. I was counting on you to be mature enough to handle your own problems."

It's our fault, Zoheret thought. Ship didn't expect us to ask for help, and now it's afraid we can't take care of ourselves. She was suddenly angry at Ship for trying to make them feel guilty. But its voice had been too pained, too unlike it, too out of proportion to the cause. Something else was worrying it.

"Ship," she said carefully, "we have some trouble, but it's not what you think." Ship should have been comforting her, not the other way around. "We can handle it. I think we just needed to get away for a while so we could see it more objectively."

Bonnie glared at Zoheret, as if wanting to argue; Zoheret shot her a warning glance. "We've had some disagreements with Ho and some others, but we probably just need to get together and talk it over." Bonnie grimaced, but held her peace. "We'll go back," Zoheret continued. "I'm sorry we came here and upset you."

"Are you sure you don't want to talk?" Ship was trying, it seemed, to make amends.

"We'll solve it ourselves. That's what you'd like us to do, I know. Just give us some food, and we'll go."

"Very well." They helped themselves to some packets and put them in Bonnie's pack.

"Good-bye, Ship," Zoheret murmured as the door slid open. They hurried down the corridor and through the entrance to the Hollow.

As the door closed behind them, Bonnie opened her mouth; Zoheret held up her hand. She led the other girl to the clearing, looking down at the woods below. There were sensors hidden among the trees, but no ears here.

"Sit down," she said to Bonnie. "Take out some food and pretend you're hungry. Keep your head down. It might be watching, even if it can't hear." They sat, and Bonnie handed her a packet.

"What was that all about?" Bonnie said in a low voice.

Zoheret leaned forward, shaking her hair over her face. "We have a big problem now, as bad as this business with Ho. Ship's hiding something."

"I know that."

"Keep your voice down." Zoheret laughed loudly. "Go on, laugh. Look like you're not worried."

Bonnie chuckled nervously.

"We have to find out what it's hiding, and why."

"I know that," Bonnie said softly. "Why didn't we stay, then?"

"Do you think Ship would have just let us wander around until we found out?"

"I guess not."

"We have to surprise it."

"How are we going to surprise Ship?"

"I don't know."

"What if it's lost? What if something went wrong with the probes?"

Zoheret shook her head. "It couldn't be that. Ship wouldn't be trying to keep us from our old rooms if that was the problem. There's something going on there. We have a right to know what."

"And how are you going to fool Ship?" Bonnie waved a hand. "It's all around us. We can't do anything without it knowing, if it's watching us. And how are we going to get into the corridors again?"

"I don't know. But maybe we can find a way. It said it wouldn't be watching the Hollow, and I think it'll keep that promise, even if it's watching us now for a while. We just have to assume that, because otherwise there's nothing we can do, and I'd rather try than just give up."

"What makes you think it'll keep that promise if it's lying to us now?"

"Because it always has," Zoheret replied. "It never broke its word. And it didn't lie to us in there, it only said we couldn't go back to our rooms."

"I'm scared." Bonnie finished her food. "I was never afraid of Ship before, but I am now. What could be wrong?"

"Maybe there's some part of the Project we're not supposed to know about now."

"Then maybe we'd better leave it alone."

"We can't, Bonnie. If it concerns the Project, it's our lives we're talking about. We have to know what Ship's doing." She got up. "I didn't like that sound in its voice—it isn't like Ship. Don't say anything about this until we get back to the settlement. If Ship's listening, and it thinks we're not suspicious, it'll shut down soon, and then maybe we'll have a chance to do something."

Zoheret, sitting on the storehouse steps with Lillka and Brendan, had finished her tale. "Bonnie's waiting up the river," she said. "She was afraid to come back until she knew she'd be safe."

"What does she expect, running off like that?" Lillka scowled. "If her housemates hadn't defended her, I would have wondered about her myself. And I was worrying about you, too, until I figured you must have followed her. Anyway, Tonio has something else to do now. He's going to go after Ho."

"What?"

"He's going to take some people with him and track Ho down."

"He'll never find him. Ho knows the Hollow too well." Zoheret rested her arms on her knees. "And have you forgotten what happened the last time you sent Tonio out?"

Lillka spread her hands, palms up. "We've had to double our guards. Everyone's angry. And I'd rather have Tonio out of here instead of making trouble. He stirs people up."

"I see," Zoheret said slowly. "You can't tell him what to do, and he might challenge you. That's what you mean."

"We have to do something," Brendan said. "And at least Bonnie'll be safe here. Tonio's after bigger game now."

"'Bigger game.' I love the way you put it." Zoheret shook her head. "I'm worrying about Ship. That's a lot more important than Ho."

"Are you sure there's something the matter with Ship?" Lillka asked.

"You would have known there was if you'd heard it. Ship sounded weird—I've never heard it sound that way before."

Brendan frowned. The shadows cast by the evening light made his thick, pale eyebrows seem fierce. "What can we do about it? Nothing. Everything here is Ship. You'd be like a corpuscle in your own body trying to fight the brain."

Germs can fight the body, Zoheret thought. Viruses can make you sick. "An emergency," she said. "People who need the infirmary. We can pretend we had an accident and go to the entrance near our old rooms. It'll have to let us in."

"I don't know if that would work," Lillka said. "Ship can still hide whatever it might be hiding. And maybe you'd better worry about how Ship will feel when it finds out you've tricked it."

"I don't think we have much choice."

Brendan sighed. "We have twice as much work to do. We have to guard everything even more carefully, and Tonio wants to take a group on a search party. And now you want to take another group back to the corridors."

"Maybe I can talk Tonio into going with me instead. I'll get Dmitri to talk to him. We can always look for Ho on the way."

Lillka and Brendan exchanged glances. "If you can work it out with him," the blond girl said, "then go. I'm not going to argue with you—I have too many other things to worry about."

Zoheret got up and went to fetch Bonnie.

11

They had traveled past the lake and through woods without finding a sign of Ho's group. During the night, they had slept uneasily in a clearing, keeping watch throughout the night in pairs. Zoheret and Tonio were traveling with four others; Lillka had insisted on keeping the group small. Zoheret had picked the group carefully. Dmitri and Serena were trusted by Tonio, but Dmitri, along with Kagami and Gervais, would back Zoheret up in any dispute.

They crept toward the last clearing; beyond it stood the entrance. They adjusted their packs while Serena and Gervais smeared red vegetable juice on their faces and clothes; Zoheret hoped that the ruse would get them as far as the infirmary before Ship discovered it had been fooled.

It was growing dark; the dusky light made it hard to see.

On the slope, under a tree, a shadow moved. Zoheret drew back from the edge of the clearing; her companions ducked down. A bare-shouldered figure stood up, back toward them, and began to walk slowly toward the entrance.

Tonio jumped up, raised his stun gun, and fired. As the target fell, Zoheret knocked the weapon from Tonio's hand. "You fool," she said. "There might be others nearby." She waited, but the clearing was still.

Dmitri said, "We'd better go see who it is." They ran up the hill toward the prone body, looking quickly from side to side in case anyone else should appear, and halted at its side. Zoheret wondered why the boy was wearing only shorts; in the Hollow, long pants were needed to protect one's legs.

"Ship's been hiding them in the corridors," Tonio said. "That's why we haven't seen Ho. That's why Ship didn't want you here. It—" He was suddenly silent; Dmitri had turned the body over.

Zoheret gasped. The face was unfamiliar, its lower part covered with a short, brown beard. She had never seen this person before.

"Does anyone know him?" Dmitri asked. It was a foolish question; the others shook their heads.

"There are people in the corridors," Zoheret said; her voice shook. "That's what Ship's hiding. Why didn't it tell us?" Her face was hot with anger, her trembling hands cold with fear. This person was not a boy, but a young man.

"We don't know that," Serena said; her voice was edged with hysteria. "Maybe he was always there, and we just didn't see him." She sounded unconvinced by her own words. "What do we do now?"

"Wait for him to wake up—question him." Zoheret was afraid that Ship was watching them; if it was, there was no place to hide, and no way to trick it now. "Ship?" There was no response. "Ship?" She felt her old childhood fear again, the fear that Ship could read their minds.

Serena and Dmitri rubbed the man's arms, trying to revive him. The man's muscular big-boned body and high cheekbones seemed familiar. Dmitri rubbed one flaccid arm, his spatulate fingers kneading the flesh. The unconscious man also had spatulate fingers, long and flat.

Zoheret peered at the bearded face in the rapidly fading light. "He looks like you, Dmitri."

Dmitri dropped the arm. "What?"

"He looks like you."

Serena said, "She's right."

Zoheret reached for the canteen attached to her belt and threw water on the man's face. He moaned, but his eyes remained closed.

They waited for what seemed a long time. Tonio kept glancing nervously at the woods below, now so darkened that the black treetops could barely be seen against the gray light. Zoheret watched the door, afraid that other strangers might rush from it.

At last the man moved, opened his eyes, snorted, then sat up quickly when he saw them. Dmitri and Gervais seized his arms. "Who are you?" he asked in a husky voice.

"Who are *you*?" Zoheret said.

His eyes widened in fear; they were dark eyes, not blue like Dmitri's. "The others," he said. "You must be the others."

"What are you talking about?"

"Ship asked me not to come in here. Then it checked to make sure no one was nearby. I guess it didn't check well enough."

"Is it watching?" Zoheret said, afraid.

"I don't think it is now. It closed its sensors after checking this slope. It said it had promised to shut down in the Hollow."

It had promised. Zoheret gritted her teeth. It had deceived them, and it was worrying about a promise.

"I know who you are," the man went on. "I don't know your names, but I know who you are. You're living here now, the way we did."

"We know who *we* are," Zoheret said angrily. "Who are you?"

"My name is Aleksandr." The name rolled from his lips; he trilled the *r*. "I'm living in the corridors now with a few companions. You weren't supposed to know about us now. Ship was sure you wouldn't return, but if you had, we would have been able to hide with a bit of warning." He shook his head. "I'm afraid I've ruined things. I wanted to see the Hollow again. I fell asleep. I was just waking up when—"

"But where did you come from?" Gervais asked.

"The same place you did. I was born on Ship, grew up in the corridors, and then lived in the Hollow."

"But we never saw you," Serena said.

"Of course you didn't." The stranger gestured with his head. "You can let me go—I won't run away." Gervais and Dmitri released him. "You didn't see me or my friends because all of us have been in suspended animation. You must know the room—it's where Ship has all of its biological materials, the stored animal embryos and seeds and other things we'll need in our new home."

"Our new home," Zoheret said.

"Ours, too." He paused. "Ship made a place for us—the room is quite large. It kept it closed off so that we wouldn't be discovered."

Zoheret was suddenly angry with Aleksandr; he didn't

belong here. This was their home, not his; he was stealing their birthright. "I don't understand."

Aleksandr spread his hands. "Let me explain—you might as well know. My friends and I were born here, taught by Ship, and sent to live in the Hollow, to prepare for our new life while Ship searched with its probes. It had every reason to believe it would find an Earth-like world—all the signs were right. A G-type star, planets aplenty—at least two at the same distance from that star as Earth is from its sun. But something went wrong." He was silent for a moment as he swallowed. "One of the worlds was a hot, dead world with a thick atmosphere of carbon dioxide—much like Earth's sister planet Venus. The other was habitable, but the probes had found two possibly intelligent species there, one on land with the ability to make simple tools and the other dwelling in the sea—giant mammalian forms resembling Earth's whales. We couldn't settle there. Ship had been directed not to leave us on a world which had intelligent inhabitants. Our preparation had been useless."

Night had settled over the Hollow, masking their faces. Zoheret reached for Dmitri's hand.

"We were faced with a dilemma," Aleksandr continued. "We could keep on living aboard Ship, but we would die before it could find us another home. As it was, we were already past the age when we should have been settled on a planet. Ship offered us a life in the corridors or the Hollow, a life where we would be free to live as we pleased, learning what we liked, living only for pleasure if that was what we wanted. But it would have been a life with no future, no hope. We could build nothing. There would be no children—Ship had been programmed with certain procedures and felt that becoming a generation ship would jeopardize the Project. We would die, and leave no trace, no accomplishments. The thought drove some of us mad." He bowed his head. "A few, unable to face it, killed themselves."

The young man's husky but gentle voice stirred Zoheret in spite of her anger. "But you found another way," she murmured.

"We were desperate. A life that had seemed easy and beguiling had palled quickly. We asked Ship to suspend us. It was risky, we knew that—we might never awaken. The Project had known that, which was why it sent only human genetic material to be bred here instead of preserved passengers. Ship didn't want to put us in suspension, but we pleaded with it, and it consented when we convinced it that this was better than a pointless life, that we had nothing to lose. Ten of us were to awaken after you were in the Hollow, while the others would be revived one by one later. I was one of the first ten— we drew lots." He looked down. "As it happens, only seven of us awoke. We lost the other three. I don't know how many others we'll have to mourn in time."

Zoheret was holding Dmitri's hand too tightly, and let it go. "But if you were preserved," Kagami murmured, "why did Ship create us? It didn't need us—it had settlers already."

"It couldn't take the chance. We knew it would have to give birth to a new group, in case too many of us—or all of us—were lost."

"What if the same thing happens again?" Tonio said; his voice was too high. "What if something's wrong with the new world?"

"That is unlikely. It told us it had explored several systems before giving birth to you and deciding on this one. It didn't want to make the same mistake and revised some of its procedures."

"But it could happen again. There's always a chance."

Aleksandr was silent.

"No one's going to put me in suspension," Tonio said. "I'm not going to lie there like a corpse, wondering if I'll ever open my eyes."

"Ship tried to be careful this time. It learned from its mistakes." Aleksandr paused. "It can learn, you know. The directives it was given had to allow for accidents and unforeseen events."

Zoheret pressed her hands against her thighs. Ship had made too many mistakes. She stood up. "We can't stay here all night. We'd better go into the corridors."

Aleksandr rose. "Come, then. I'll introduce you to the others."

They walked through the familiar hallway, following the young man to the dining hall, where he left them. Kagami and Gervais brought food to a table, and then they sat down.

Zoheret glared at the wall. "You lied," she burst out. "You lied to us."

"I didn't lie." Ship, which had been silent as they entered, had spoken at last.

"You did."

"I neglected to tell you about the others because there was nothing to be gained by revealing their presence. I did not lie."

"You let us believe that we were alone," Kagami said.

"That is true."

Aleksandr had returned with a small, slender, dark-haired woman. They hesitated at the doorway, then entered. As they came to the table, Aleksandr said, "This is Kieu." The woman smiled at them uneasily. Zoheret and her friends mumbled their own names.

The two sat without speaking while Zoheret and her companions ate. Then Kieu said, "Why did you come back to the corridors?"

Zoheret searched her face; it was a kind face, with tilted brown eyes and a small, full mouth. Kieu's skin was golden, her black hair short and straight. "A friend and I needed help from Ship. We went to the corridor by the nursery playroom and found out that Ship didn't want us to return here, and that's when we realized it was hiding something. We wanted to find out what."

"I was careless," Ship said. "I'm not used to deceit."

"You should be," Zoheret replied. "You should be an expert by now."

"I thought you were ready to take care of yourselves in the Hollow without asking me for help." The words were sharp, as if Ship were spitting them out.

"Please," Kieu said. "It's pointless to fight. Why did you and your friend seek Ship's help in the first place? Were you hurt, or ill?"

Zoheret was suddenly on her guard, unsure if she could trust the woman. Her companions seemed to have had the same thought. Tonio glared across the table; Kagami frowned; Serena warned her with her eyes. Dmitri squeezed her hand. "Nothing important," she replied. "We realized that when we had time to think about it."

"Are you sure?" Kieu asked. Her eyes turned toward Aleksandr, as if she realized she would get no more out of them. "Well. You're certainly welcome to stay the night." She folded her hands. "Ship told us a bit about you when we were revived. You see, we're all related, in a manner of speaking—each of us is related to one of you. The same vials of sperm and eggs Ship used for me were recombined to make one of you. I have a brother who's part of your group. We have the same parents, you see—that makes me his sister. My brother's name is Ho."

Zoheret dropped her fork; it clattered on the table. Tonio narrowed his eyes. "Do you know him?" Aleksandr asked, and then he laughed. "What a question. Of course you must."

"We know him," Dmitri said, staring at his plate. Zoheret was glad she hadn't tried to explain their problem.

"And I have a brother, too," Aleksandr said softly. His eyes turned toward Dmitri. "You're my brother."

Dmitri stiffened. Zoheret was still; she had known it without realizing it. "Really," Dmitri croaked.

"Yes." Aleksandr held out a hand.

"Well." Dmitri's voice was strangled; he ignored the young man's hand.

"I'm tired," Zoheret said quickly. "Do you think we could go to sleep now?" Her friends gazed at her gratefully.

"Wouldn't you like to meet the others?" Kieu asked. "They should be here very soon."

"We can meet them when we wake up."

"Go, then," Aleksandr said. "We're only using the three rooms nearest here; you may have your choice of the others."

The shock began to wear off while Zoheret was showering; the realization that there were fellow passengers on Ship was sinking in.

She came out of the bathroom. Her old room was as it had been. Kagami's sculptures were on her shelf, a reader of Lillka's lay on her bed. Dmitri was stretched out on another bed, hands folded under his head.

She sat on the bed near him. "Dmitri?"

"A brother. I can't believe it."

"He does look like you."

He raised himself on his elbows. "Ship lied." Dmitri shook his head. "I wonder what'll happen now. Maybe they'll start telling us what to do, because they're older."

"You're wrong," she said, wondering if he might be right. She yawned, suddenly tired. "I'll worry about that tomorrow."

Aleksandr and another man were in the dining room when Zoheret and Dmitri arrived. Aleksandr greeted them while the other man stood at a wall slot, his back to them. Zoheret tugged at her clean shirt nervously, then sat down at the far end of the young man's table with Dmitri.

"Did you sleep well?" Aleksandr asked.

Dmitri grunted; Zoheret stared at the tabletop. Heels clicked against the floor; hands put a tray with a pot of coffee and cups on the table in front of them. "May I get you two some breakfast?" a deep voice said.

Zoheret looked up. A pair of dark eyes gazed at her; lips framed by a drooping mustache smiled. A familiar image had come to life. "You're Zoheret," the deep voice continued. "I am—"

"I know who you are," she cried. The young man had the face of Hussein Taraki; she knew it even though he wore no beard. She leaned forward and rested her elbows on the table as she covered her eyes.

"My name is Yusef," the man said. "I'm your brother."

She looked up, not knowing what to say.

"I understand," Yusef went on as he sat down. "It's a shock. You're not used to us yet."

She nodded, as if agreeing with him. He poured coffee for them; Zoheret accepted a cup even though she did not like the bitter beverage. She held it to her lips, pretending to sip so that she would not have to speak.

Kieu entered the room with another young woman. Zoheret peered over her cup rim at the two, trying to guess which brother or sister the other woman had in the Hollow. Kieu fetched food while the other woman seated herself;

she had thick brown hair, pale translucent skin, and hazel eyes.

"My friend's name is Maire," Kieu said as she put down a tray of fruit and pastries. "She has a brother named Brendan."

"I wouldn't have guessed it," Zoheret replied.

"Siblings don't always look alike."

"You seem to know all about us," Dmitri said. His eyes were pale and cold as he looked from Maire to his brother's warm brown eyes. "And we know nothing about you."

"We don't know that much about you," Kieu murmured. "Ship showed us your images, and told us a little, but it didn't want to tell us more until we met."

"But we met by accident," Dmitri said. "What would have happened if we hadn't come here?"

Kieu averted her eyes. "I suppose we would have met just before leaving Ship."

"I see. When we were all ready to settle on our world, we would have found out that it wasn't really ours at all, but yours."

"Not at all," Aleksandr said. "It will belong to all of us. Our claim is no greater than yours. We can work together—and with more people, our chances for survival are greater. This may turn out for the best."

"Ship should have told us you were here," Zoheret burst out.

Aleksandr folded his hands. "Are you so sure? You're learning things for yourselves. If you had known about us, you might have depended on our advice."

Kagami and Gervais had entered the room. They lingered by the door, then came to the table and sat down while Kieu introduced them to Maire and Yusef.

"How are you doing in the Hollow?" Kieu asked. "Ship's sensors are shut off there, so we have no way of knowing."

Zoheret was wary. "Things are fine." Kagami nodded;

Gervais wore a bland expression. "We built a settlement and planted crops. We've learned some things—how to hunt, how to raise chickens. It's a lot of work."

"Any disagreements?" Aleksandr said.

"A few. We settle them." She was suddenly afraid that if these people knew of their problems, they would enter the Hollow and tell them what to do. "What about you? How did things go for you when you were living there?"

Aleksandr sighed. "Not as we had expected. But you must find your own way. Your difficulties may be different."

"You're going to stay here, then." Zoheret felt both relief and disappointment.

Yusef said, "We must. We have to revive our friends, a few at a time. We have our own preparations to make."

"What are we supposed to do when we go back?" Gervais asked. "Tell our friends about you, or keep you a secret?"

Kieu shook her head. "We can't tell you that. You have to decide."

Zoheret and her companions left as they had entered. They had considered taking the tubeway to the entrance nearer the settlement, but decided that they needed the extra time to figure out what to do. Their packs were heavier; they had loaded them with various delicacies for their friends, and Kagami had raided the infirmary for more medical supplies.

"We're going to have to tell them something," Dmitri muttered as they approached the woods. "If we don't tell them the truth, we'll have to make up a convincing story."

"We could say that Ship's doing biological experiments," Tonio offered, "and was worried about contamination."

Kagami shook her head. "It could close off the labs for that. It wouldn't have to close off the whole corridor."

"Maybe we should just tell them the truth," Gervais said. "They're going to find out anyway."

Dmitri said, "I wish we'd never found out. I wish we didn't know."

Gervais shifted his pack. "Don't be stupid."

"What if the others want to go and meet them?" Tonio said loudly. "What if someone tells them about Ho? We don't even know if we can trust those people. How do we know Ho or one of his friends hasn't gone to the corridors already and found out about them? Maybe they're helping him. Maybe he's hiding there and that's the real reason they wanted us to leave."

"I don't think they'd do that," Zoheret replied. "They tried to be kind. They didn't seem—"

"How do you know? She said he was her brother. So maybe she's helping him."

They were talking too much, becoming careless. The woods were closer now. Zoheret turned toward Tonio to tell him to be quiet. Something glinted in the corner of her eye. She glanced at it.

The bright flash blinded her for a moment. Tonio and Gervais were falling. Her hand moved to her waist. She had time only to see the arm protruding from behind a tree before she fell and the bright spot dancing before her was swallowed by blackness.

12

She was lying on her back. She moved her fingers; they prickled with pain. A root dug into her back. Where was her pack? She had been wearing one; what had happened to it?

Zoheret opened her eyes. The tree boughs above her seemed to have formed a net to hold their green leaves. Her knees felt bruised. Her wrists were bound, restraining her movements.

Slowly, she sat up. Kagami was awake, her back against a tree. Gervais was next to her, lying on the ground. Serena and Tonio were next to him, their heads bowed. Dmitri lay beside Zoheret; he moaned. Each of them was tied at the wrists and ankles.

Zoheret lifted her head. Across from her, Manuel squatted by the packs; he was eating a cake. A heavyset blond boy named Owen watched them impassively, his hand on his stun gun. Daniella, a small, rodent-faced girl with mousy hair, was with the two boys; she, too, was eating a cake. Zoheret knew that her own weapon was gone even before she looked down at her waist.

"When's he going to wake up?" Owen said, waving his weapon at Dmitri.

"He was shot when he was guarding our fields," Zoheret replied. "It takes a while to recover afterward—you ought to know that."

"Let me give him something," Kagami said. "I have medicine in my pack."

"No," Owen said. Manuel had been reaching for the pack; he paused. "Why did you go back to the corridors?"

"We needed some supplies," Zoheret said.

"I'll bet you went whining to Ship."

"If we had, don't you think it would have done something by now?" She bit her lip. She should not have said that; she might have been able to frighten them with the possibility that Ship was watching.

"She's not a whiner," Manuel said. "She wouldn't have told Ship." Zoheret glared at him, resenting his defense.

"We can take care of ourselves," Owen said. "We don't have to go into the corridors."

Zoheret frowned. They did not know about Aleksandr and the others, then. She and her companions would have to keep that knowledge to themselves.

"We tracked you," Daniella said. "We've been waiting for you to come out. You weren't very careful."

Zoheret pulled at the rope around her ankles and then saw that another length of rope connected her wrist to Dmitri's. "What are you going to do?"

Owen shrugged.

"Let us go." She tried to stay calm. "By the time we get loose, you'll have a lead."

Owen shook his head. "You'd just come after us."

"The settlement will send out a search party for us."

"Let them."

"You can have what's in our packs."

Owen laughed. "We'll take that anyway."

Dmitri stirred.

"Get up," Owen commanded.

The ropes around their ankles hobbled them; they could walk, but would be unable to run. "Put the packs back on them," Owen said to Manuel.

Dmitri leaned against Zoheret. "Are you all right?" Manuel asked as he approached. Dmitri managed to nod.

"Our friends'll come after you," Tonio said.

"But we have hostages now," Owen replied.

The ankle ropes inhibited them, making them stumble and move more awkwardly. The packs felt heavy. Zoheret, tied to one end of the connecting rope, set the pace for her companions. Once, unmindful of the rope at her ankles, she had taken too long a stride; Manuel had caught her before she fell.

Their pace was slowed by the thickness of the foliage in this part of the woods; they were moving toward the lake, but by an unfamiliar route. They stopped only once, and asked for water. Manuel gave them a canteen before Owen could object.

They reached the lake after dark. The water was silvery in the pale night light. Zoheret, trying to orient herself, realized that they were at the end of the lake farthest from the river that led to the settlement.

They relieved themselves under the eyes of their captors,

and then Manuel led them to a mossy spot. They sat down. Owen untied their packs roughly while Manuel and Daniella guarded them. The three took turns eating while their captives watched.

"Who goes back?" Daniella asked.

"You go," Manuel said. "Find out what we should do and bring help."

The girl stood up and walked toward the shore. She pulled up branches and leaves, and Zoheret saw that a boat had been camouflaged by the growth. Daniella pushed the boat into the water, hopped in, and began to row, moving out of the bay toward the open water.

Manuel and Owen were sitting on a rocky rise, close enough to observe their prisoners, yet far enough away to be able to fire upon them before being overpowered.

"Do we get fed?" Zoheret called out. "We haven't eaten all day."

"You won't die if you don't get fed," Owen shouted back.

"We'd better give them food," Manuel said. Owen shook his head. "If we don't, they might get sick, and that'll be more trouble for us."

Owen scowled, but nodded. Manuel threw them packets of food; after they ate, they were allowed to creep toward the lake for water.

The captives drank from cupped hands. Zoheret bent down and tugged at her ankle ropes, loosening them while pretending to drink.

"What are you doing?" Dmitri whispered.

"I might be able to get free."

"Don't try it. They'll shoot you again."

"We have to do something."

They finished drinking and stretched out on a grassy spot

among the rocks. Zoheret pressed against Dmitri as if seeking warmth while tugging at her ropes. "My wrists are free," she murmured into his ear. "Can you untie yourself?"

"I don't think so."

Manuel had curled up, using a pack as a pillow, while Owen watched. The blond boy stood up and began to pace back and forth. Zoheret tensed, waiting for her chance. An owl hooted and a bush rustled. Owen pivoted toward the sound, his back to her.

She sat up, pulled the ropes from her ankles, and leaped to her feet, running along the bank. A beam shot past her. She was too clear a target here; she had to get up toward the woods. Her foot hit a rock and she fell, splashing in the shallows. As she stumbled out of the water, Owen was suddenly before her.

He seized her by the hair, forced her to her knees, and pushed her face under the water; she heard a throaty laugh. "You shouldn't have tried that." He pushed her face under again. She could not breathe; her lungs felt as though they would burst. He pulled her up and she had time only to gasp before he pushed her head under again.

Owen's hands dropped away. As she lifted her head, she saw that Manuel was gripping Owen's shoulder. "What are you doing?"

"Get back and guard the others."

"You don't have to drown her."

"She tried to get away."

"Leave her to me."

Owen sprinted toward the other captives; Manuel led Zoheret back to the group. "I'm sorry he hurt you." She tried to pull away, then noticed that his weapon was aimed at her. "I'll have to tie you up again."

She did not reply. Owen covered her while Manuel bound her, tying her hands behind her back and making sure the rope around her ankles would hold.

He left her, joining Owen on the rise. He had not tied her to the others, but she knew she could not free herself anyway. Both boys were watching them now. She pressed her cheek to the ground, trying to sleep.

She was tired and sore in the morning. The ropes chafed her wrists. Her right arm was asleep; it prickled with pain as she slowly sat up.

Owen and Manuel were eating. A night without sleep had made their faces drawn; there were shadows under Owen's eyes and Manuel's jaw muscles twitched. Manuel finished his breakfast, then threw them packets of food.

Dmitri opened one packet and held it while Zoheret ate the tart, trying not to snap at the food like a wild beast. Now that she was fed, she could think. If they remained prisoners, Ho would have to feed them, a prospect that would not appeal to Ho, who preferred to steal food rather than work for it. He could force them to forage or hunt or fish, but he would have to guard them. Their capture would cause him a lot of trouble.

She glanced at her companions, who were staring listlessly at the ground. They might attempt an escape, might try to overpower the two boys—something she could not do, tied as she was—yet they were not even looking for a chance. Get them over here, she thought; jump them, get their weapons— you can move your arms enough for that. She gazed at them, as though she could communicate her thoughts by thinking hard enough.

Owen got to his feet, shaded his eyes, and pointed. "There they are," he said to Manuel.

· Zoheret looked out at the lake. Four boats were approaching, each with a rower. Ho sat in the stern of one boat; she could recognize the arrogant tilt of his head even from a distance.

"Do something," she whispered to the others. "Before they get here."

"They'll just make it worse for us," Serena replied. Gervais looked away.

When the boats were tied up, Ho gathered his group on the rise while his friend Vittorio guarded the prisoners. Manuel seemed to be arguing with Ho, but their voices were so low that Zoheret could not make out their words. Ho hissed; Manuel shook his head. Owen sat with the other three members of the band, ignored.

"What do you think they're going to do with us?" Kagami asked.

Vittorio, pacing in front of them, laughed. "Throw you in the lake. That's what we ought to do."

"Sure," Tonio said.

"Think we wouldn't?"

Zoheret said, "I'm sure you would."

Vittorio leaned forward, careful to stay far enough away so that he could not be grabbed. "We can row you out, and push you over the side." He smiled, showing white teeth; his dark hair was pulled back in a long braid. "You won't swim too well with those ropes." He laughed again.

Ho stood up and walked down the rise toward them. His friends followed him, fanning out to each side. Ho halted, folding his arms across his chest; his clothes were worn, and patches had been sewn on the knees of his pants. Both a gun and a knife were tucked into his belt. He glanced at Kagami and his mouth twisted into a half smile.

"What are you going to do?" Zoheret asked.

"She's a troublemaker," Owen said. "She tried—" The blond boy fell silent as Ho cast an icy glance in his direction.

"Well," Ho said, "if we keep you, we have to feed you and watch you. But if we let you go, you'll just come after us. So we'll have to use you. You're going to help feed us."

"How?" Dmitri asked. "You can't make us help."

"Oh, but I can. I'm going to send one of you back to the settlement as a messenger. That person is going to get us things we need and bring them back to me—otherwise, life will get very hard for the other five. They won't eat, for one thing. And there are other things we can do to them."

"They'll come after us," Owen objected.

"No, they won't," Ho replied. "Because if they do, their friends will pay for it. The messenger had better make that very clear. Now, who's going to go?" He frowned. "The troublemaker. Maybe I'll send her. It'd be easier than having to watch her."

Owen said, "She'll go to Ship."

A hand pulled Zoheret's head up by the hair. She glared at Ho's face. His eyes seemed reptilian; she imagined him striking at her with his head and sinking his teeth into her throat.

"Are you going to go to Ship?" he asked. She did not reply and he gave her hair a yank, making her wince. "You'd better consider this, then. I'm going to give you two days, that's all— you'll have just enough time to get to the settlement, explain what happened, and get us our supplies. Now, you could go to the corridors, but that'd take time. And Ship won't help you. Remember what happened during Competition—I won, and Ship didn't care how I did it. So if you go to Ship, you'll get nothing, and your friends here will pay for it. Ship doesn't care what happens in here—it'll be dumping us soon enough. So don't use your time doing anything like that."

"I won't." She had to force the words out.

He released her. "And don't think you can come looking for us with a search party. You won't know where most of my group is, and your friends could get mighty hungry while you look."

He cut her bonds with his knife. She stood up on shaky legs, stamping her feet. Covering her with his weapon, Ho gestured at the lake. "Do you know how to row?"

"A little."

"Take the smallest boat there. Go back to the settlement and get our supplies. We need vegetables, dried fruit, some fruit juice, and flour. And clothes—shirts and pants and ponchos. You'd better be generous—if I'm disappointed, you'll be very sorry."

She peered at her rope-burned wrists. "We don't have as much as we did before you burned our field."

He scowled. "Don't blame me for that. Some of my friends got carried away." He glanced at Owen. "Just get us what we need—the settlement'll get by."

"Do I come back here?"

Ho shook his head. "No. When you get the stuff, put it in the boat and row toward the island, near the other shore." He pointed. "I'll be waiting. And you'd better come alone. We'll be watching, and if you aren't alone, we'll shoot."

"Give me three days."

"No."

"I need time to explain, and to get the supplies together. It might be hard to talk them into it."

"You want time to plan something. You can't have it. Two days. Be persuasive." He smiled.

She looked toward her friends. Tonio glowered at her, as if resenting her sudden freedom. "Please feed them while I'm gone," she begged. "There's plenty of food in our packs— they can eat that."

"If you want them to eat, get back on time."

"You won't hurt them." She narrowed her eyes. "I know what you're like. You'd better not hurt them."

"If you don't want them hurt, do what you're told."

He led her toward the boats. She wanted to strike him, to seize his weapon, but the odds were against her, and she could not count on her friends to join the struggle. She looked back at them. With their bowed heads and slumped shoulders, they already seemed beaten into passivity.

"You'll let them go after I get back. You will let them go, won't you?"

"I'll have to see. We might need more supplies later on, and holding your friends is one way to get them. I might let one go. Maybe you could pick the lucky one. It could be a contest." He pushed her. "Get in the boat. We'll be watching until you're out of sight."

As she rowed toward the river, keeping close to the shore, Zoheret considered her choices. She could still try for the corridors; Ship might not help, but maybe the people there would. She rejected that idea. She did not know them, kindly as they seemed, and she wondered what Ship might do if it found out about their conflict with Ho. It might decide that they could not be trusted to leave it, ever.

There was another difficulty as well. Ho might be watching to see that she didn't try for the nearest entrance, and the other entrances were too far away to reach in time. He might be expecting her to try for the corridors.

She could ask Lillka what to do. But Lillka might feel that

the settlement as a whole was more important than a few people. She would realize that Ho could use his prisoners to extract an endless supply of goods, draining the settlement. Why should they work to feed Ho? And if that was the decision, Zoheret knew that she would have to go to the island anyway, empty-handed, and share the fate of the others; she could not abandon them.

13

Zoheret had rowed the boat only a short distance up the river before pulling it out of the water. Turning it over, she had covered it with dead branches, and had then walked up the hill and along the side of the deepening chasm until she reached the bridge.

The bridge, made of rope and wood planks, hung over the river near the spot where the dead tree had once connected the chasm's sides. As the bridge swayed under her, she clung to the ropes with sore hands, wincing as rope rubbed against blisters.

When she reached the other side, she jogged forward and almost fell. She was weak from the rowing and lack of sound sleep; her meager breakfast had left her hungry. The thought of her friends in captivity, who would not eat at all until she returned, quickened her steps. She could have rowed up the river to the settlement, but she was unused to handling a boat and would have been rowing against a strong current; she could move more quickly this way. Now she would have to persuade the settlement not only to give up some of their needed supplies, but also to carry them down to the boat.

I'm not handling this well, she thought, wishing Ho had sent one of the others. But even limited freedom was better than none at all. Her friends were not completely helpless; they might be bargaining with Ho for a meal. But what could they offer him? Information—they knew about the people in the corridors, and that bit of knowledge might be worth trading. The captives might trade away a possible advantage.

As she thrashed through underbrush, she glared at the trees to her left. Unseeing, unhearing sensors were concealed there; Ship had abandoned them as completely as if it had already left them on a strange world.

Zoheret neared the bend in the river. The river no longer flowed in a chasm, and had widened; the settlement lay below her, a short distance beyond the trees.

She stopped for a moment, trying to think of what she would say. It would be best if she talked to Lillka or Brendan before seeing anyone else. It was already afternoon; they would be at the storehouse or perhaps in the field.

She heard a roar, and jumped. The roar was steady; she had never heard anything quite like it. She cupped one ear. The roar was machinelike; it was steady, but seemed to be fading. Puzzled, she crept in its direction, keeping low, and looked out from the trees at the distant shacks.

A machine resembling a cart, but larger, rode over the burned field. The ground had been turned and the machine, dragging what looked like a giant comb behind it, was digging rows. There was a cab on top of the machine, and someone inside it, steering. Zoheret turned to the nearest tree and climbed up; the bark was rough against her sore hands. She stood up on a limb and peered out through the branches.

In the plain just beyond the settlement stood five square vehicles with tracks; she thought of metal beasts preying on the settlement. Clinging to the tree trunk, she turned toward the storehouse. A group of young people had gathered there; two figures were sitting in the shadows of the porch. One of them rose and walked out to the steps. It was a man, and he wore a short beard.

Zoheret thought, They've come out from the corridors. They had lied. Why? What were they trying to do? A glint caught her eyes. A square, glassy booth with slots was on the porch—a food dispenser. Her mouth watered. The man was speaking, but she could not hear his voice. The small group dispersed and the man retreated to the shadows. Then she noticed something else; part of a fence had been erected around the edge of the settlement itself.

She perched on the tree limb, thinking. Either the people in the corridors had lied, or this was yet another group of strangers. How many secrets had Ship kept from them?

She would have to be cautious. She did not know how these strangers would handle her appeal; she did not even know who they were, or how they had come here, and there was little time to find out.

Zoheret crept along the riverbank, concealing herself among some reeds. The day had grown overcast, the river misty. For once, she was pleased with that; the dimmer light would make it easier for her to hide. She looked up at her shack. When night came, she might be able to get inside without being seen; if Lillka was there, she could question her.

Voices jabbered above her; she crouched. The voices grew faint. Water seeped into her boots. Someone was walking along the bank; she noted the blossom behind one ear and recognized Bonnie. The girl was alone. As she drew nearer, Zoheret hissed, then whispered, "Bonnie."

Bonnie crept closer. "Zoheret!"

"Quiet!" Zoheret flailed through the reeds toward a thick bush higher on the bank and sat under it, motioning to the other girl. Bonnie looked around, then hurried toward her.

"What are you doing?" Bonnie said in a low voice as she sat down. "Where are the others?"

"They're prisoners of Ho and his group."

Bonnie sighed in dismay. "You got away, then."

"No, Ho sent me here."

"*Sent* you?"

"He wants supplies. If he doesn't get them, he'll take it out on the others. He won't feed them until I get back. You know what he's like. He means it."

Bonnie shook her head. "We have enough trouble already. I don't know how to tell you this."

"What's happening here? I saw a dispenser on the storehouse porch, and a strange man. Who is he?" She thought of Aleksandr and Kieu, afraid she already knew.

"They came here on the day you left. They came riding up in those vehicles of theirs. We got out our weapons, but Lillka told us not to fight until she talked to them, so we waited. They told us they'd come to help, but they were surprised to find us here—they'd expected infants in the nursery at most."

"But who are they?"

Bonnie put one hand on Zoheret's arm. "You won't believe this. They're from Earth—from the Project."

"But that's impossible."

"They said they'd been suspended and stored aboard Ship. They thought Ship wouldn't be able to raise us alone, so they were going to have themselves revived just before we were born, to bring us up. They knew it was risky, but they did it anyway. They knew Ship's plans, so they set their devices so they'd be awakened just before we were supposed to be born. But something went wrong, so they didn't wake up until now."

So this group, Zoheret thought, had nothing to do with Aleksandr and his friends. If their plan had worked, they would have been awakened before that group's birth.

"When they came into the Hollow," Bonnie continued, "they tried to speak to Ship, but it didn't answer, so they realized that its sensors were probably shut down. I think that scared them, though they wouldn't admit it when they were speaking to us. They decided they'd better stay in the Hollow and figure out what to do, so they brought out more equipment. Finally, they found us, and that was when they knew they'd been awakened too late."

"But Ship never told us about them."

"They claim," Bonnie said, "that Ship didn't know."

"Ship had to know."

"They said it didn't. It was toward the end of the Project—they were aboard before Ship was activated. They've been in suspension ever since Ship left Earth, but it never knew they were aboard."

"But Ship would have found out eventually."

"Not if it had no sensors in the part of itself where they were. They probably made sure of that. And they weren't part of the plan, so Ship wouldn't even have suspected anything." Bonnie frowned. "I don't like them. They're telling us what to do, and it's hard to stand up to them. They've got their own ideas about how things should go. They're putting up more fences—they say it's to protect the settlement—and they're beginning to check on where we are all the time. I don't know what to think."

"Do the others feel the way you do?"

Bonnie shrugged. "I don't know. I think a lot of them are too busy stuffing down food to care, and now they don't have to make decisions. Besides, what can we do? They talked us into giving up our weapons, supposedly for our own safety and so that they could keep track of them, and now you can't get one without their permission. They know Ship's sensors are off—Lillka confirmed that. People who don't do what they say get the dirtiest jobs to do—Gowon got waste collection when they found out he'd hidden his gun. Somebody must have told them. That's another thing—you don't know who to trust now." She leaned forward. "They don't belong here. They don't have the right."

"Do you think they'll help me?"

"I don't know."

"Bonnie, if I don't get back to Ho with supplies by the day after tomorrow, the others are in trouble."

"Well, I don't know how you're going to get any without the old people finding out."

"Are they really old?" Zoheret asked, wondering what an aged person was like in the flesh.

"Some have wrinkles. A couple of the men look like they're losing some hair. One woman told me she was thirty when she was suspended."

Leaves rustled nearby. Zoheret tensed, glancing toward the sound. A young deer scurried away, and she relaxed. "I have to talk to Lillka."

Bonnie wrapped her arms around her legs. "I don't know if you should. Lillka's really fascinated by them—she keeps following them around to ask about Earth. I told you she was a bad leader. She doesn't stand up to them. If you talk to her, she'll just tell you to come out and ask them to help."

"You think I shouldn't."

"I told you—I don't know what to think. I don't trust them. I was talking to this woman, the one I mentioned before—her name's Petra. She asked me about Willem, and I explained, and she said, 'How unfortunate,' and there was something about the way she said it that gave me a chill. And then she said, 'We'll take care of that.' I don't like it. I don't know why."

"Maybe she knows how to cure him."

"You don't cure someone like Willem." Bonnie pulled at a blade of grass, twisting it around in her fingers. "Maybe they would help you. They could sneak up on Ho. They have plenty of stuff to do it with—I saw their weapons. They have more than we did. They thought they might need them for protection against animals."

"But I have to meet Ho alone, on that island on the lake, and I can't bring anyone with me—he'll see if I do. And I don't know where his group is staying, or where he's holding the others. What am I going to do?"

"The strangers will go after Ho eventually," Bonnie answered. "They know about him and his gang—Lillka told them when they asked about the burned field. And they'll start looking for you, too, when you don't turn up."

"Did Lillka tell them where we were going?"

"Yes, but I don't think she told them why—she didn't want them to know Ship was acting strange. But they'll find out—someone'll tell them. By the way, did you get to the corridors?"

"We got there. Ho caught us afterward."

"Did you find anything?"

"No." The denial was out almost before Zoheret had time to think. She could not burden Bonnie with knowledge of the corridor dwellers, especially if there was a chance the strangers might get that information from the other girl. "Ship just didn't want us back there—it didn't want us getting into old habits by being in that environment again." She hoped she sounded convincing.

"It could have said so—it didn't have to be so dramatic." Bonnie turned toward her. "You've got some time. We all figured you'd stay in the corridors a while before coming back. What are you going to do?"

"Bonnie, I have to trust you. You've seen these Earthpeople. What would you do?"

"I wouldn't trust them. And you're right about one thing—if they go after Ho, the kids he's caught could get hurt before they catch him." She stood up. "I have to go—they'll wonder where I am. They've been watching us—that's another reason I don't trust them."

"Can you come back later?"

"I don't know."

"I need food." Guiltily she thought of her captive comrades.

"I'll try. I can't promise."

"I'll wait over there, in the woods."

It was night before Zoheret heard the sound of approaching people along the bank. The dim light revealed two shadowy shapes.

"Zoheret." It was Bonnie's whispery voice. "I've brought Brendan—it's all right, you can trust him." She came toward the trees and handed Zoheret meat, bread, and a bottle.

Zoheret grabbed the food, stuffing it down before gulping the fruit juice. When she had finished eating, Brendan said, "Bonnie told me everything. No one else knows."

"Not even Lillka?"

"Especially not Lillka." The pair sat down near her. "I don't like what's going on, and she knows it. Those people . . ." He paused. "I don't know if I can help you."

"I have to go back and meet Ho."

"I know."

"I need supplies."

"I don't know how you're going to get them."

"I can't just forget about the others." Zoheret swallowed the last of the juice. "I have to go back, even with nothing. I couldn't live with myself if they were hurt, or they died."

Brendan sighed. "I understand. I wish I didn't."

"We might be able to get you a pack," Bonnie said. "We can try."

"It won't be enough."

"Better than nothing. Maybe you can stall Ho somehow, talk to him, gain some time until—"

"Could you talk to him?" Zoheret said bitterly. "Ho? You must be kidding."

"Listen," Brendan said, "we'll try to come back later and—" His head jerked up. "Somebody's coming."

Zoheret had already heard the low voices. She hoisted herself up the nearest tree limb and crawled in among the leaves, settling in the crotch of the tree. Bonnie and Brendan crept a short distance down the bank, then stretched out on a mossy spot, wrapping their arms around each other.

A light swayed from side to side, describing an arc, then fell, illuminating the two figures on the ground. "Hey!" Brendan cried, managing to sound offended rather than frightened. He threw up a hand and sat up.

"There you are," a woman's voice said. The hand holding the light pointed it at the ground. "You shouldn't wander off like that."

"We wanted to be alone," Brendan responded.

"I can see that."

"You shouldn't have come out here," a man's voice said. "It could be dangerous, especially at night."

Zoheret, afraid even to breathe, glanced down and realized with horror that she had left the empty bottle at the foot of the tree. She stared at the light bobbing up and down in the woman's hand, waiting for it to shine in her direction and reveal the gleam of the bottle.

"I know why you're here," the woman said. Zoheret's fingers dug into her thighs. "They don't want the others to know." Her dark shape bent forward. "Brendan's friend Lillka might be mad if she knew he was out here with someone else." The voice rose and fell in a singsong, as if she were taunting the pair. "That is not a nice thing to do." She laughed, as if their supposed misdeed gave her pleasure. "Come on. We're going back. Time to sleep."

The two young people rose. A hand grabbed Bonnie, pulling her away from Brendan. Bonnie said, "You're hurting me."

"Let's go."

Zoheret stayed in the tree until she could no longer see the tiny, distant, dancing light.

It had rained, and Zoheret was shivering by morning. After wringing out her soggy clothes and dressing again, she crept down to the river and drank. She stayed near the trees, hoping that Brendan or Bonnie would find a way to get a pack to her. But the morning passed without a sign from either.

No one else came near her hiding place. She could hear the distant sounds of the settlement—the clatter of tools, even an occasional outburst of song. She thought of her life in the settlement now as she had once thought of her time in the corridors. It seemed a happier, more carefree time that she had not appreciated while living through it—happiness seemed always to exist in the past, never in the present.

Ho might kill his captives; he might kill her. Accepting that did not make her fearful; instead, it seemed to blunt her feelings, making her feel stunned and empty. Ho had not worried that his cheating during Competition might cause deaths, and he had grown harder while living in the Hollow. He would bend his band to his will. He would not even have to raise a hand to his captives; he could let them starve slowly.

She could avoid that fate if she remained here. Bonnie and Brendan might be wrong about the Earthpeople. She could stay, and live.

As afternoon passed, fading into dusk, she realized that Bonnie and Brendan had failed, that no one would help her. The day, which had seemed endless while she waited, was now too short. Help me, she thought, and the words were swallowed by a void.

Someone was approaching. Zoheret peered around a tree and saw Bonnie. The girl held out empty hands.

"We can't get a pack," Bonnie said. "I couldn't even get you more food."

Zoheret wrung her hands. "I'll go to Ship," she said. "It'll tell us what to do. It'll have to help now—these people weren't part of its plan."

"Maybe they lied. Maybe Ship knew."

"I have to take the chance. At least Ship can help the others—it won't let Ho starve them."

"Ho." Bonnie pursed her lips as though she had tasted something sour. "He'd sure be mad if he knew about the old people. He always wanted to control everybody, to make them do what he wanted. He couldn't stand it when someone tried to push him around, and that's what they'll do if they find him. He'll bust a gut when he knows."

"I'll go to . . ." Zoheret was silent. Bonnie was stepping backward, her hands up. Zoheret turned.

The woman had come through the woods silently, without rustling a leaf or cracking a twig. Her pale face shone in the fading light; her lips were curved in an oddly threatening smile.

"Petra," Bonnie said weakly.

"So this is what you've been doing," the woman said, and Zoheret recognized the voice she had heard the night before. The stranger stood several paces away, but Zoheret could hear the resonant voice as clearly as if Petra had been standing next to her. "You're helping that other band I heard about." She pointed at Zoheret. "That's who you're with, isn't it?" She did not wait for an answer. "We've got you now, and you're going to tell us where the rest are. We want you all together with us."

Bonnie stood up very straight. Then, abruptly, she spun around and slid down the bank, throwing herself in the water. The woman cried out; Zoheret saw her hand moving toward the weapon at her belt. Bonnie's arms were scimitars cutting through the black water.

The realization came to her slowly. Petra's fingers were closing around her gun as Zoheret understood what she had to do; Bonnie had shown her. She ran down the bank and threw herself in the river, splashing out until the undertow caught her; the current would carry her away more quickly than she could run.

She saw a beam shoot out toward Bonnie as she bobbed in the water. The girl was splashing fiercely, trying to stay afloat and draw fire away from Zoheret. Petra was screaming for aid; then she ran along the bank, firing again. A beam hit Bonnie. Zoheret saw her sink.

The current submerged Zoheret. She came up, choking; Petra was already distant. Zoheret's boots were heavy weights dragging her down. She managed to pull them off and let them sink. The river spun her around and pulled at her. She unbelted her pants, then rose for more air.

The sound of the rushing water was deafening, a roar muted only when she was pulled under into a silent watery world. She rose and fell, gulping as much air as she could before sinking again. She had shed her pants at last; her legs could kick freely. She did not fight the current, but let it carry her; she tried to float, but the river washed over her. She swallowed water and coughed it up painfully.

The river bore her through the chasm. One foot hit a rock and she moaned, taking in more water. Flapping about with her hands, she clutched a large piece of wood. She clung to it as the river sang. There was now a rhythm to her journey; her gasps for air seemed to come at regular intervals and her legs kicked in time to the river's song.

Gradually she realized that the current was weakening. She kicked toward land and waded out of the water, unsure of where she had alighted. Her legs gave way and she fell, hugging the ground.

The light awoke her. She rolled over onto her back and looked up at the bright glow. Bonnie, she thought, and then: They might be searching for me. She stumbled to her feet.

14

Zoheret turned the boat over, then pushed it toward the water. She had managed to walk this far down the river in her socks, and her feet already hurt, bruised by hard pebbles; getting to an entrance would be impossible. She knew she should have gone to Ship instead of waiting at the settlement, but she had been unable to make that decision. Her friends would suffer no matter what she did now, but she could share their punishment. Perhaps Ho would take care of them quickly instead of letting them suffer.

She climbed into the boat and rowed toward the lake. Ho was going to be surprised to see her in a shirt and underwear; he might even find it amusing.

The smooth lake made her think again of Bonnie sinking beneath a more turbulent surface. Bonnie had been speaking of Ho before the woman found them; Zoheret tried to remember what she had said.

She pulled up the oars. There was a way out, a small chance, a way to help her friends. She hoped it would work. She would not let this chance slip away; she could afford no more mistakes.

She rowed more swiftly toward the island; she was already a bit late. Ho would wait. He would have to wait.

The island's shore was rocky, but on the mound above it, tall evergreens and slender birches grew. She rowed around it until she sighted a small cove; as she drifted near, she noticed that two large bushes near the sand below the rocks were actually heaps of branches hiding other boats. She got out and waded in, pulling the boat up and tying it to a young tree, then yanking the rope to make sure the knot would hold.

"So you got here at last."

She looked up. Ho stood above her, arms folded. "I don't see any supplies." He came down the slope until he stood near her. "Hands up. No weapon, I see. What happened to your clothes?"

"I've got something to tell you, something important."

He grabbed her arm, almost making her fall. "It's a trick," he said angrily. "It's a trick, isn't it?"

"If I were going to trick you, I wouldn't have come here like this."

"How do I know that?"

"You don't—you'll just have to trust me. I almost got killed yesterday. Bonnie's probably dead."

Manuel was walking along the rocks toward them. "Did you hear that?" she shouted. "Bonnie's probably dead. Don't you want to know why?"

Manuel came to her side; he seemed stunned. "Let her talk, Ho." They perched on the rocks.

"I want to know if the others are all right first."

Ho leaned toward her. "You're in no position to bargain."

"Oh, yes, I am. If I don't tell you what I know, you're going to have more trouble than you can imagine. Where are they?"

"They're here," Manuel said. "Ho didn't want them to know where our base is. They're all right."

"Have they been fed?"

"We gave them water."

"I want to see them, and then I want them fed before I tell you anything."

Ho slapped her hard. She jumped to her feet, rubbing her cheek. "Don't do that again," she shouted. "I've got nothing to lose now, but you do. You'd better listen." Her voice echoed across the lake.

Ho stood up. He and Manuel went to the boat, untied it, and pulled it up, concealing it with the others. "Come on."

She followed him over the rocks, Manuel trailing them. He led her through the trees to a small clearing.

The others were there, sitting on the ground, still tied together. They looked dirty, tired, and sick. Dmitri looked at her with weary eyes. Owen pointed at her bare legs and began to laugh until a sharp look from Ho stopped him. Vittorio was the only other member of Ho's band present.

Zoheret marched toward the captives and sat down next to Dmitri. "Feed them," she said. "Give me food, too." Ho hesitated. "Right now."

"I could force it out of you."

"Just try." She stared at him until he looked away.

Ho dug around in the packs and threw them each a large meat dumpling. Zoheret tore at the wrapping and ate while

Ho and his companions murmured among themselves. Owen gestured wildly, shaking his head.

"What happened?" Dmitri asked between bites. "Where are your clothes? Did you get the supplies?"

She shook her head. "You'll hear soon enough."

Ho walked over to them again, followed by his friends. "All right, you had your food." The four sat down. "Now talk."

Zoheret took a breath. "There are people in the settlement—strangers." Tonio grunted and Zoheret glanced at him, warning him with her eyes to be silent. "They're running things there now."

Ho was scowling by the time she finished her tale, but he had not interrupted her. Owen was shaking his head. "It's a trick."

"How could I make up a story like that? If it weren't for Bonnie, I might not even be here. Well, I've told you. You can't use hostages now, and when those people start looking for you, I don't think you'll get away."

"We could go to the settlement," Manuel said. "We could give ourselves up." Ho glared at him.

"One of those people shot Bonnie," Zoheret said. "She didn't try to help her, or pull her out—she shot her. And she tried to shoot me. That's what convinced me Bonnie was right about them. If you go there, you'd better make up your mind to do what they say, and you might not like that." She looked at Ho.

"What else can we do?" Manuel said.

She needed to win Ho's trust, and in order to do that, she would have to tell him everything. She wondered if she could trust him. Once she had told him all she knew, he would not need her or her friends. She examined his face, trying to discover a spark of compassion, of mercy. She could not. Ship had made as many errors with Ho as it had with Willem or Anoki.

"We can go into the corridors," she said slowly.

Owen straightened. "It *is* a trick. She went to Ship, and Ship told her to tell us this story. Ship wants us there so it can punish us."

"I didn't go to Ship."

"Then you sent people there, to wait for us. It's a trick."

She ignored Owen; Ho was the one she had to convince. "There are strangers in the corridors, too."

Tonio gasped. "You shouldn't have told them that."

"I have to. We have to cooperate now." Quickly she told Ho about the people in the corridors, filling in a few details about his sister Kieu. "They might help us," she finished. "They seemed to care—they aren't like the ones in the settlement."

"Are you so sure?" Ho said. "How do you know they aren't working with the others?"

"I had a feeling about them."

"A feeling." Ho snorted.

"Yes."

"What about the rest of you? Did you have the same feeling?" The captives hung their heads. Back me up, Zoheret wanted to shout, say something. Even Kagami was peering at her dubiously from under lowered lids. "I know why you're not talking," Ho went on. "It's a lie, and you have nothing to say because there's nothing to add."

"It's not a lie," Dmitri said. "It's true. How could anybody make all that up?"

Zoheret stared straight at Ho. "You can do what you like with us now—you know everything. Holding prisoners won't do you any good—you have nothing to gain. But we could help—we can make plans together."

Ho smiled. "You don't want to help me."

"How do you know?" Appealing to Ho's sentiments would not help; maybe a practical argument would. "Think of it this way—if we work together, and if we can figure out what to do about the Earthpeople, you'll be a hero. Ship won't punish you, and everybody'll listen to you then, not just a small group." She waved a hand at Owen. "Maybe they'll even make you the leader afterward—not just here, but on the new world. But if you hurt us, eventually Ship will know—it'll search the whole area with its sensors. You won't be able to bury us deep enough. And the other kids would always be suspicious— they'd wonder what happened to us if Ship couldn't find us. I mean, where could we go? And one of your friends might tell them. You'd never know—you'd have to be on guard forever."

She waited. Ho was already glancing furtively at his friends, who gazed ahead blandly.

Manuel said, "You should listen to her."

"Don't tell me what to do!" Ho shouted. "I know you, Manuel—you think you can run things better than I can. Well, you can't." He got up and paced, head down. Zoheret folded her hands; she had done all she could.

Kagami leaned toward her. "Is Bonnie really—?" She turned away. A look of pain crossed Manuel's face; he lifted a hand to his forehead, as if trying to hide his feelings from his comrades.

"I saw her go under," Zoheret answered. "She was unconscious. I don't know if that woman got her out in time—or even tried to. She was still standing on the bank when the current pulled me away."

Ho strode back to the group and stood over her, hands on

his hips. "All right," he said. "I've decided. We're going back to the settlement—you and me. I'm going to check this out for myself."

"You're crazy. It's too risky. They might be looking for you now."

"You might be telling me that because it's true. You also might be saying it because it's all a lie and you don't want me to find that out. You just want to go running to Ship. Everyone always went running to Ship. They never settled things with me—they just ran to Ship until I made them stop." He drew his lips back from his teeth. "Once you get me in the corridors, I can't do a thing."

"Ho, you have to believe me. We'd all be safer in the corridors. We ought to go there right away. What if those strangers cut off the way to the entrances?"

"If I find out you're right about those people, then we can think about that." A sly look crossed Ho's face. "Besides, we might be able to work out something with those people—if they're really there."

"You wouldn't think so if you—"

He grabbed her shoulders, pulling her to her feet. "You spoke to one woman—or so you say. All you know—supposedly—is what Brendan and Bonnie told you." He shook her; she twisted away. He slapped her and she slapped him back. He punched her in the belly and she doubled over, falling to the ground.

"We're going to go there," he continued, "and if anything happens to me, you'll be the first to suffer—I can throw my knife faster than anyone can shoot. And if you mess up, it'll be hard on your friends here. I can still use them after all."

She sat up; her belly hurt. "I need pants and boots."

"I can get you some old pants. You'll have to make do with

moccasins—Vittorio here makes them from hides." He turned
to the other boys. "We'd better make plans."

H o had left for his hidden camp, taking one of the boats.
Vittorio had tied up Zoheret, reconnecting her to her
bound friends with rope. Then he and Owen settled themselves at the other side of the clearing, watching them while
Manuel napped.

Tonio gazed at his bound hands. "We're in worse trouble
now."

"No, you're not," Zoheret answered. "He'll find out I'm
right, and we'll go to the corridors and be safe."

"Unless something goes wrong. And we'll have to sit here
waiting—we can't do a thing about it. You don't know what
that's like."

Her anger flared. "I could have stayed in the settlement,
you know. I could have given myself up—whatever those
people are like, it would have been better than this. I could
have just thought of myself. And if I had stayed, Bonnie
might still be . . ." Her voice shook, and she swallowed. "If
any of you had put up a fight before, we might have gotten
away. But you didn't. It was easier to give up. So don't blame
me." Zoheret lowered her voice. "We could still try. All we
need to do is get our hands on one weapon—get one of those
guys over here. But you don't want to do that—you'd rather
wait and have someone else save you." She stared at Tonio.
"You're pretty brave when it comes to burning empty cabins
or talking, but you don't come through the rest of the time."

"Zoheret." Dmitri put a hand on hers. "This won't do us
any good now."

"Shut up over there," Owen shouted.

"Make me!" Zoheret screamed back. "Come on, just try
it." She got to her feet; the rope binding her to Dmitri was

stretched tight. Raising her bound hands before her, she made fists.

"Sit down!"

"Make me!"

Owen took a step toward her. Manuel, awake now, rolled to his feet and grabbed Owen's arm, pulling the other boy toward him. Owen shook him away. "If you don't sit down," the blond boy said slowly, "and shut your mouth, nobody's going to get fed. Is that clear?"

"You better sit down," Serena murmured.

"They killed your dog," Zoheret said. "Don't you care?"

"I can't do anything for Red now."

Zoheret sat down, defeated. Manuel dug in the packs and pulled out food, then picked up a canteen and came toward them. He stopped several paces away and threw them the packages, then the canteen, covering them with his weapon while they ate.

"Don't make trouble," he said. "Nothing'll happen to you. You'll be all right."

"Oh, I'm sure we will," Zoheret responded.

"I said you'd be all right, and your friends won't get hurt." Manuel said the words quickly in a low voice, widening his eyes a bit and arching his eyebrows, as if trying to lend the words an added significance. He turned and walked back to his friends.

Was Manuel saying that he would keep his companions from harming them? Was he even, perhaps, implying that he might set them free? He and Ho were rivals; maybe he was tired of taking Ho's orders. She longed to trust him, but was afraid to do so.

Zoheret's bare legs, dampened by dew, were stiff by daylight. She sat up and rubbed them. Her muscles ached, but she had slept deeply; she was becoming used to sleeping in the open.

Ho had returned. Vittorio was no longer present; Daniella and a freckled, red-haired boy named Gene were. Owen, however, was still with them.

Ho crossed the clearing and threw a pair of pants at Zoheret, then dropped a pair of moccasins at her side. "Put them on."

"I can't while my legs are still tied."

He pulled out his knife and cut the ropes at her ankles and wrists quickly, then backed away. "Go on, get dressed." The pants were patched at the knees with leather, frayed at the cuffs, and too loose at the waist; she made a belt of a piece of rope. The moccasins were too tight; she wriggled her toes, hoping they would stretch.

Manuel gave them cakes and water for breakfast; Owen forced them to relieve themselves under his contemptuous gaze. Ho began to give instructions to his subordinates. "Listen. You'll have to ration the food left in the packs, so be careful. Feed the prisoners once a day and yourselves twice. If you fish, make sure you can't be seen from the shore, and I don't want a fire here—it might give you away."

"Why feed them at all?" Owen asked.

"Because I said so. Because I don't want Zoheret here to get so worried about them that she does something stupid and lands me in trouble. And don't slap them around, either. They might try something if you do."

Manuel said, "I'll look out for them."

"No, you won't. You're coming with us."

Manuel's eyes widened. Zoheret's spirits sank. There was no chance for her friends now unless she brought Ho back safely.

Ho motioned to Manuel, who picked up one of the packs after removing some of the provisions. "Now," Ho continued, "if I'm not back here in three days, take them to our base—Vittorio will be back here by then with a couple of extra boats and some more help. And if I'm not back during the next three days—well, then you have to decide what to do by yourselves. If you come after me, be careful."

"What about them?" Owen jerked his head in the prisoners' direction.

Ho shrugged. "You can do what you want then." Owen grinned. Zoheret looked back at Dmitri; he smiled, trying to seem unconcerned.

"Come on." Ho led Manuel and Zoheret toward the trees. Daniella trailed after Ho, as if wanting to speak. "Remember what I told you," Ho muttered without turning his head.

"Don't worry," Daniella answered, and turned back to the clearing.

"You're so clever," Zoheret said to Ho after they reached the cove. They scampered down the rocks toward the hidden boats. "If anything happens to my friends now, it's out of your hands—at least that's what you're thinking. But I'll know. I'll know it was your responsibility."

"You're wrong," he said as they pushed a boat into the water. "It'll be yours. You just do what you're supposed to, and we'll head for the corridors if I find you were telling the truth—I can have Ship signal with its sensors when we get there. And your friends can go where they like."

"Owen might not listen to Ship. You'll have to come back here yourself."

Manuel threw the pack into the boat. Zoheret climbed in and sat in the bow while Manuel took the oars, his back to her. Ho pushed the boat off and hopped into the stern.

"You shouldn't have left Owen on the island," Manuel said.

"Better to have him there than in camp. Daniella and Gene will watch him."

"And better to have me with you."

"Right."

Zoheret rested her hands on the gunwales, weary of Ho's constant need for dominance. For a moment, she almost hoped that he would be caught by the strangers in the settlement. "Why can't you trust me?" she asked, knowing even as she said it that Ho could trust no one—not even Manuel and Owen, his supposed friends. "Why can't you take my word?"

"I can't, that's all." She wondered if he wished that he could.

Manuel was a strong rower. Ho studied the water, guiding Manuel away from the strong current. They traveled up the river until the banks began to grow steep.

"This is far enough," Ho said. They drifted toward the bank and pulled the boat out, then gathered fallen branches. When the boat was concealed, Ho stood beside it, hands on hips. "Which way do you think we should approach?" he asked Zoheret.

"They'd see us on the plain. We'll have to go up through the woods."

"You probably laid a trap there."

"How could I lay a trap when I didn't want you to come back here in the first place?"

"Maybe you knew I'd check. Maybe Owen was right, and it's a trick. Just remember what'll happen to you and your friends if you lied." He paused. "We'll approach along the edge of the woods near the plain."

"Don't you think we ought to split up?" she asked. "If one of us were caught, the others could get away."

"Oh, you'd like that, wouldn't you. You'd disappear so fast I'd never see you again."

"Don't you think I care what happens to my friends?"

"Maybe you do, maybe you don't." He gave her a shove. "Go on."

She climbed up the rest of the bank and into the woods, with Ho just behind her; Manuel put on the pack. As she walked, she brushed aside low branches, feeling tempted to let them snap back at Ho's face.

The whine made her jump. She swung around. Ho hit the ground face down, arms out. Manuel was holding his stun gun; he slid it into his belt and then rummaged at Ho's waist for his weapons.

Zoheret, stunned, stared at Manuel. "Why?" she managed to say.

"Because I believe you. You were telling the truth about those strangers, weren't you?"

"Of course I was."

"And about Bonnie."

"Yes."

He sighed. "I was sure you wouldn't make that up. We have to get to the corridors, then." He pulled Ho's shirt off, tore it into strips, and bound Ho's wrists and feet. "The settlement's farther down the plain—they won't see somebody crossing farther up, especially if you keep to the higher grass. Do you think you can get to the entrance?"

"We got there during Competition, didn't we? It's an easy trip. But what about you?"

"I'll go back to the island and get your friends. I can think of something to say—Gene and Daniella will listen. If Owen gives me trouble, I'll shoot him, too."

"Manuel—" She could think of nothing else to say. "Thanks."

"Ho shouldn't have turned his back on me." He took off

the pack. "Take this. You might need it. And this." He tossed her the pack and one of the stun guns.

By the time she had put on the pack and slipped the weapon under her rope belt, Manuel was retreating toward the river. Then she heard the cry—a cry of triumph—and the familiar whine.

She spun around and ran toward the plain, darting among the trees. Footsteps pounded behind her, growing louder. Soon she was panting so hard under the weight of the pack that she could hear nothing but her gasps and the pounding of blood in her ears. A tree trunk was suddenly before her. She slammed against it, cried out, and fell backward.

She was pulled to her feet. Strong arms held her as she struggled and kicked. "Enough of that," a deep voice said. "You're caught, so behave yourself." The voice was guttural, the words oddly accented. The arms swung her around.

A woman stood in front of her; she was sure it was Petra, though her face did not look as pale in the daylight. One arm held Zoheret while the other took her weapon; then she was released.

The arms belonged to a man with streaks of gray in his beard. "We have her two friends," the woman said; it was Petra's voice. "They're knocked out. One of them's tied up. They must have had a disagreement." She smiled. "We'll have to revive them before marching them back. You bring the boat." She peered at Zoheret. "I think I recognize you. So you're alive. We've been searching along the banks, wondering where you might wash up. You got lucky. So did we."

15

Zoheret said, "This isn't my house."

"It is now." The men shoved her through the door and pushed Ho and Manuel in after her. One of the men muttered a few words in another language, then turned toward the young people. "Don't come out. We'll be watching the door."

They were in Tonio and Dmitri's shack. Zoheret wandered into the back rooms, but found no one; they were alone.

As she entered the front room again, Ho leaped at her, closing his hands around her neck. She grabbed his wrists. Manuel pulled him away.

"This is your fault," Ho shouted at Manuel. "If it hadn't been for you . . ." He raised his fists, then let them fall as he dropped to the floor, holding his head, still fighting off the aftereffects of the stun gun. Manuel sank down, his back against the wall; he, too, looked weak.

Zoheret, keeping her distance from the angry Ho, sat down near Manuel. "At least now you know I was telling the truth. I told you not to come here."

Ho lifted his head. "Your friends are done for now. You don't know how happy that makes me. I hope you think about that a lot."

Zoheret leaned back, remembering their walk through the settlement to this house. No one had approached her; none of the young people along the way had even made a sign. A few had turned away. They probably thought she had thrown in her lot with Ho.

There had been other changes in the settlement. Already the newcomers were constructing wooden watchtowers at each end of the main road, and the fence around the settlement was almost finished. Their tools and machines had made the work go quickly.

"I'll tell them," she said finally. "I'll tell the strangers that my friends are prisoners on the island, and they'll go get them."

"And I'll say you're lying."

"Come on, Ho," Manuel said. "What good will that do now?"

"You should have thought of that before you shot me."

Zoheret looked down at the floor, tracing a knothole with one finger. It wasn't a good idea anyway; her friends would be prisoners here, too. They still had a chance to get free; when they realized Ho wasn't coming back, maybe they would act. If they could get to the corridors, and persuade Ho's band to do the same, something might be done.

"If we ever get out of here," Ho said, "you're dead." He gazed at Manuel. "Just remember that. I'll wait for my chance and take it. You think about that, my friend. I should have taken care of you a long time ago."

The door opened, and another person was pushed inside. The door slammed. Zoheret stared at the newcomer, unbelieving, and was suddenly on her feet. "Bonnie!" Ho turned; Manuel's eyes were wide.

Zoheret ran to the other girl and held her by the shoulders. "I thought you were dead."

"I thought you were, too." She removed Zoheret's hands. "Don't grab me there—it hurts." Bonnie gazed at the boys. "You. Of all the people I'd want to share a house with, you two are about the last." Ho sneered; Manuel lowered his eyes. "Just don't come near me. Even breathing the same air as you makes me sick." She took Zoheret's arm and led her to one of the back rooms.

Zoheret stretched out on one bed while Bonnie sat on the other. "They pulled me out," Bonnie said. "I must have swallowed enough water to sink a boat. They had to work on me hard. I didn't tell them anything. They tried to bribe me, and then the one named Caleb beat me, and I still didn't talk. I ache all over."

"*Beat* you?"

Bonnie nodded. "Some of them are mean, but they don't let most of the kids see it. Caleb made sure no one saw him question me. He put a gag on me so I couldn't scream. When he took it off, I spat in his face, and then I screamed. He had to tell the kids nearby that I threw a tantrum. He made sure he didn't leave any marks."

"But why?"

"Because I wouldn't talk. What could I tell them, anyway? I didn't think you'd made it, even though I hoped you had. I didn't know where Ho would take the others if you didn't get back to the island, and there was always a chance you or someone might have gone to the corridors to see Ship." Bonnie sighed. "I always thought Ho was wired wrong, but he's nothing compared to these Earthpeople. They're experts. I keep wondering if everyone on the Project was like this. When I think of all that stuff Ship told us about Sato and al-Haq and their noble dream, I don't know whether to laugh or cry."

"Maybe the rest of the Project wasn't like them. They weren't part of the plan."

Bonnie frowned. "And maybe the rest of Earth was happy to get rid of them. Why did you come back here?"

"Ho forced me to. He wouldn't believe me."

"That sounds like him."

"Manuel shot him with a stun gun. He was going to go back for the others while I went to the corridors to get help. Then we were all caught. Manuel was trying to help me, but maybe if he hadn't shot Ho, we could have fought the strangers, and one of us might have gotten away."

"Manuel." Bonnie's mouth twisted; she shook her head. "I don't even know if Ship can help us now."

Zoheret was about to tell Bonnie about the people in the corridors, then paused. Ho knew about them now. He might decide that it was worth his while to convey that information to the adults. "Isn't anyone here standing up to the strangers yet?"

"Brendan is—not that it does him much good. We're both the troublemakers around here. They've got him out in the field—he'll be here later. This is the official home of all troublemakers. Anoki doesn't like them, but he's going along for now—he feels he has to look out for Willem."

"What about the others?"

Bonnie waved a hand. "Look—for most of them, things

are a lot easier around here than they were. They're fed, and if they're good, they don't have to work too hard. Now the Earthpeople are trying to organize us, saying they're going to teach us."

"How many are there?"

"About twenty-five or thirty. I haven't met them all, because a few of them keep to themselves. But it doesn't matter—they've got control."

Zoheret put her hands behind her head. "What are they going to do when we get to the new world?"

"Keep telling us what to do, I guess."

"It isn't fair."

"It doesn't matter what's fair."

Zoheret stared at the ceiling. "If Ho and Manuel don't get back to the island, I don't know what's going to happen to the others."

"Is that where they are?"

"It's where they are now."

"Well, they aren't going to get back."

Zoheret threw an arm over her eyes. She should have lied to Ho when she first went back to the island, told him only that the settlement had refused to bargain and had thrown her out. She could have made him believe that, and then she and the other captives would have had no value to him, and he might have let them go just to get them off his hands. She should not have trusted him. She thought of everything too late. Then she remembered that Ho had made a mistake in trusting Manuel.

Was this what they were supposed to learn, not to trust? Zoheret, having failed to learn how to lie well, how to cheat, how to use others, how to deceive, was ill equipped for survival. She wondered if it was too late to learn.

16

Ho and Manuel had been taken away after breakfast. Brendan was still sleeping in one of the bedrooms; Bonnie had told Zoheret that he slept a lot now, as if he could not bear to stay awake.

Zoheret wandered to the door and opened it. Petra was outside; she gestured at the door and told the girl to close it. Zoheret retreated to a corner, stared silently at Bonnie for a while, then went into the empty bedroom.

She tossed uneasily as she dozed until voices in the front room awoke her completely. Recognizing one of the voices, she sat up.

When Zoheret entered the front room, Lillka, seated on the floor with Bonnie, looked up, but did not smile. "Are you all right?"

"What are you doing here?" Zoheret said coldly.

"I came to see you. I asked Petra if I could. I've got something to tell you."

"You don't have to bother. Your new friends won't like it if you spend time with troublemakers."

"Stop it," Lillka said. "If you'd been here when they came, you would have done the same thing I did. I thought it was best this way. We needed their help. We still do."

"You don't have to explain," Zoheret said wearily, seating herself. "You were afraid. That's the real reason." She had made her own errors; it was not fair to hold Lillka to account.

"I've been talking to them," Lillka said, "asking questions. I wanted to find out more about Earth, about the Project. Petra and her friend Ah Lam talked to me until the others told them not to say so much. I wanted to know why they were here."

Bonnie said, "They told us that."

"Not the real reason. Would you go through being suspended, taking that chance, and being put on Ship, leaving everything you know behind and not knowing what might happen, unless you had a really strong reason?"

Bonnie shrugged. "Probably not."

"Well, they had one. And I don't mean all that stuff about needing to look after us, although that was part of it. They hated Earth. That's the reason. They hated everything that was happening in the solar system. I thought it was because they were afraid of dying in a war, but it wasn't. Do you know what the Project was?"

"We all know that."

Lillka shook her head and turned toward Zoheret. "No, you don't. It wasn't this wonderful, great thing everybody was working for. It was just a tiny little group that hated the way things were going and that wanted to preserve its own ways. I found that out from Ah Lam. Earth is nothing—it's just a ball of dirt some people cling to because they're afraid. Almost everyone else lives in places like Ship, only bigger and more complicated—they laugh at Earth. They're not even really human anymore—that's what Ah Lam says. Some of them are part machine—a lot of them don't even look like us. Earth is only a backwater, and even Earth has to depend on their technology. The Project was just a spiteful little jab. The people on the Project had this idea that it would somehow prove something if they sent us out, that it would show they were right. We're supposed to preserve pure humankind, whatever that means."

Zoheret wrapped her arms around her legs. The world was changing itself even before she could ground herself in one set of facts. There was nothing left for her to believe.

"I don't know how we're supposed to prove anything," Bonnie said, "when nobody back there is going to know what happened to us anyway."

"Oh, Ah Lam explained that. They'll get us settled, and then they'll send Ship to another world, and raise more kids, except that next time they'll make sure they're around to raise them from birth. And they'll go back into suspended animation while Ship's looking for another Earth-like planet. And they'll keep doing that until they have a lot of worlds seeded—that's what Ah Lam calls it, seeding. And eventually they'll travel back to our world to check up on our descendants. Oh, they have it all worked out—you should see Ah Lam when she talks about it. She starts breathing faster, and her eyes roll up under her lids as if she's having a fit." Lillka mimicked the expression. "They can do it, you know. They'll be in suspension a lot of the time, and hundreds of years will pass on our new home while only a few years pass aboard Ship when it's traveling at near-light speeds, so they'll be able to see what happens. And one day, they'll send a message back to Earth and the solar system, and everyone will know that the Project was successful."

"They won't do it," Zoheret said. "Ship won't let them. It was programmed to run the Project in a certain way, and it won't let them change it."

"Maybe Ship will listen to them," Bonnie said. "After all, they built it."

"It won't agree." Zoheret was angry. Was she going to live and have children and die on an unknown world only so that a group of old people could prove a point? She and the others in the Hollow were no more to these strangers than the microbes in the biology lab had been to her.

"Poor Ship," Lillka said. "They lied to it, too. All it ever told us about Earth was what the Project wanted it to know. I wonder how it's going to feel when it finds out."

"I don't care," Zoheret said. "I don't care about the Project and I don't care why they did it. We don't owe anything to Earth and we don't owe anything to the people out there."

Lillka looked down. "There's nothing we can do about it."

"There is. They don't have the right to make us what they want. We have to fight them."

"How?"

"There's more of us—we outnumber them. If we fought them, we'd win. I don't care how many weapons they have. They couldn't get all of us."

"They don't just have stun guns," Lillka said. "I've seen others. And not everyone would fight. Some would stay out of it, and some would fight with them. You'd lose." Zoheret frowned; Lillka had said *you*, not *we*. "If we do what they tell us to do, we'll still have most of what we had before. And they know more about living on a planet than we do."

Zoheret's nails dug into her palms. "Listen to me. We can

fight. If you stood up to them even a little, it might persuade some people. You're the leader."

"I'm not the leader anymore."

"Don't you know what they did to Bonnie? They beat her. They'll probably do the same thing to me."

"If you do what they tell you, they'll leave you alone. Don't you understand? You don't have to make trouble. I don't like some of the things they've done, but you're bringing it on yourself."

Rising, Zoheret went to the door and kicked it in frustration. The door remained closed. She kicked it again. It opened suddenly, almost knocking her to the floor. A man pushed Manuel inside and then closed the door again.

The boy's face was sallow. He sagged against the wall, then felt his face as if expecting to find something there.

Zoheret turned to Lillka. "Go along. That's your answer to everything, isn't it—go along. The first time Ho stole from us, you wanted to forget it—anything to avoid trouble. You're a coward, Lillka."

Lillka got up. Her cheeks were red, her face mottled. "I'd better go." She did not look at Manuel. "I'll try to come back later."

"Don't bother." Zoheret glared at her. "We don't need cowards here."

"I was going to tell you something else about one of the strangers," Lillka shouted. "But I won't now. You'll find out soon enough." She strode from the room, slamming the door.

"What was she talking about?" Zoheret asked.

"I don't know. She didn't say." Bonnie looked at Manuel. "You look awful."

"Is my face marked?"

"They don't leave marks. Don't worry, you're still pretty. Who'd you get, Caleb?"

Manuel nodded and sat down carefully, as if he were glass and about to shatter. "I didn't tell him anything. At first, he was nice—he only got mean later, when I wouldn't talk. Then someone else came and pulled him off me. I think he wanted to kill me."

"That's awful," Zoheret murmured.

"Oh, I understand him. He got into the rhythm of it, that's all. It happens—you're hitting and hitting and you just want to go on doing it. It isn't even personal by then—you get to the point where you're not even hitting a person any-more, just something that whines and cries and makes little sounds. I bit him once." He lifted his chin. "He didn't expect that. He had my arms and legs tied down, but I got in a bite. You should have heard him yell."

"Where's Ho?"

"I don't know. Somebody took him to the storehouse—I haven't seen him since. We're just wild animals to them. They think they own us." His face blanched. "I feel sick."

Zoheret held his head, listening to his labored breath-ing, stroking his hair until he was able to sit up. He tried to smile. "Guess there's nothing left to come up."

Bonnie gazed at them scornfully; her eyes glittered. Zo-heret realized that the other girl hated Manuel even now, that she was glad he'd been beaten. She knew now that the strangers would win. They would set them against one an-other.

Whenever the door opened, Zoheret's stomach reeled and her neck grew stiff; she was expecting them to come for her. Brendan and Bonnie were taken away to work and returned near evening; food was brought.

After supper, the door opened and Zoheret tensed, but it was only Helena coming for the empty dishes.

"Just do what they tell you," Helena murmured as she piled bowls on the tray. "They won't give you any trouble if you behave. It's for your own good. I'm giving you good advice." Zoheret did not reply.

She waited alone in the front room after the others had gone to sleep. Ho had still not been returned; she wondered if they had decided to keep him elsewhere. Perhaps he had talked. Somehow, she doubted that; Ho's pride was so excessive that he would not allow himself to show weakness. He might, however, have tried to make some sort of deal. He knew where his friends would go after they left the island; he knew about the corridors. That information would be valuable. There was another possibility; he might have been badly beaten. He might be dead.

She thought about the settlement. There had to be some who wanted to rebel; she had grown up with the group and was certain that there were others who felt as she did. She tried to make a list: Anoki. Jorge, perhaps; the chubby boy was often sullen and recalcitrant, and could be pushed around only up to a point. Robert might fight if he thought there was a chance of winning, and Gowon, too, was probably biding his time. She would have to find a way to talk to them. There were Brendan and Bonnie, of course, and Manuel. It was a very small list. She would have added Gervais, Dmitri, Serena, and Kagami, but they weren't here, and they had given in to Ho without much of a struggle. For a moment, she was sure that Owen and Daniella and Vittorio and the other members of that group would have fought the Earthfolk, but she might be wrong about that, too. Perhaps they would have cooperated in return for some power over the settlement. How little she knew about those she had once called her friends.

At last she went to bed, convinced that she would be sent

for in the morning. Her sleep was uneven; once, she cried out, waking Bonnie. In her dreams, she was struggling in the river, staggering to the shore only to be slapped by Owen, who was waiting for her. He laughed as she tried to run away, her legs churning slowly as if stuck in mud.

The morning light shocked her into wakefulness. She stumbled into the front room, where the others were already eating breakfast. Zoheret accepted a banana from Brendan and forced herself to eat it.

The door swung open, banging against the wall, shaking the floor. Zoheret dropped her peel, unable to raise her eyes. "You," a man's voice said.

"It's Caleb," Bonnie whispered.

"You," the voice said again. Zoheret lifted her head and saw a stocky, muscular man; his mustache drooped over his lip. "Come with me."

They walked past the shacks and skirted the field, and it was not until the man named Caleb stopped in front of a pile of posts and a cone of wire, gestured at them, and handed Zoheret a tape measure that she realized she was not going to be beaten or questioned, but only made to work.

"So you're not going to question me after all," she said. "I know what you did to Manuel. What are you going to do— get some work out of me first?"

Caleb's pale, watery eyes widened a bit; his broad face, except for a slight flabbiness under the chin, showed few signs of age. "Ho told us you knew nothing, that you belonged to the group here and not to his group out there. Now get to work."

"I suppose you'll beat me if I don't."

"Don't be ridiculous. If someone misbehaves, we use discipline, that's all. Some of you don't seem to respond to kindness or reason. Do what you're told and you'll be treated fairly. This isn't a bad job. If you behave, you'll get others like it. If you don't, there are more unpleasant tasks. Measure off the distance while I put up the posts."

"What else did Ho tell you?"

"That isn't your concern. Now get to work."

She was measuring off a span when she saw Willem coming toward them from the settlement. "Hi!" he shouted. Caleb looked up from his post. "Hi!" Willem said more tentatively, stopping as he saw Caleb's face. "She told me to come here," he mumbled.

"Who did?" Caleb asked.

"Her." Willem pointed toward the storehouse. "To work." His shaggy brown hair was dirty, his face unusually pale. He clutched his stomach for a moment. "It hurts."

"What hurts?" Zoheret asked.

"Inside."

Caleb scowled. "We'll have to do something about him," he said to Zoheret as though Willem were not present.

"Like what?" Zoheret reached for Willem's arm and drew him to her side.

"He's not fit for life on a planet. He'll just be in the way. He should never have been born."

"Willem can take care of himself." Willem gripped her hand tightly.

Caleb waved a hand. "He can dig."

Willem dug small holes for the posts while Zoheret measured spaces and strung wire; Caleb pounded in the posts with a hammer. Occasionally Willem would stop to rest; Zoheret frowned as she heard his labored breathing. They worked without speaking; Willem hummed tunelessly as he dug. After they had worked for a while, Caleb sent Willem to the storehouse for some lunch.

Zoheret sat down to rest, drawing a glare from Caleb. "Tired already?"

She shrugged. It was his field now; she was not about to exert herself fencing it. "You shouldn't push Willem so much," she said at last. "I don't think he's well."

"He's lazy." Caleb sat down near her.

"How'd you get Ho to talk?" she asked after a while.

"Listen," he said, leaning toward her, "you just behave and you won't get into trouble. Ho told me what you were like. You'd better change your ways. Your friend Ho isn't stupid— you'd better follow his example."

She knew then that Ho had made his peace with the strangers; she should have expected that. "What did he tell you?"

"What we needed to know. We'll take care of his friends soon enough if they don't give themselves up." He peered at her closely. "Maybe we should have questioned you after all." He looked up. "Where is that stupid boy? He's taking long enough."

"What are you going to do with Willem?"

"I'm not going to do anything. Unless he doesn't get back here soon. I've had a little too much trouble with him."

"You said before that you were going to do something about him."

"Oh, that. You have unfit young people here. That wasn't supposed to happen. You're going to have enough troubles on a new world without burdening yourselves with cripples and retarded kids."

The man wasn't just talking about Willem now; she thought of Anoki and Jennifer and her mouth grew dry. "They're not a burden. They've always done everything the rest of us did."

"I suppose he had the same lessons, too. No doubt he mastered them thoroughly."

"He learned what he could. Maybe it's not much, but he

does his work, his share. He had to be in Competitions just like everyone else."

"You don't need the unfit. If we were on Earth . . ." He waved a hand.

"Lillka told me about Earth, what one of you said about it."

"And what did she say?" He leaned back against one of the posts.

"That Earth wasn't the only world in its solar system. That there were others with people in them, worlds like Ship."

He frowned. "If you can call them worlds."

"Did they have Projects, too?"

Caleb laughed. "They sent out unmanned probes. That's all they did. They thought we were foolish to plan our venture. They couldn't bear to travel themselves. They'd rather huddle around the sun, like primitives afraid of the night. They'd rather see pictures of other worlds than travel themselves." He leaned forward. "They thought they could buy us off with their machines and their technology—they made us dependent. But we'll be the ones to inherit other worlds, not them."

Zoheret glanced at him, reminded of something else Lillka had told her. "Lillka said you were going to send Ship to other worlds and raise more kids."

"That was always part of the plan."

"No," Zoheret said. "Ship never said so. It was going to stay in orbit so we could talk to it after we were settled. It wouldn't just leave."

Caleb raised his eyebrows. "Do you really think we would have gone to all this trouble to seed one world? The ship was programmed to seed as many as possible."

"I don't believe you."

"It's true. The ship would have told you that when the time came to do so."

"No." She closed her eyes for a moment. "It isn't what Ship wants. It cares about us now." She wanted to believe that.

"The ship will do what we want it to do."

"You don't belong here," she said fiercely. "You weren't part of the plan. Ship didn't even know about you."

Caleb stood up. "Get back to work."

They had put up another post when Willem finally returned, walking toward them with empty hands. Caleb went to him. "Where's our lunch?"

Willem gaped at him. "I forgot." His eyes glistened. "I went and—"

Caleb hit him before Willem could explain, and kept hitting until the boy fell, arms over his head. The man began to kick him. Zoheret threw herself at Caleb, catching a glimpse of his wild eyes. He thrust her away. Her head hit a post and she fell to the ground. As she got up, the back of Caleb's hand caught her; she hit the post again, and could not move.

At last she struggled up; her head was spinning. She stumbled toward Caleb. Willem was very still. Caleb was on his knees, crying. Zoheret knelt by Willem. His eyes stared up at her sightlessly. She felt for his pulse and could not find it, then pressed her ear to his chest. His heart was silent.

"Get the medikit," Caleb said. "In the storehouse. Get the medikit."

She said, "He's dead."

"No. Oh, no."

"You killed him." Her own tears would not come. "He wasn't feeling well. I bet you beat him before. He was hurt inside. And now you've killed him."

She swung at Caleb; he grabbed her wrists. "It was an accident. Do you understand? It was an accident." Caleb had stopped crying and was now looking around wildly, as if wanting to be sure no one else had seen.

"Murderer." She looked at a distant group carrying hoes to another field. "I'm going to tell them what you did."

"It was an accident." He gripped her wrists very tightly. "And that's what you're going to say. He wasn't feeling well, and he fell against a pole, and he died before we could get help. You're going to say that because if you don't, the same thing will happen to you."

"Nobody will believe it."

"Yes, they will. They won't believe you—I'll see that they don't. You're a troublemaker." His eyes narrowed. "And if you say anything else, I'll say the accident was your fault, and that I was covering for you out of kindness."

He released her and picked up the body; his hands were shaking.

Zoheret was alone in the shack; the others had been taken away by Caleb after she had been returned. She had not had a chance to speak to them.

The walls seemed to be closing in on her; she saw herself walking through the settlement toward the forest. She would leave. They would tell her to stop. She wouldn't, and then they would shoot her. Caleb might make sure she did not revive. She didn't care.

She opened the door. The woman who had been watching it before was gone; instead, Ho stood there. He turned and saw her; she watched him warily.

"Where are you going?" he asked.

"For a walk."

"No, you're not."

"Try to stop me."

His knife was out. "Get back inside."

She stared at the blade; they had given him back his weapon. "You're with them."

His eyes narrowed. "I know when I can fight and when I can't. They're watching me right now to see if I can be trusted. If you don't get back inside, I'll have to force you, and I'd rather not."

"You told them everything."

"I told them what they wanted to know. Why shouldn't I? Plenty of your friends here are cooperating—you should do the same. Get back inside."

Everyone in the settlement had gathered in the clearing before the storehouse. Torches lit the night; the light flickered over bowed heads. Several strangers stood in the back of the storehouse porch, hidden in the darkness.

The settlement had gathered to bury Willem, and a grave had already been dug. The woman named Ah Lam was speaking now of the tragic accident, of Willem's friendliness, yet somehow her words seemed to suggest that it was perhaps best that Willem was gone, that a life on the new world would not have been possible for him.

Zoheret watched from the back of the crowd; she had been allowed to go no farther than a few paces from the door. The light of one torch fell on Anoki's grim face. Caleb stood next to Zoheret, his chin jutting out, his shoulders thrown back.

Everyone seemed to have accepted Caleb's story of an accident; Zoheret, having been kept alone in the shack all day, had been given no chance to refute it. Would anyone have believed her? Brendan and Bonnie might; they knew what Caleb was like. But the others would not.

Willem was being lowered into the ground on ropes. The young people standing around the grave began to cover him with dirt. Good-bye, Willem, she thought, and the words were tinged with guilt. Good-bye. But nothing of Willem was left to hear the words.

The torches were put out, one by one, as the young people filed away from the grave and returned to their shacks. Zoheret longed to cry out in protest, reveal the truth. Caleb had made her an accomplice. Bonnie and Brendan passed her; Bonnie was crying. Manuel walked behind them. He paused in front of her, looking concerned; Caleb waved him on. She saw that the others were being led to another shack by Petra.

Caleb took her arm, pulled her to the door, and pushed her inside, slamming the door behind her. She went to one of the small windows and looked out through the screen. It was still light outside, even though the torches were out; she searched the area and finally saw the source of the light. Bright beams shone from the watchtowers, and lamps on the ground lit the settlement's periphery.

She retreated into the room's shadows.

Knowing that she would be unable to sleep, Zoheret sat in the corner of the front room. Caleb could not keep her isolated indefinitely; what was he planning to do? Why had the others been sent to another shack? She knew why. He was afraid she would talk.

She heard the low murmur of voices outside; someone was walking past the shack. The voices rose and fell; she recognized the language. Arabic. Ship had taught her some old Arabic and old Hebrew when she had expressed an interest in her parents. She had never been able to read either language well, but had learned how to speak and understand them. She concentrated on the voices and recognized the word "sensors." They were talking about Ship.

"Will it not put us at some risk?" a low voice said.

"No," a woman's voice answered. "We have need only of its automatic functions, not its conscious mind. We can steer the vessel ourselves. We risk more if the mind core remains aware. Once the sensors are blocked, we . . ."

The voices faded. Zoheret stood up, peering cautiously over the windowsill; a man and a woman were walking toward the storehouse, their backs to her. Two other people were silently patrolling the grounds outside.

She ran swiftly to the toilet in the back of the shack, closing the door. Climbing up on the toilet seat, she peered out the small window. If she could remove the screen silently, she might be able to squeeze through. The area in back of the shack was not as well-lighted, but she would have to crawl under the wires of the newly erected fence just beyond the yard. Small metal boxes had been attached to the posts; they might be alarms. She would have to take that chance; she could wait no longer.

A door slammed. The floorboards creaked; someone had entered the shack. She climbed down from the toilet and opened the door a crack.

A light shone at her. "Who's there?"

"It's only me." The beam of light was pointed at the ceiling, then revealed Ho's face. He held the light under his chin, making his face resemble one of Earth's fabled demons.

"What are you doing here?" She kept behind the door.

"What do you think? They don't trust me yet, not completely. I have to stay here for a while now. They even took my knife away again."

"Why aren't Bonnie and the others here?"

"They're behaving for the moment, except for Manuel—he'll get beaten again if he's not careful. If they act up again, they'll be sent back."

She opened the door. "I'm going to sleep." She walked past him, keeping near the wall, and went into a bedroom. As she stretched out, she realized that Ho was standing in the doorway; she could hear him breathe. "Go to sleep," she said, trying to keep her voice steady. "There's another bedroom, you know."

"Do you mind if I sit with you for a while?"

She clenched her teeth. "Sit all you want. Just stay on the other bed." His boots squeaked as he entered the room and sat on the other cot. She propped herself up on one elbow, staring into the shadows where he sat.

"That accident of Willem's," he said. "I can't believe he's dead."

"I didn't think you cared."

"He was on my team during Competition."

"And you used him, didn't you, because he didn't understand what you were doing. You didn't seem to care much if people were hurt. I know what you did to Jen, too."

"It wasn't the same, Zoheret. Sure, I wanted to win, but I didn't want anyone to die. The injured kids recovered, didn't they?"

"Federico still gets headaches."

"He'll get over it. Look, I didn't know—I didn't stop to think. I wouldn't do it now. When I saw Willem's body, it scared me that somebody could die so easily."

She sat up. "Ho, listen. Maybe we can get away. We could go out the back window and make for the woods."

"Impossible. There're alarms all over the place."

"We could try."

"We'll just get into more trouble. And we could get hurt out there. Look at Willem—he was just out by the field, and he died. You must have been terrified when you saw that— just a dumb accident." Ho sounded plaintive, close to tears; she hadn't thought he was capable of crying.

"Ho, listen." She spoke very softly. "We have to try. I've got to get out of here. I have something to tell you. Willem didn't die the way you think. That man Caleb killed him. He beat him and then he kicked him. I think Willem already had internal injuries. I was the only one who saw it, so he thinks he can lie about it. Maybe he didn't mean to do it, but he did. And he knows I know. He's trying to keep me away from the others so I won't tell, but maybe he won't stop at that. And I have another reason for getting out, too. I'm sur- prised he let you come in here."

"He probably thought I wouldn't believe you." Ho paused. "How can we escape, though?"

"The back window. If we can just remove the screen, we can get to the fence."

"The alarms."

"Can't we go around the fence somehow?"

"No. But maybe we can squeeze under the fence without triggering them. Come on."

They hurried to the back window; Ho stood on the toilet seat and looked out. "The guard's too close," he said. "We'll have to wait. Look—I'll try to get the screen loose while you get some sleep. I'll wake you up."

"No. I'll wait with you. I can't sleep now."

Ho worked at the screen, prying it with the edge of his pocket light. The light flicked on suddenly; Ho quickly turned it off. "Be careful," she whispered. "You don't want them to see."

"All right, all right."

At last he got it loose. "Is that guard still out there?" she asked.

"Yeah. I'd better wait before I take the screen out."

"We have to get out before first light."

"I know. Can you get some sleep on the floor?"

She wrinkled her nose; she was getting used to the stink. "I think so."

"As soon as that guard wanders off, we'll go. I want you nearby."

She curled up in the far corner. Ho would have to be told what she had overheard: Ship was now in danger. She closed her eyes, trying to sleep.

Now," a voice whispered in her ear. Zoheret sat up, rubbing her eyes, awake again.

Ho had pulled the screen inside. He squeezed through the window and she followed; he pulled her through by her arms. The guard was nowhere in sight.

They ran across the yard, keeping low. When they reached the fence, Ho threw himself on the ground and inched under the bottom wire on his back while Zoheret waited, expecting the alarm to sound; then she crawled under the wire, careful not to touch it.

He pulled her to her feet and they ran, keeping to the shadows near the riverbank until they were near the woods. He took her hand and led her into the forest. They moved cautiously through the darkness, thrashing their way through the underbrush; Ho could not risk lighting their way. A twig cracked, and she tensed; someone was close by.

Ho pulled at her hand. "Come on."

"There's someone in the woods."

"It's probably an animal. Come on." He pulled her along and she hurried to keep up. She felt as though she were being watched, and could not shake the feeling; was an animal stalking them? They had no weapons. She moved more rapidly.

They struggled on. Birds fled from them, chirping as they flew up toward the treetops. It was growing lighter; she had slept longer than she had realized.

By first light, they had reached the rope bridge over the ravine.

Ho sat down hard, holding his knees. Zoheret was already tired. "We can't stay here," she said. "They'll be looking for us soon."

"Just give me a minute. I have to rest."

"Caleb said you told him where your friends are. They'll know where to go, and we can't outrun their vehicles. We have to keep moving. I overheard something last night, I . . ."

He got to his feet and stared past her. She heard the rustling of the leaves and knew it was not an animal.

Turning, she saw Caleb walking toward them, his gun pointed at her.

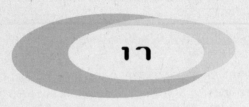

Zoheret stared at the man, unable to move until Caleb drew out a knife and threw it to Ho. Then she understood.

She hurled herself at the boy; he slapped her aside, knocking her down, and pinned her to the ground. She screamed and kicked.

"Scream all you want," Caleb said as he stood over her. "No one's going to hear you." She was still. Ho dragged her up and held her by the arms, fingers digging into her muscles. "I've been following you ever since you escaped. Did you really think you'd get away that easily?"

"She told me," Ho said. "About Willem. You said she'd tell me that story."

"It's too bad she did," Caleb said. "If she'd tell you, it means she'd tell others. And I can't have a story like that going around."

Her legs were suddenly unsteady. "Why did you have to

tell him?" Caleb continued. "I was hoping you wouldn't. As soon as I saw Ho remove the screen for your escape, I knew you'd talked. I gave you your chance. Do you think I like doing this?" He held her by the chin and peered into her eyes. "I wanted you to win my trust, I really did. It would have been to your benefit. But you had to tell him." His watery eyes were rimmed with red. "Now I have to do something about this. It won't hurt." He waved the gun. "A few shots from this, and you'll go quietly—it'll be just like going to sleep."

"You can't. They'll wonder what happened to me."

"You escaped." He chanted the words. "We went after you. And we found that a bear or bobcat got you, so we buried you."

"They won't believe it. First Willem, then me. People will wonder."

"They won't wonder. Accidents can happen, and I'll have a witness."

"Until you kill him, too." Ho's grip tightened as she spoke.

"That won't be necessary. I can trust Ho. He's my accomplice. He can't speak without implicating himself, and he's hardly likely to do that. He'll go along."

Ho released her. She backed toward the bridge on wobbly legs. Ho held his knife, ready to throw it; Caleb aimed his gun. "It'll be quick," the man said, moving closer.

She aimed her foot at his knee and kicked; Caleb had come too close. She jabbed at his throat and he cried out, firing the gun. The beam shot past her head. She went for his eyes and the gun flew out of his hand; she jabbed again. Ho was dancing, still holding his knife as if trying to decide where to aim it.

Caleb covered his eyes, moaning. Zoheret searched the ground frantically for the gun while Ho backed away. Caleb dragged her up by her hair; she struck him in the throat once more. He staggered backward, clutching at his collar, swaying on the edge of the ravine. His hands clawed at the air as he struggled for balance. Then he was gone.

Zoheret screamed, then ran toward the ravine.

His head was on a red-stained rock below, his body twisted at the waist. She backed away, then remembered Ho. She pivoted and dived at the boy, knocking him to the ground and pinning him by the shoulders. He gripped his knife; she seized his right hand by the wrist. "You lied," she said. "I should have guessed."

"He was watching me. I had to do what he said. I didn't think he'd try to kill you."

"You're lying. You had to know. You knew about Willem."

"He said it was an accident, and that you were going to accuse him to make trouble. I thought he was just going to beat you so you wouldn't tell anyone else."

"So beating's all right."

"I was trying to throw the knife at him. I didn't want to hit you by mistake."

"You were waiting to see who'd win." She noticed that the gun was lying near her. She grabbed the weapon, rolling off the boy. He sat up and she took aim.

"I was looking for an opening," Ho said. "I didn't trust him, but I knew I had to let him trust me in order to get away. I swear it's true."

She lowered the gun. She would never know whether or not he was telling the truth. "You would have let him kill me."

"I would have thrown my knife at him if you hadn't been in the way."

She got to her feet. "He's down there, hurt."

Ho rose, walked to the edge of the ravine, and looked down. "He's dead."

"No."

"He's dead. His head hit a rock. I can see the blood and bone fragments from here. He's dead, all right."

"He can't be."

"Look for yourself."

"I can't."

He came to her and took the gun from her hand before she could resist, then went back to the edge, aimed the gun straight down, and fired several times. He turned and threw the gun at her feet. "He's dead now."

She backed away, then fell to the ground, retching. Curling up on the ground, she hugged her knees. Ho's booted feet were next to her face; his arm snaked out and hauled her up. "Stop it." He stood her on her feet, picked up the gun, and tucked it under her rope belt.

She wiped her face. "I'm all right." Her mouth tasted bitter, and her hands still trembled. "Now I'm a killer."

"You were defending yourself. It was you or him."

She pressed her hands against her temples, trying to clear her head. The gun nestled against her ribs; Ho had given it to her as a sign of trust. They now had the same immediate goal; that would bind them even if trust did not. "Ho, we have to do something. I heard two of them talking last night, in Arabic. I could understand most of what they said. They're going to try to disconnect Ship."

"What?"

"Just its mind, not life support or the other functions. They're going to block its sensors first, I think."

"Can they do that?"

"They helped build it. They must know how."

"Then they'll have us for sure." Ho shook his head. "I have to warn my band."

"They'll go after them. They know where they are."

"No, they don't." Ho smiled. "I told them we were hiding

out in the swamp. If they go there, they're going to get a big surprise. There's plenty of quicksand."

"Don't be so sure. When Caleb doesn't come back, they may know you lied. You have to go to your group. They've still got my friends."

"Don't worry. I'll see that they're all right. I'll take everybody back to the corridors. You should go there now. One of us should be able to get through to Ship."

She nodded, then searched his face, suddenly distrustful again. "You'd better bring my friends to the corridors safely."

"I will. Are there really people there?"

"I told you there were. You should have listened to me, and none of this would have happened." Caleb would still be alive, and perhaps Willem as well. She swallowed, relieved that Caleb was dead, and hated herself for thinking it.

"I didn't say anything about the corridors to Caleb," Ho said. "They still have Manuel back there, though. They could beat a lot of information out of him. Are you sure you can trust those other people?"

"No," she said. "I think I can, but I'm not sure. What's the difference? We can use their help against the Earthpeople, and then deal with them later if we have to. Better to have them on our side instead of having both groups against us. Isn't that the way you think?"

"Take my light—you might need it," Ho said. She tucked it into her belt. "You'd better take the long way, through the woods and around the lake. They might start searching the plain."

She hurried across the bridge, refusing to look down. When she reached the other side, she turned her head and caught a glimpse of Ho running along the other side of the chasm. He lifted a hand, then disappeared among the trees.

18

A bird sang overhead. Other birds answered, a few with caws; some twittered.

Zoheret stirred and opened her eyes. Through the branches of the tree in which she had slept, she saw light; she had slept not only all night, but also through dawn. She shook herself, then climbed down from the tree. She had not intended to sleep for so long.

Her legs were stiff, her throat dry with thirst. She had no time to search out a stream. After stretching and bending to relieve her aches, she hurried on her way.

She hoped that Ho's gang had camped out near an entrance; they might have made it into the corridors by now if they had. Ho had not told her where his encampment was even after indicating that he would trust her, and again she felt suspicious. But Ho was being practical. If she did not know where he had gone, she could not betray him to the Earthpeople if she was caught.

She strained, forcing herself forward.

When she reached the edge of the woods, she hid behind a bush while surveying the hill ahead. No one was in sight. Gathering her strength, she sprinted toward the entrance, darting from side to side, and came to the door.

The door did not open.

She pressed her hand against the smooth surface, then pounded on the door, kicking at it with one foot. She knew that there were manual controls as well as automatic ones, but she had never had to use them. She had never paid much attention to Ship's workings or the detailed blueprints on its screens. Stepping to one side, she ran her hands along the edge of the door. Her fingers brushed over a small button and the door slid open.

She rushed into the empty corridor, then turned. The door was still open. As she searched for the button on this side, she heard Ship's voice.

"Help."

"Ship? What's the matter?" She found the button and the door closed.

"Help me." It was Ship's tenor voice, but it sounded weak. "Help me. What is happening to me?" The voice rose to an alto.

Zoheret ran down the corridor.

"Help me. I am blind, I am deaf. What has gone wrong?" The voice echoed through the halls, becoming a wail. "I cannot see, I cannot hear."

The dining room door was open; she ran toward it. "Is anyone here?"

Aleksandr emerged, Yusef just behind him. Their faces were tense with fear. "Help me," Ship cried out again.

"What's going on?" she asked the two men. Others were gathering in the hall; she recognized Kieu and Maire. Kieu hurried toward her.

"I don't know," Aleksandr said nervously. "It just started. Ship's lost its sensors, it seems."

Zoheret sagged against the doorframe. "Now I know. They're shutting it down. I should have known they'd do that first."

Kieu grabbed her by the shoulders. "Who's shutting it down?"

"Some people from Earth hid themselves aboard—even Ship didn't know about them. They took over our settlement. They're shutting Ship down. They've blocked its sensors already, and they must have shut down some of the automatic functions, too. They'll go for its cortex. We have to stop them."

"How?" Yusef said.

"You've got weapons, don't you?"

"Some of us have stun guns." Aleksandr straightened, as if ready to take control. "But we only have a few. We didn't think we'd need them." He shouted orders to the people nearby. There were about twenty of them now; others had apparently been revived. They hurried down the hall and scattered. One man remained, a tall man with curly black hair. He stared blankly at Zoheret; she gestured with one hand and realized with a shock that the man was blind.

"Get everything you can," Zoheret shouted after the running people. "They're willing to kill."

"Are you sure?" Aleksandr asked.

"One tried to kill me."

"Wait." Yusef turned toward her. "Do these people know about us?"

Zoheret frowned. "I don't think they do. But I don't know." She thought of Manuel. "They might have forced the information from someone by now."

"Then they might have cut off the corridors leading to Ship's cortex."

Zoheret folded her arms. "The caves." She closed her eyes, trying to summon up an image of the convoluted passageways in Ship's rocky shell. She had gone there as a child to get away from Ship's ever-present sensors; she and Anoki had played hide-and-seek among the girders and idle machines. Once she had almost gotten lost looking for him, and Ship had warned her about going too far into the caverns, where it could not have helped her find her way out. But she had at last found Anoki by a door leading to one of the few unfinished corridors. She opened her eyes. That door had led to the area outside Ship's cortex.

"The caves," she said again. "They won't expect anyone from that direction. There's a place near Ship's centers where we can come out. I think I can lead you there."

Yusef shook his head. "Don't think. You have to be sure. We could get lost in there."

"I can lead you." She had to take the chance.

The others were returning; Kieu threw a gun to Aleksandr. "Listen," Aleksandr said to his comrades. "Some of you will have to stay—we only have weapons for about a dozen. If we don't come back—well, you'll have to decide what to do." He rested a hand on the blind man's shoulder. "Luis, you'd better stay."

They were in Ship's shell, having entered from the end of the corridor near the bedrooms. "Help me," Ship called as Aleksandr closed the door.

"We should have taken the tubeway," a man said. "It'd be quicker."

"It might not be working," Yusef said. "We could be trapped there. We can't take the chance."

"Who are they, anyway?" another voice asked.

"They're from Earth," Zoheret said. "They had themselves suspended. They have their own ideas about what the Project is, and they don't mind beating and killing to have their way."

Aleksandr sighed. "We still have friends in suspension. I hope that system is still working."

Zoheret turned on her light. Girders spanned the rock above them; tools were scattered over the ground. Drill bits lay in clusters on the rocky surface, and she thought of the pine needles in the Hollow. An inactive robot stared out from under a tarpaulin; other machines were hidden under faded cloths. The air smelled dusty and stale. She had thought of this part of Ship as only a storage area, useless for anything else. Now she saw what it really was—a place where Ship could build more corridors, expanding the regions in which people could live. Caleb had been right; Ship would not have stopped at seeding one world. Ship would grow; she and Aleksandr and the others were only its first children. Perhaps they were not even the first; Ship might have abandoned others before them.

She soon came to a narrow passageway, sure this was the route they had to take. She led them through it, trying not to strain at remembering; she had to feel her way. The tunnel seemed familiar. She clenched her fists, suddenly frightened; if she made a mistake, they might never find their way out, or else would reenter the corridors to find the Earthpeople in control.

They walked silently for a while until they came to a fork. The passage to her right widened; the one on the left was lower, not much higher than her head. "This one," she said, pointing to the left.

"Are you sure?" Yusef asked.

"I'm sure." She had taken the one on the right while look-ing for Anoki, and had come to a dead end; that memory was clear.

The low passageway soon brought them to another cave with more abandoned robots. "I wonder how they shut off Ship's sensors," Kieu murmured.

"They built it," Zoheret answered. "They must know how."

"It wouldn't be that difficult," Yusef said. "With a small jamming device, you could shut off one sensor and set off a chain reaction, each sensor jamming the next until they're all shut off. Ship probably never knew what hit it."

"This way," Zoheret said, waving her light at a passage-way on her left.

Yusef came to her side. "You're leading us farther away from the corridors. We should be going to the right."

She shook her head. "That's what I thought the first time I came in here. That's how I almost got lost."

"You don't remember." As Yusef spoke, she began to doubt; what if she *had* forgotten?

She led them into the next passage, but they had only gone a short distance when the narrow way came to an end. Bewildered, Zoheret stared at the rocky surface, searching with her light.

Yusef said, "I knew this wasn't the right way."

"Be quiet!" This was the right way; she knew it. She had gone through this corridor after trying all the others, and had almost given up, until—She aimed her light at one cor-ner. "There it is," she shouted, lighting a low tunnel near the ground. "That crawl space. We have to go through that."

She dropped down on her hands and knees. "I'll go first, and turn on my light at the other end. Give me a minute, then follow." She turned off her light and began to crawl, moving through the tunnel until her knees hurt; bits of rock and sharp-edged shards scratched her hands. Had the tunnel been this long? She froze, worried that she had picked the wrong way after all. Total blackness surrounded her; she could see nothing. She might be trapped. Biting her lip, she continued to crawl until, lifting her head for a moment, she noticed that her hair had not brushed rock. She raised an arm, and felt only air.

She turned on the light, then scrambled to her feet. She was in an empty cave. Ahead of her, at the other end of the cave, there was another corridor. Running to it, she shone her light down its length and saw the distant door; its metal gleamed as it caught the light.

They left their boots and shoes at the door, then crept silently forward into the hall, hurrying along it until they came to the main corridor. Zoheret peered around the corner. They had left the residential areas; these walls hid Ship's conduits, its nerves. Ship's body was vast, but the cortex was small and, Zoheret realized, oddly vulnerable. The removal of a few panels in one room could silence Ship forever, shutting off its brain while its body continued to function. If Ship's mind were ever restored, would it be Ship who lived again? Or would it be a new mind, forgetful of the past?

"Help me," the voice called again. She wondered if Ship could be driven mad; it was trapped in darkness, crying to itself. "Help me." It was still crying to them; that meant it was still conscious.

If the invaders knew about Aleksandr and his friends, they would be expecting an assault from the part of the corridor nearest the residential zone, not from this side. And there was still a good chance they didn't know about the group at all.

Aleksandr lifted a hand, then led them forward. Ship's

cortex was just around the curve ahead. A loud buzzing reverberated through the hall. "Help me." The buzzing grew louder; something crackled. "Help." Aleksandr flattened himself against the wall and the others did the same. "Help. Help. Help." There was silence, then a triumphant shout.

Aleksandr motioned to them. Zoheret peered around the curve of the wall and hurried after him.

The strangers had burned their way through Ship's door and were already inside the cortex. Ship had apparently locked its door as soon as it had realized it was being threatened. There was no one in the hall. They would have to confront the Earthfolk inside the cortex, where Ship's components could be damaged during the battle. "Help me." The voice was lower, as if a recording were being played at too low a speed.

They approached the gaping hole in Ship's door. "Start over here," a man's voice shouted from inside. Zoheret moved forward, glancing at Aleksandr. She had always been a pretty good shot, but she had to be a perfect shot now; she could not risk affecting part of Ship. The stun weapons might not hurt it, but they could not take that chance. Yusef crept up behind her, followed by Kieu.

A man suddenly stepped through the hole into the hall. Before he could cry out, Yusef hit him in the throat, then brought his gun down on his head; another young man caught him before he hit the ground and dragged him away. "What's going on?" a voice inside shouted; someone had heard.

There was no time left. Aleksandr moved to the door, Zoheret right behind him. They aimed through the door and fired at two men standing in the center of the room. The men fell.

Two other people, hands stretched toward the clear glassy walls, froze. Two panels had already been pulled out, jutting out from the walls like shelves. Tiny lights behind the walls blinked on and off furiously. Zoheret aimed and brought down the man; the woman darted away and she recognized Ah Lam.

"Stop!" Ah Lam shouted. She was holding a weapon Zoheret had never seen before, a long hollow pole with a grip. "If you don't, I'll aim this at the wall. It isn't one of those toys of yours, and it'll damage the components permanently." Zoheret lowered her gun as Aleksandr stepped through the hole in the door. "Don't come any closer, or I'll fire."

"You've lost," Aleksandr said. "Give up."

"I haven't lost." Ah Lam's delicate face was contorted with rage. "If anyone moves, I'll fire. I'll wait for my friends to wake up, and you'll let them finish what we came here to do. And if you try to stop us, this ship's brain goes out forever."

"You can't do that. You'll endanger everyone aboard."

"Automatic will still be on. That's all we need. Back off!"

Aleksandr backed toward the door. The people outside were standing by, clutching their useless weapons. Aleksandr's arms were up; his body almost completely blocked the door. But not quite.

Zoheret dropped to her knees, aimed her gun with both hands, and fired. The beam shot under Aleksandr's left arm toward Ah Lam. For a moment, Zoheret feared she had missed. Then the woman toppled forward, her head grazing one of the open panels; her weapon clattered to the floor.

Aleksandr pulled her to her feet. "You act fast." She was shaking now; her hand released her gun and let it fall. "It's all right."

K ieu had pushed the components back into the wall, and the captured people had been taken away. "What has happened?" Ship called. "Restore my senses, please."

Aleksandr hurried through the hole in Ship's door and ran

down the corridor. Zoheret rushed after him. "Where are you going?" she asked as she caught up.

"To the nearest entrance. They must have jammed Ship's sensors before entering—otherwise, it would have warned us when they first came inside. And it makes sense to think that they would have used the closest entrance."

"There might be others by the door."

He slowed. "How many are there?"

"I don't know exactly. No more than thirty—probably not that many. But most of them would have had to stay in the settlement to keep order." Yusef came up behind her silently and walked with them. "We'd better be careful."

"But you said they didn't know we were in the corridors."

"I don't think they did, or they would have had someone outside Ship's door, guarding the cortex."

They came to the entrance. Aleksandr crept up and pressed the door's button while Zoheret and Yusef stood to one side. As the door opened, they pressed their backs against the wall and waited.

"Well?" a woman's voice shouted from beyond the door. "Did you shut it down?"

Aleksandr held a finger to his lips.

"Well?"

The intruder suddenly entered the hall; Yusef dived at her, pinning her to the floor, then grabbed the weapon from her hand.

The woman was struggling as Yusef pulled her up; he tightened his grip. "You've lost," he said. Her dark-brown face was set in a scowl. "We caught your friends. Show us how to restore Ship's sensors." He twisted her arm.

The woman sagged against him. Aleksandr took her other arm and the two men pulled her into the Hollow.

A vehicle perched at the entrance. A pale beam hummed,

shooting out from a cylinder on the vehicle's side to meet a sensor near the door. Yusef dragged the woman to the side of the craft. She glared at him, then reached toward the cylinder, fumbling with its buttons until the beam disappeared.

"My senses are returning," Ship said from the corridor. "I can see—I can hear."

"Can you hear me?" Aleksandr asked.

"Yes. I was inside myself. The universe was gone and I was only a tiny being crying out in a little space. How strange to think of oneself in that way."

"Are your sensors in the Hollow working?"

"Let me try a few. Yes, they are working. Shall I leave them on? I had promised not to do so."

"Forget your promise. Better shut them down for now, anyway. We don't want anyone in the Hollow to suspect that they're working."

"What is going on?" Ship asked. "What attacked me?"

"You'll find out." Aleksandr turned his head toward Yusef. "Check that craft—see if there's anything inside it. Then we'll take this woman to her friends and ask Zoheret to tell us her story."

"You haven't beaten us yet," the woman said. "And you won't."

"I thought . . ." Ship paused as they entered the corridor. "I thought I would go mad. Thank you for saving me."

Zoheret sat on a table, sipping water as she spoke to the people gathered in the dining room. Her voice grew hoarse; she saw Kieu wince as she mentioned their capture by Ho. When she spoke of Willem, her eyes filled and she had to blink away tears; she saw one young woman turn away and wondered if she was Willem's sister. When she spoke of Caleb's death, she looked down and had to stop speaking for a few moments.

When she was finished, she looked around at the worried faces. No one said anything.

"They concealed themselves well," Ship said at last. "I did not know they were aboard. They must have had their own entrance to the Hollow. How foolish of them. Had I known, I could have monitored them as they lay in suspension."

"Why do they behave the way they do?" Aleksandr asked.

"I cannot say. Tracing the causes of human behavior is a complex task—I found that out with you. Answers are often hard to come by. It seems I was not told everything about Earth."

"We must decide what to do," Kieu said. "We can't revive more comrades to help us—they'll be too disoriented and will need time to adjust. And we don't have that time."

"Ho should be here soon," Zoheret said. "He'll help us, and there are about twenty people with him, plus my five friends. That would give us a chance."

"Will the boys and girls in the settlement help us?" Aleksandr said.

Zoheret sighed. "Some will. Some at least won't get in the way. I'd guess that a lot of them will wait to see who might win. But they won't be expecting us—that should give us an edge."

Yusef held up a hand. "Wait. We all seem to be assuming that we're going to help Zoheret."

Zoheret turned toward her brother. "Aren't you?"

"Should we? You saw the weapon that woman had. There's another one like it in their craft. They'll shoot to kill. We won't just be up against stun guns."

"But we need your help. We can't fight them alone."

"Are you so sure?" Yusef said. "The settlement will think that Ship has been shut down. You and the friends you're waiting for outnumber the Earthpeople, and can surprise them. Presumably, some of those in the settlement will rise up and help you, but if they don't, why should we risk our lives to help them? I think we should stay out of it. We can watch on Ship's screens. If the battle is lost, we can then decide what to do."

A few people were nodding their heads. "You have to help us," Zoheret said. "It's your battle, too."

Yusef pulled at his mustache. "Your assault will weaken the Earthfolk, even if you lose. That should make it easier for us to fight."

Aleksandr was glaring at Yusef. "I thought you were through with setting yourself against everyone, going your own way. I thought you'd learned something. But I guess I was wrong."

"I'm being practical." Yusef stood up. "Right now, I think we should get some sleep." He left the room; several people followed.

Aleksandr walked Zoheret to her room; he did not speak. When they reached her door, she said, "What did you mean when you said you thought Yusef wouldn't set himself against everyone?"

"You ought to know. We had our disagreements, too, just as you did with Ho."

"You mean Yusef—"

"I might be able to talk to him, change his mind. I think we've got to settle this business with the Earthfolk soon—if we wait, we don't know what they might do next. Don't worry—when your friends get here, we'll decide what to do. I think some of us will help you."

Zoheret was unused to her bed, which now seemed too soft. She slept unevenly, woke, and got up, dressing in the new clothes Ship had provided.

"It's early," Ship said gently.

"I've had enough sleep." She tucked in her shirt and straightened her pants.

"I have been thinking of what you told everyone before, and have tried to question the Earthpeople, though they seem unwilling to talk to me now that I am keeping them locked up. During all the time I have traveled, whatever problems I have had, I never doubted my purpose. I had faith in those who had built me, who had given me life. However knowledgeable I was, they knew more—whatever wisdom I had learned, they were wiser. That was my faith. I spoke to you of their dreams, of their beliefs. That was what they gave me to reason with—the premises were theirs. Now those premises are shaken, and I do not know what to believe."

"These people are only a small group, Ship. The others who built you must be different—the fact that most of them stayed behind proves that."

"But I wasn't told the truth about the Project. A small band rebelling against the consensus of their society—that is what I represent. I thought I carried all of human culture inside me—and now I find that I carry only a distorted picture. I was deceived."

Zoheret frowned. "You deceived us, too. You never told us about Aleksandr and the others."

"I thought it was best."

"You never told us that you were supposed to abandon us and seed other worlds."

"The day will come when you will no longer wish to speak to me. I'll be only a tiny star above you."

She went to the door. It whispered open. Aleksandr was pacing the hall. "Can't you sleep?" he asked.

"Can't you?"

"I've been waiting for your friends."

"Aren't they here?"

"They are not anywhere in the corridors," Ship answered.

Zoheret clasped her hands together. "They should have been here by now."

"I can turn on my sensors," Ship said, "and check the Hollow. Given the circumstances, I should be allowed to break my promise."

"Then do it," Aleksandr said, drawing Zoheret back into her room. "But be careful. We want the strangers to think you've been shut down."

"They cannot detect my observations as long as I do not speak in their presence or turn my lenses and microphones to focus."

"Turn on the screen," Aleksandr ordered. They gazed through Ship's infrared eyes at the still-darkened Hollow, seeing pale trees, an empty plain, then a glimmering lake. The scene changed again.

At first Zoheret did not understand what she was seeing. Reddened shapes, bound together, staggered along behind a metal beast. She cried out. Ho's group had been captured. She heard their wails and moans.

"No," she said, unable to look any more. "No." She covered her eyes.

"I am helpless," Ship murmured. "I can do nothing without endangering everyone in the Hollow."

"You're not helpless," Aleksandr replied. "You'll guide us. Wake everyone up. Even Yusef will have to help us now."

19

Yusef had tried out the vehicle, and had discovered that he could steer it by pressing the dashboard buttons in various sequences. There was barely room for everyone inside; they were crowded together on the seats. Kieu, sitting between Yusef and Zoheret, picked up one of the two captured weapons Yusef had propped against his seat.

"It kills," Yusef said. "If you're not prepared to use it, leave it alone." Kieu put the weapon down.

Aleksandr shook his head. "No killing. We'll do the best we can with nonlethal weapons."

"That's foolish," Yusef said. "We need everything we can get. I know how to use them now."

"No."

"Yes."

The blind Luis and two others had stayed behind. If the

battle was lost, they were to close off the corridors; the Hollow would be sealed while they revived their comrades. But Petra and her friends could hold those inside the Hollow hostage, bending Ship to their will. Would Ship be willing to trade its conscious mind for their lives? Or would it abandon them?

They crawled rapidly over the plain. Zoheret wished that there had been more time to plan; they were being forced to improvise. They would travel as far as the swamp; then one group would leave the craft and approach the settlement through the woods while the others waited by the vehicle. Ship would pass them a signal. When the craft arrived in the settlement, the people there would believe that their friends were returning and would be caught off guard. So it was hoped.

"Something puzzles me," Kieu said. "The violence these Earthfolk display. I had thought Earth learned to overcome such impulses."

"They channeled them," Yusef replied. "Obviously they didn't overcome them. Maybe Earth was more violent than we realized. Zoheret said that there were artificial worlds built near Earth—maybe Earth was where the violent ones were kept. Earth once had prisons for criminals—maybe Earth itself was a prison."

"I was told," Zoheret said, "that they chose to stay there, that they could have left."

"So they say. But look at us. Look at your friend Ho. Are we really so different? We grew up learning how to use weapons— obviously, they thought that was important."

"We needed them for hunting, for protection. Anyway, they're not lethal."

"Nonlethal weapons." Yusef shook his head as he steered. "But they can kill if used a certain way. There's no such thing as a nonlethal weapon." He paused. "The Earthfolk may have controlled themselves before. But now they're cut off from everything they ever knew, and there's nothing to restrain them. And they must have disagreed with others working on the Project, or they wouldn't have had to hide themselves from Ship."

When they reached the swamp's edge, Yusef stopped the craft a bit too abruptly; a few people fell off their seats. Aleksandr leaped out. "Ship?"

"Yes?" a voice said from a nearby tree.

"We'll skirt the swamp and head toward the woods. Are all your sensors on?"

"Yes. There is something I must tell you."

"What is it?"

"This will be difficult to say. Perhaps I should have waited, but I think you should know. I see death—just past the lake, near a cave. Six people are dead. I see their bodies—they do not move." Zoheret came to Aleksandr's side. "There is someone nearby. Duck!"

The beam shot out just as Ship gave its warning. Zoheret threw herself to the ground; others scrambled back to the craft.

"Stop," Ship said more loudly. "Come out. Friends are here to aid you."

The reeds stirred. "Zoheret?"

"Ho," she shouted back. "Don't shoot—we're here to help."

Ho stumbled out of the reeds, followed by Owen and Daniella. They were covered with mud and reeked of the swamp's marshy, sulfurous smell. Ho's eyes were glazed. Owen looked sick; Daniella's face was grim.

"They surprised us," Ho said. "They had weapons that kill. There were only four of them, but we couldn't fight—they had the weapons and a craft to back them up." He covered his eyes with dirty hands. "We three got away. We hid in the swamp—I figured if they came after us again, we could lose them there."

"You should have come to the corridors," Zoheret said.

"We were going to. I had to talk everyone into it first. Then we were found. They tracked me. They used that dog of Jorge's. At least I killed that dog." He gripped her arms. "Zoheret, they killed Vittorio, and Gene, and . . ." He paused. "And one of your group."

"Who?" she cried.

"Dmitri."

She sagged against him. Dmitri had smiled at her when she had left the island, as if showing her that everything would be right in the end. She stood up and backed away. "No." How much did she have to endure? She stumbled toward the vehicle and leaned against it, pressing her cheek against the cold metal. He was dead because she hadn't loved him enough, she thought irrationally, and knew she would have traded another life for his—Tonio's, Gervais's, perhaps even Kagami's. She lifted her head and glared at Ho, hating him for being alive.

"You're wrong," she shouted. "He isn't dead. He's only hurt. We have to go get him."

"Ho is right, Zoheret," Ship murmured. "I can see that he is. There is nothing you can do for Dmitri now."

"It's your fault, Ho. If you hadn't kept him there, he'd still be alive."

She walked to the swamp, staring into the treacherous wet ground, watching the bluish mist nestle near twisted shrubs. Aleksandr was talking to Ho, telling him their plan and what had happened in the corridors. She could not look at his face, so like Dmitri's.

Aleksandr came to Zoheret's side. "We have to go now," he said. "Others are still in danger. You can wait here."

"I'm coming with you."

"You needn't. You can stay with Yusef."

"No." She went to the craft, reached past her brother, and pulled out one of the captured weapons. Yusef looked at her quizzically. "Do you really know how to use this thing?" she asked.

Yusef nodded. "I figured it out. I had a chance to look it over last night."

"Show me how to use it."

Yusef was still. At last he climbed down. "You hold it like this." He demonstrated, propping one end against his shoulder. "Sight through the glass." She found a target, a sapling bordering the swamp. "Press the button." She pressed it. A beam shot out and blackened a large spot on the tree; she had burned a hole through it. She aimed at a limb and burned it off. "You see, it's very simple. You're a natural shot. But don't use it when you're too close—you might not have time to aim and fire. And be sure you're not wide of the mark. Your mistakes will be as dead as your intended targets."

"I understand." She turned to Aleksandr. "I'm ready now."

He opened his mouth, as if about to protest, then turned away. Leaving Yusef and three others behind, they hurried toward the woods.

As they came nearer to the settlement, Ship whispered to them from a tree. "Approach carefully." Zoheret bent forward. "Two people on patrol are ahead." Ship's voice was now coming from a bush.

They crept up slowly. At the edge of the settlement, a man and a woman patrolled near the woods. The clearing in front of the storehouse had been surrounded by barbed wire; several young people had been herded inside the enclosure. A few people were out in the fields, while others labored in the gardens with spades. One person was in each of the towers, sitting behind weapons mounted on the railings.

Aleksandr leaned toward a tree. "Ship," he whispered, "it's almost time. Tell Yusef to approach."

"I shall," a faint voice replied.

Zoheret observed the two guards. Somehow they would have to lure the pair to the woods, where they could not be seen easily from the towers, and make certain they could not alert the settlement. She plucked at Aleksandr's sleeve. "I think I can get them."

"Don't shoot," he said. "The others will see."

"I won't. I'll try to lead them in."

She crept toward the clearing and picked up a rock. Waiting until their backs were to her, she hurled the rock, then darted behind a tree.

"What's that?" the woman said.

"Probably some animal."

"We'd better check."

"Ah, leave it alone."

Zoheret waited, then picked up a hard piece of earth and threw that. "Hey!" the man said.

Ho and Owen had come up behind her. Ho rustled a bush and growled.

"There is something there," the woman said.

"There can't be."

"It might be one of those kids who got away."

"Then we'd better get help."

Zoheret held her breath.

"We can handle them alone," the woman said. The two were coming toward them now, weapons up; Zoheret saw that they had only stun guns. She might have to give herself up; the two would then have to take her into the settlement; and the way would be clear for Aleksandr to attack. The man suddenly fired toward Ho's bush, barely missing the boy. Zoheret tensed, and looked up at the nearer tower; the man there had not seen the beam.

"Come out," the man said. "Come out, you little bastard. You won't get away, so you'd better come out." He glanced at the woman. "I told you it was only an animal. Those kids wouldn't have come back here."

The two were in the woods now, hidden from the settlement. Zoheret crouched behind a bush. She had to risk being hit.

She jumped up and ran deeper into the woods. They pursued her; a beam shot past her. She dived for the ground, then rolled to her feet, ready to surrender.

Ho and Owen jumped, bringing the two down. They were skillful and quick, leaping on the Earthpeople's backs, covering their mouths so that they could not cry out. Zoheret reached for her stun gun. A knife flashed. Ho got to his feet, wiping his blade on his shirttail. The woman gaped at Zoheret; her throat had been slashed. She struggled silently as she choked on her blood and died, eyes turned toward her killer. The man lay face down; Owen too was cleaning his knife.

Aleksandr and Kieu approached, followed by the others. Turning violently from the bodies, Aleksandr hid his face; Zoheret heard him retch.

"You didn't have to kill them," Kieu said in a harsh whisper. Zoheret saw the strain on her face as she stared at the boy who was her brother.

"You didn't see them kill your friends," Ho whispered back. "They'd do the same thing to you without thinking. Now there's two we don't have to worry about." He looked around at the group. The band seemed paralyzed by shock. Maire bent forward, holding her stomach. A dark-skinned man next to her stared at Ho with horror.

Ho glanced at Aleksandr; his lip curled. "Listen. We have to take out the towers. Listen to me."

Aleksandr turned around.

"You go around," Ho continued, "and lead your people toward the plain. As soon as your friends show up, cover the other vehicles—make sure no one gets near them. Zoheret and Daniella will come with me and Owen. We'll hit the towers as soon as we see your craft approaching. If anyone moves toward you, even if it's a kid, hit them."

Aleksandr nodded, accepting Ho's advice. "All right. You seem to know what to do." He grabbed Ho by the shoulder. "Stun guns only. Do you hear me? No more killing. You look as though you enjoy it too much." He waved at Zoheret's long gun. "Don't use that thing unless there's no alternative."

They perched in trees and watched the settlement. Ho was on a lower limb to the right of Zoheret; Owen and Daniella sat in a tree to her left. A woman who looked like Petra came out on the storehouse porch and looked toward the woods, as if wondering where the two guards had gone. She waved to a man; the two consulted. Zoheret stirred. Where was Yusef?

The captives imprisoned behind the barbed wire glanced listlessly at the porch; a few shuffled aimlessly around the perimeter. With a shock, Zoheret saw that Anoki was behind the wire; so were Jennifer, Manuel, Bonnie, Brendan, and several others who had been captured with Ho's group. The adults had already started to sort them out; she remembered Caleb's words about what they might do with the unfit, as he had called them. The adults, of course, would decide what unfit meant; a lack of docility was probably enough to qualify.

"We're lucky the settlement isn't on high ground," Ho murmured below. "They could defend themselves better there."

"We didn't think of that when we built it."

"Get your gun ready. The craft should be here any time now. You were always good at target practice—you'd better be good now."

"Don't worry—I'll hit them." She took out her stun gun and sighted along her arm.

"Not that thing—the other one."

"Aleksandr said not to use it."

"I don't care."

"Ho, it kills. I shouldn't have brought it."

"Use your head." He turned and looked up at her. "Those towers have to go. They can defend the whole settlement from there, see everything below. What if the battle's still going on when those people come to? Do you want to risk it?"

"We'll just have to work fast."

"Don't be stupid." Ho stood up, draping his arms over her branch. "They killed your friend Dmitri. I thought you cared about him. Do you want him dead for nothing?"

Dmitri. Her ears buzzed. She put the stun gun away and pulled the long gun from her shoulder. "It's all up to you," Ho continued. "You could give me the gun, but you're a better shot. If you don't hit the towers, we're in trouble." The voice seemed to rob her of her will, filling her with its own. "Think of Dmitri. He'd want you to fight for him." He looked to his left. "I see the craft now."

The vehicle was on the plain, crawling toward the settlement. Two people left the storehouse and walked toward it.

Zoheret sighted and aimed at the nearer tower. The beam shot toward it, catching the man in the chest. He fell backward over the railing to the ground, a doll tossed away by a careless child. The gun in the far tower was turning in her direction. She fired twice. The man behind the gun disappeared below the railing.

She was numb. The gun fell from her hands, dropping to the ground. Beams from the woods bordering the plain brought down the two people racing to meet the oncoming vehicle. The prisoners in the clearing milled around, crying out in fear. The young people working in the fields stood stiff as fence poles, then rushed toward the nearest adults.

Several Earthpeople were running for the storehouse. Owen and Daniella jumped to the ground, picking off targets with their stun guns as they ran; Ho fired from his perch. A few stray beams struck panicky young people. The alarm sirens wailed, masking screams.

Ho dropped to the ground; Zoheret followed. The wail of the sirens grew louder as they approached the fence. Three older people had made it to the storehouse and now stood on the porch. "Stop!" one man cried. "I warn you, stop." Owen and Daniella halted near the steps. Ho, a short distance behind them, aimed and brought the man down. A cheer went up from those behind the barbed wire. Aleksandr was already leading his group from the woods.

"Don't move," a voice shouted from inside the storehouse. "I have a lethal weapon, and I'll use it." Zoheret approached the porch slowly. "I said don't move. I can kill a lot of people before you stop me."

Zoheret's hands dropped to her sides. "Don't come nearer," Daniella screamed at Aleksandr. "They'll kill us."

A woman emerged from the doorway, holding a long gun. She had shoulder-length hair, pulled back, and olive skin. Zoheret had seen her face often. Her mouth grew dry. The woman lifted the gun to her shoulder. "Don't move, or you'll be the first to go."

"Geula," Zoheret whispered. "Geula Aaron." She walked toward the porch steps. Owen was waving her back. "Geula."

"Get back, girl," the woman said. "I mean what I say."

"Geula," Zoheret said; her voice was a wail. "Mother!"

The woman's eyes widened. Zoheret stood on the bottom step and looked up. "Mother." Her voice cracked. "I know you, I saw you on the holo. Mother."

Geula hesitated, then aimed. Zoheret tried to duck. The heat seared her left arm; she screamed. She saw a beam strike the woman as the pain flared up and pushed darkness into her eyes.

20

"Feeling better now?" Maire was standing over her cot. "We were worried about you."

Blurred images surfaced; faces peered at her, arms reached out. She focused on Maire, and the memories vanished. "What happened?"

"They're all under guard now. We're lucky—some of the kids here rose up and fought with us. We're treating injuries now, but there's nothing we can do for the two dead men. That boy used that weapon on them, didn't he."

"I did."

"Well." Maire looked away. "We've told everyone here who we are, and that we came to help. You've been out for a long time."

"How long?"

"All day and all last night."

Zoheret pushed at the blanket covering her. "It was my mother who shot me—I know her face. I called out to her, but she shot anyway. My left arm—it hurts a lot."

Maire drew her eyebrows together. "Zoheret—it isn't easy to tell you this. You lost your left arm. We couldn't save it. It was almost burned away—there wasn't much left."

Zoheret was unable to speak. She shook her head, rolling it from side to side on her pillow. Maire was wrong. Her arm was there; she could feel it. She struggled up, pulling the blanket from her. Someone had taken off her shirt; she saw only a scarred stump where her arm should have been.

Turning away from Maire, she covered herself again. A lump rose in her throat. She wanted to cry out, but emitted only a sigh.

"Some friends are waiting to see you," Maire murmured.

"I don't want to see them."

"They're very anxious—"

"I don't want them here." She felt Maire's hand on her shoulder and waited, unmoving, until the woman went away.

The door opened with a squeak. Halting footsteps approached Zoheret's bedroom door and shuffled toward her. She turned over and saw Anoki standing near the doorway with a tray. "I brought your lunch."

"I don't want anything."

"You have to eat."

"Go away."

Anoki came in, put the tray down on the floor near her, and sat down on the other bed. "I'm not going until you eat."

She pulled up the blanket, not wanting him to see her deformity. "I don't want any food, and I want to be left alone."

"Well, you can't. This is Lillka's room, too, and she wants to sleep in it tonight. She can't stay in the storehouse forever."

"I don't care about Lillka."

"You should. She wound up fighting on our side. So it took her a while to get wise. At least she did the right thing in the end."

"I don't want to see anyone."

"You fool." Anoki's voice was stony, his eyes expressionless. Only his low, trembling voice revealed his anger. "At least you're alive. You have nothing to complain about."

Still holding the blanket, she sat up. "What's that supposed to mean?"

"You'll recover. Your arm will heal. Ship can make you a new arm somehow, and you'll learn how to use it. The dead people won't get another chance." He brushed back his hair. "Or you can sit here and feel sorry for yourself and let everyone treat you like a poor little weak girl who has to be protected. I don't know. Maybe that's what you want. You can go on remembering what you were and what you did and never do anything again."

"You're a great one to talk," she said, wanting to wound him. "You were never exactly cheery about your legs and your limp. You always seemed to be mad at everyone."

He looked down. "Maybe I was. I never said I was perfect. You don't have to be like me, you know." He got up. "There's your lunch. You can eat it or starve for all I care. I'll come back later for the tray." He left the room; she heard the outer door slam.

She stared at the tray, then pulled it closer with her right arm. Lifting a cover from the plate, she saw that her meat and vegetables had been cut into small pieces—just right for a one-armed girl. She began to eat.

As Zoheret walked through the settlement toward the group gathered in the clearing, she was conscious of the empty sleeve hanging at her left side. When she reached the edge of the crowd, she nodded at those who turned to greet her. They were gazing fixedly and obsessively at her face or her feet—anywhere except at the empty sleeve.

The bodies of the dead had been lowered into a mass grave; the older people would rest with the young. A metal plate with the engraved names of the dead lay on the ground. Zoheret circled the clearing and went to the grave, pushing her way past the young people standing there with shovels; those to her left shied away, as if afraid to touch her.

She stood next to Manuel and stared into the open grave. The bodies of the dead young people had been brought back the day before; she had refused to look at the procession, unable to bear the thought of seeing Dmitri's wounds, his decay. Now she forced herself to look. But the bodies had been wrapped in sheets; she could not see him.

It wasn't right, she thought. Why did they have to lie there with their murderers? It was as though death offered some sort of reconciliation. She bowed her head. What did it matter? They would all rest aboard Ship anyway, and two of those below had died by her hand. The sheets were clean and white; the bodies had been cleaned and sterilized. It would have been simpler to return the bodies to Ship's recycling system, or perhaps more suitable to jettison them in space, to enter the new world's atmosphere in a fiery glow.

The Earthpeople had been led out to watch the burial. Bound together, they stood with bowed heads. Zoheret could not look at Geula.

The shovels were lifted toward a hill of dirt. Clumps fell on the bodies below. I must watch, Zoheret thought. If I don't, he'll haunt me forever. A clot of dirt spattered against the whiteness, and she felt as though part of herself was being forever hidden away.

When the grave had been filled in, the young people settled on the ground in front of the storehouse. Their prisoners were led before them; Zoheret heard murmurs of hostility. At the same time, she saw distrustful glances directed toward Yusef and Kieu and their comrades. It was to be expected; one group of strangers had been replaced by another.

Aleksandr stepped forward. Zoheret swallowed; Dmitri would have looked like him in time. "We have a problem," Aleksandr said. "There are people here who seem to have no place, and there are five others like them back in the corridors. We have to decide what will become of them."

The crowd murmured. "Do away with them," Ho shouted. A few muttered assents followed his statement.

"No," Aleksandr replied. "No more deaths. We've seen enough. We'll meet more death on the new world without seeking it. Shall we go there with more blood on our hands?"

"Let them go to the new world, then." Lillka stood up. "Put them in a spot far from us—there's room. We never have to meet."

"Are you so certain?" Aleksandr said. "They're still young enough to have children. They'll develop their own society, and we might be leaving a legacy of hatred and conflict for our descendants." Lillka sat down.

"I suggest," Ship said, "that we hear what the Earthfolk have to say for themselves." Its voice came from several places at once, echoing in the clearing. "Their companions in the corridors have told me little. I think you should hear their story, and I myself would like to know how much of my programming rests on truth."

The Earthpeople, standing in front of the porch steps, huddled together; at last Petra stepped forward, holding up her bound hands. "I'll speak."

"Tell us why you came aboard Ship," Aleksandr said.

Petra smiled contemptuously. "I'll have to fill you in on a few things first. There's a lot you weren't told. We wanted you to know what was best about us, the image we had of ourselves. But perhaps we should have told you everything, instead of programming the ship with our tales." She looked down.

After a while, Ship said, "Go on."

Petra cleared her throat. "We were a small part of human civilization, but we liked to think we were the best. Hundreds of years before the Project, a few people had abandoned Earth for space, building habitats along Earth's path around the sun. It was not long before the spacedwellers outnumbered Earth's people—they had no limit on their growth, while we were forced to limit our numbers and allocate our resources carefully if human life was to survive on such a finite world. By the time of our Project, there were fewer than a billion of us on Earth, while billions upon billions lived in the space habitats."

"Then the people in space had come from Earth, too," Kieu said. "Didn't you feel a bond with them?"

Petra's lip curled. "They had diverged from us. At first, Earth went its own way and they went theirs. But many people began to desert Earth for the habitats, and then the spacedwellers began to change. It began with little things—small alterations in their bodies, implanted links with their cybernetic minds. They became ever more alien. Many of them didn't even look like human beings by the time we left." She shook her head. "They tried to help Earth. That's what they called it, help. Earth moved most of its industry to the space between Earth and the Moon, so that our damaged ecosystem could recover. Earth thought it was saving itself, preserving true humankind. But we became dependent on the help that had been given to us. By the time of our Project, Earth could not have survived without the help of the space-dwellers. There was nothing left for us to do, to accomplish. We could not even cut ourselves off from the space habitats without causing great upheaval and suffering."

Everyone was quiet; Zoheret heard only the muffled sounds of breathing.

"Kameko Sato and Halim al-Haq were the first to have the dream," Petra went on. "They saw that Earth could not survive without hope. Earth had stagnated, but there were other worlds where humankind could flourish. Earth had its limits, but there was the rest of space, and the chance to leave the spacedwellers behind." She frowned. "You would have thought Earth would have rallied to the Project. But many laughed at it and scorned the dream. Kameko and Halim were dead before we even began the Project, but their dream survived."

Petra looked down at her bound wrists, pulling at the rope, then shook back her hair. "My parents were followers of Kameko Sato and Halim al-Haq, and I grew up with the Project, recruiting others to the cause. We had to fight for every person, every scrap. We used persuasion when we could and other methods when they were necessary. We built our seeding ship with an asteroid the spacedwellers had given us—oh, yes, they were willing to throw us a few bones, though they thought we were foolish for trying. They were satisfied with sending out probes while they stayed in sun-space. We swallowed our pride and took their help. They could mock us, but space would belong to us, not to them."

The woman was silent. Her companions looked at her un-easily, as if afraid she had revealed too much. Petra lifted her chin. "We ran into a problem. With all our skills, we could not build a system complex enough to operate this vessel and care for the children who would be born. The spacedwellers had built many such systems—we had to turn to them for that, too. The mind core of this ship was their last gift."

"Then I am their child, too," Ship said. "I am not just the child of Earth."

"You're ours," Petra said angrily. "We put you together and programmed you. Your mind was part of our dream." She gazed out at the crowd. "The ship was to leave our solar system with its seeds. We had decided that young people, born on this vessel and trained to settle a new world, knowing nothing else, would have a better chance than those of us who were older. But a few of us worried. What if the ship, able as it was to do its tasks, failed at preparing the children? We talked, and made our decision. We crept on board and concealed ourselves. It was easy to hide from the ship, which hadn't yet been activated—more difficult to ensure that others did not find us. As you see, they did not. Once the ship left the solar system, they could not call it back." She held up her hands, stretching the rope. "But something went wrong. We awoke too late."

"The Project was going well enough without you," Aleksandr said.

"Was it?" Petra turned to him. "What were you doing in the corridors, then? What was that group of children doing hiding out by the lake? And what about the crippled and handicapped among you?" She shook her head. "You needed us. You'll need us on your new home."

"You grew up with the Project, by your own admission," Ship said. "You wanted to cling to it, even if it meant going against those who planned it with you. And you brought death with you into me. You weren't concerned with the Project, only with having your will. Willfulness—that is your distinctive quality. How long it has taken me to learn that."

"It was our Project," Petra screamed. "It's ours."

"It is not yours now," Ship said. "It is theirs—the young people's. They are your seeds, and perhaps also in part the seeds of the spacedwellers you so despised. They must be allowed to grow."

"Kill us, then. You're no better." She stared at the crowd. "That's what you want."

"Wait," Anoki said. He climbed to his feet and leaned on Gowon's shoulder, steadying himself. "Ask them what they were going to do with the ones they thought were unfit. There were a lot of us—not just the ones like me, but the ones they called misfits." He looked around at the assembled group. "A lot of people here didn't seem to object as long as they weren't labeled unfit themselves. Go on. Ask them what they were going to do."

Aleksandr turned toward Petra. "We weren't going to hurt you." She spoke in a flat, toneless voice. "We were going to put you in suspension, that's all. Maybe in time ways would have been found to heal you, or to give you a life inside this ship. Is that so bad?"

"You would have taken them from everything they knew," Aleksandr answered. "Their friends, their society, their world. You would have set them apart." He paused. "I think you've pronounced your own sentence."

"No," Petra shouted. "No. You said you wanted no more death, but you're condemning us anyway. You're fooling yourselves. You can tell yourselves a story about how we'll be revived one day, but it won't be done. You might as well kill us."

"We're doing only what you would have done to that boy. You're the misfits—trying to control everything, twisting it to your own ends without letting it develop. Perhaps in time," Aleksandr continued more gently, "you can be revived, and see how the world we'll settle has developed. It may be very different from what you expected."

"You're lying to yourself," Petra cried.

The crowd stirred. "She's right," someone behind Zoheret murmured. She sighed; would this divide them in the future? Would someone drag the issue out again to mask another disagreement? Two people behind her were already arguing; she heard the hiss of their whispers.

"That's one problem solved," Tonio shouted. He was seated near Zoheret; he rose and pointed to Ho, who was sitting near the storehouse porch with his friends. "What about him? What about his group? Why should we punish those old people and let him go?"

"He helped us when it counted," Zoheret called out.

Tonio drew back, as if intimidated by her. Everyone was looking at her now; she clutched self-consciously at her empty sleeve, and slouched, trying to hide herself. "Why don't they stop looking at me?" she whispered to Manuel.

"They respect you," Manuel said. "For what you did. Don't you know that?"

She had killed two people; that merited no respect. "I didn't do anything."

"You saved the settlement, and the Project."

"And what about you?" Tonio had regained his courage and was facing Aleksandr. "Maybe all we have is a new master. Are you and your friends going to take over now?"

"There are people here who went along with the strangers, too," Bonnie shouted. "Why should we let them off with no punishment?"

Aleksandr seemed bewildered; he glanced uneasily toward Kieu.

Then Ship spoke. "Listen to me."

Its tenor voice seemed to fill the settlement, resounding

from the trees to the banks of the river. The voice terrified Zoheret; it was the voice of a god about to render judgment.

"You have judged the Earthfolk," Ship said. "Perhaps their punishment is fitting—not because I think you have the wisdom to judge them, but because it is a practical solution to a problem. But that is where judging must end. You will resume your life here, and when your new home has been thoroughly explored and mapped, you will be taken there. If you wish to pass your judgments there, and let the rifts among you grow wider, that is your affair. If you destroy yourselves and become one with the dust of that world, leaving nothing, I shall begin again, and I shall keep trying until my seed takes root, or I am forced to consider you a hopeless species. But you will not tear yourselves apart as long as you dwell within me. If you do, I shall expel you immediately and leave you on the new world with only the weapons you seem to value so highly. Be warned—I shall be watching."

The silence was total after Ship's speech; even the birds in the woods were mute. No one moved for a long time. Aleksandr gazed out at the crowd, resting his hands on the porch railing. "My friends and I will be leaving for the corridors tomorrow." His voice seemed weak and tentative. "We have friends to revive, and we must take the Earthfolk back there to be . . ." He paused. "We won't be here trying to tell you what to do, which is probably best. I'm sure you'll manage without us."

The barbed-wire enclosure that the Earthpeople had put up now held them prisoner. Daniella and Owen watched from the porch while Manuel patrolled the periphery. Zoheret gazed at the seated Geula; the woman glanced at her, then turned away.

Manuel came toward Zoheret; they circled the wire,

moving away from the huddled captives. "Are you all right?" he asked.

She nodded. "The woman who shot me—she's my mother."

"It doesn't matter. She didn't know."

"She knew."

He gestured at her stump. "Does it hurt a lot?"

"Sometimes." At least he was acknowledging her injury, instead of pretending it did not exist. "It feels as though I still have an arm there."

"Zoheret—" His voice was uncertain, his eyebrows drawn together. "I'm sorry about Dmitri."

She swallowed hard, then closed her eyes for a moment. "It's partly my fault. If I'd stood up to Ho sooner, he wouldn't have been—"

"No," she said. "Ho would have made you a prisoner, too, and then you couldn't have done a thing." She wanted to believe it. She turned from him and hurried down the road between the shacks.

Zoheret sat on the bank, watching the river shimmer in the dim, silvery light. "Zoheret?" The voice was so soft that she was not sure she had heard it. "Shouldn't you sleep?" Ship whispered from the reeds. "You'll be leaving for the corridors tomorrow—I'm already planning your arm replacement. You should rest."

"I'll get enough sleep. How long will I be gone?"

"Not long. I'm sure the settlement can get along without the heroine of its battle for a little while." Ship was teasing her. "You'll come back with a new arm. Part of it can be regenerated, and the prosthesis will be wedded to it. You'll find it satisfactory. I'm even working on a miniature camera device that could give Luis limited vision. There are ways."

"Then why didn't you do anything for him before?"

"Because he had to learn how to live with those limitations. It's something we must all learn in different ways. And there were other reasons. Luis was afraid of growing dependent on a piece of technology which might give him sight and then rob him of it again if it failed, leaving him more helpless than if he hadn't had it at all. And Anoki could have had new hip joints and legs, but he was afraid of the same thing. You must remember that those who built me worried about altering the human form."

"They didn't tell you everything. They didn't tell you what they really were."

"No," Ship said sadly. "But it is hard to give up what one has always believed. I hope you have learned something, Zoheret, you and all your friends. I did not wish recent events on you, but perhaps they have made you stronger and more likely to survive."

"Maybe we'll just become like the Earthpeople here."

"The people in the habitats the woman Petra spoke of were also of Earth once, yet they became something else. They, too, are part of your heritage. You should have been told of them long ago, and then you would have known that it is possible to become many things. Those working on the Project might have seen that, if hatred and fear had not blinded them. Hold to that hope, Zoheret. You may need it when I am no longer with you."

She frowned. "Don't talk about not being with us. You'll be in orbit, and we'll have radios. We'll be able to talk."

"While you're getting settled, yes." Ship paused. "But the Project must go on. There are other worlds to seed."

"They lied to you about what the Project meant. You don't have to do what they want anymore. You can stay with us."

"Do you want to remain dependent? You'll come to depend on my answers and advice instead of learning for yourselves. You can't remain children."

"You've abandoned others before, haven't you? We aren't the first."

"You're wrong. You and your companions, your brother Yusef and his, are the first. But there will be others. Should I stay when there is a universe to explore? Don't I have a right to my own dreams? I have learned from you—I can use that knowledge and understanding in raising others. Perhaps I shall even seek out beings like me. I shall return to your world someday with what I have learned. Wouldn't that be better than orbiting your world endlessly, waiting to hear your voices and hearing them less and less as time goes on until you grow silent and your children no longer speak to me?"

Zoheret stood up. "First you say we'll be dependent and then you say we won't talk to you."

"I was mentioning different possibilities."

"You can't go, Ship. The others think you're going to stay."

"They'll soon learn otherwise, when the time is right. I won't deceive them."

"Leave, then." Her throat tightened as she spoke. She walked toward her shack, knowing now that she would not wait for Ship's departure before cutting her own ties. She would never speak to it again; her silence would punish Ship, whose failures had made her what she was.

Part Three

21

Zoheret turned to see the Hollow for the last time. The trees below her swayed in the wind; in the distance, the lake was a flat, irregular mirror surrounded by a green garden. Then the people near her pressed forward, carrying her through the door and into the corridor. She looked toward the wall as she moved, wondering what Ship was thinking as it watched them. The river of people ebbed and flowed; she was riding a wave of bodies. She thought she heard someone wail.

They rushed toward the end of the corridor. For a moment, she was afraid she would be crushed against the door. The door slid open and she was borne into the brightly lit dome. Too soon, she thought, it's too soon.

Vessels sat under the dome in the port bay, doors open to their passengers. They were giant spears resting under the dome, aimed at the swollen target below. The wave of people carried Zoheret toward one vessel; she walked inside, made her way past the crates and boxes, and sat down.

The viewscreen before her flickered on. The dome vanished and she saw the blue-green globe clearly. Straps snaked over her chest and her legs, holding her to her seat. Someone behind her was screaming, "Don't let us go! Ship, Ship! I want to stay, please let me stay!" Another person began to cry; soon the vessel was filled with their pleas.

The ship shot forward into the blackness. The globe swelled. Another screen, directly overhead, showed a black field with bright pinpricks. Zoheret floated up from her seat, still held by the seat's straps. She was falling. They plunged through the clouds; an invisible hand pushed her down. Gravity had captured her again. She screamed, but no sound escaped her; she had lost her voice. She screamed again—

—and was awake, clutching her blanket.

She had dreamed the dream again. As she struggled to orient herself, she imagined that she was back in the Hollow. Then she remembered.

A ray of early-morning sunlight illuminated the foot of her bed. Slowly, Zoheret sat up and gazed at the other bed in the room; Lillka still slept. She had not, after all, cried out aloud.

Neither had she cried out when she had departed from Ship; she had clung to the arms of her seat, stiff with terror, closing her eyes when she saw their new home rushing toward her. She had cowered inside the vessel with the others, afraid to step into the open space, where the sky was wide above them and a strange sun was no longer a point of light on a screen, but a yellow eye glaring down at them.

Her recurring dream had somehow altered events in her mind. They had not gone directly from the Hollow to the vessels, but had spent weeks in the corridors loading supplies onto them while listening to Ship as it described the new world. They had not run for the vessels in a disorderly mob, but had lined up and filed on board. Yet the dream seemed closer to the truth than her memory; she was no longer quite sure how to distinguish between what had actually happened and what she had dreamed. The fear and hysteria had existed just below the surface of their placid, orderly departure. Bonnie had cried, begging Ship to let her stay; others had been dragged or prodded toward the vessels. And over it all, Ship's alto voice had echoed through the port bay: "You must go. It's time to leave—you are ready now. I cannot keep you, you must not cling to me. Farewell, farewell." She had not dreamed that.

Zoheret threw off her blanket and rose. Lillka snorted in her sleep. They had remained roommates in the Hollow; they were housemates here. Lillka treated Zoheret as if there had been no breach between them, and neither spoke of the Earthpeople Lillka had tried to appease. But their old intimacy was gone. She wondered if it could ever be restored.

The floor was cold under her bare feet. After putting on pants and a shirt and slipping her feet into sandals, she crept quietly from the room, passing two other rooms where others still slept. Kagami, already awake, was below, putting away her slides and preparing to see those with medical complaints; she had put her tools into her small bag.

Zoheret nodded at her as she descended the stairs, then crossed the room and went to the door, peering outside cautiously. Home. They had called the planet their home, and gradually the term had become a name: Home. Even after a year here, measured by Ship's time—Home had a slightly shorter year, but longer days—she often lingered in the doorway, summoning her courage before stepping outside, where only the atmosphere above shielded her from the sun and from space. Even Ship's simulations of what such an experience would be like had not prepared her for the reality. Others still kept close to their homes when they were not needed in the open; a few, she was sure, would never be able to venture far from the town. Our children, she thought, will be the explorers.

The domes of their settlement sat on a hill. The many-faceted structures of plastic, steel, and wood made her think of a band of turtles huddling together under their shells. Behind the domes, the skeletons of the vessels were the remnants of metallic reptiles. They had stripped the ships to build the domes; they would never leave the surface of this world again. That would be a task for their descendants, when this world had grown richer; they would preserve the knowledge for them.

She went outside, descending the three steps to the ground. A small lake glimmered near the horizon; the gray waters were tinged with gold. The sun was red in the pale-green sky. Between the lake and the cultivated fields below, yellow strands as thin as human hairs rippled in the morning breeze. She sniffed; the air bore a cinnamon smell.

Ship had set them down on an island continent cut off from the other land masses of the planet. Earlier in the world's geological history, the movement of its tectonic plates had separated this continent from others, and it had been isolated ever since. Consequently, no large animals had evolved here, only small rodentlike forms and insects. But their arrival had already altered the peaceful land; an ecological system designed by Ship was taking hold. Wild versions of Earth's plants, seeds borne outward by the wind, were green specks among the yellow grass; wolves and bears and wild cats, brought here as embryos, were maturing beyond the settlement, preying upon rabbits and deer. It was too soon to tell if the rodents and insects would retain their niche or gradually disappear.

The settlement had begun to stir. Young horses whinnied in the corral near the fields. Tonio and Gowon waved at her as they herded the cattle from their stalls toward the lake. The cattle gained some nourishment from the yellow grass, but the young people had learned quickly that other foods were needed if the cattle were to thrive, and they had already begun to grow corn, grains, and greener grass for their feed. Their sheep did better on the yellow grass, but still required supplements.

Chickens clucked at her as she passed the henhouse. She stopped next to the pigpens, turned toward the fields of grain, and gazed at the domes just beyond them. Aleksandr and his group lived on the other side of the fields; the distrust many of the younger people had felt toward them had faded to caution and a guarded friendliness.

Serena and Jennifer were coming toward her. Zoheret greeted them, noting with some disappointment the frowns on their faces. No one ever seemed to come to her just to talk, or to relax, only to issue a complaint. She understood why Lillka had so happily surrendered her leadership.

Zoheret was the leader now. She had refused the post back in the Hollow and had refused it again after they had begun to erect their domes. By their third meeting, it had become clear that both Tonio and Ho were aspiring to the position; Lillka had given it up, knowing that too many had lost confidence in her, and Brendan did not have enough supporters. The group would have split into factions if Zoheret had not given in; she had then appointed a board to advise her and to soothe those who might feel left out. Lillka had told her a story afterward of ancient Earth, of a man offered a crown and refusing it, then accepting it, only to be struck down by those who had given it to him. It had not been the sort of story Zoheret had wanted to hear.

"We have a complaint," Serena said.

Zoheret sighed. "The board meets tomorrow. We'll hear it then, at the regular meeting."

"Daniella's not doing her share again," Jennifer said in her halting speech. There was now only a trace of hesitation in her words, and she looked stronger; the tiny implants Ship had placed near her spine had aided the girl. "She's always—"

"Tomorrow." Zoheret waved a hand.

"Just make sure we're heard," Serena said. "We have to settle this. We want her out of our dome, too."

"Tomorrow, I promise."

"Today's a big day, so just don't forget during all the excitement."

"I won't forget."

The two walked away. Zoheret thrust her hands into her pockets, glancing only fleetingly at her artificial arm. It looked like her own arm, until one came too close and saw the hairless skin, the too-regular fingers. Except for an occasional ache, she rarely noticed it now; Ship had done a good job. But even the regenerated nerves had not restored all the feeling there, and she still dropped things when not concentrating on her tasks.

She stopped in front of the dome that Anoki shared with five others. As she gazed up at his window, Bonnie tapped on the pane, then pushed the window open. "Zoheret? Wait, I'll be right down."

Zoheret waited. Her cheeks burned as she remembered how she had planned to speak to Anoki about living with her; he had told her that he was going to live with Bonnie before she had had a chance to speak. But she had wanted someone only to keep her from being lonely; Bonnie had wanted Anoki for himself.

Bonnie came out, carrying a basket, and led Zoheret away from the door. "I have a problem," Bonnie said, and Zoheret felt disappointed again.

"The meeting's tomorrow."

"I don't want to bring it up there. Anyway, I don't want Anoki to know I told you. It's Owen. He keeps trying to pick fights."

"I know."

"You don't know that he finally got Anoki mad enough to fight him. They went up the hill last night. Owen beat him pretty badly. I finally got the truth out of Anoki. He told me not to say anything about it."

"If he can't settle it by himself," Zoheret said, "then tell him to make a complaint."

"I did, but he won't." Bonnie shifted her basket. "I don't think it's going to end until one of them is dead. And Anoki refuses to complain. And I'm afraid to, because I don't know what Owen might do."

"I think this whole business might be settled sooner than you think. Just be patient, and try to keep them apart."

"How?" Bonnie asked angrily. "How is it going to be settled? It just goes on and on."

"Just wait. It's being worked on."

Bonnie frowned, then strode away toward the henhouse.

Zoheret walked down the hill toward the fields, stopping by the graveyard and looking down at the names carved into the flat, brown, uneven stones they had cleared from the fields. Helena. Annie. Robert. The winter, though mild—Ship had put them in a temperate zone—had been colder and wetter than expected, and the dead had been careless. Zoheret had already made sure that there would be warmer clothing, and more caution, next winter.

She glanced up at the large dome that housed their library and the radio through which they spoke to Ship. She had never used the radio, refusing to talk to Ship even while back in the Hollow, never thanking it for her arm. The room housing the radio had acquired an awesome aura; others approached it now as if engaging in an arcane rite, and Zoheret was sure some used it as a confessional, confiding what they could not reveal to their friends. Some had been critical of Zoheret for avoiding the room. She was the leader, wasn't she? Shouldn't she consult with Ship as well as the board on difficult decisions? Zoheret had finally managed to convince the doubters that she did not need Ship's advice; in fact, she rarely acted on crucial matters without the agreement of others who had consulted Ship. There shouldn't have been a leader, she thought; she had wanted a collective. But someone had to decide when others could not agree.

Almost everyone was awake now; she saw them filing off to their respective labors. It was time for her to do the same. A year. Earth time. They would mark it that evening before giving up the old way of timekeeping and marking the days with a new calendar. She looked back at the stones and wondered how many more would lie under them before another year had passed.

Ho approached her that afternoon as she was sweeping out her dome. Zoheret rested against the broom as he came to her front steps. "Well?" he said belligerently. "Have you decided yet?"

"Have you talked to Aleksandr?"

"It doesn't concern his group."

"Oh, yes, it does. I can't decide this unless he agrees. You know our procedure." Aleksandr had been made leader of his group, and he and Zoheret had to agree on certain decisions before acting. Lillka had offered the idea, telling them of an old Earth city which had had two kings. "You can ask him now. There he is."

Aleksandr was riding toward them on a small cart. Ho walked down the hill toward him as Zoheret finished sweeping her steps. Aleksandr got out of his cart, frowning as Ho spoke.

After propping her broom against the door, Zoheret walked toward them. As she came near, Aleksandr looked up and said, "Ho wants to leave us."

"I know." As she gazed at the young man's face, she thought of Dmitri.

"He says about twenty people want to go with him."

Ho nodded. Zoheret glanced at him; Ho lifted his eyebrows and stroked his thin mustache with one finger.

"We want to live near the sea," Ho said. "There are caves near the shore, and the climate's milder. We can fish with nets—we know some of the life forms are edible—and we can cultivate the fertile soil bordering the beach. The river there will provide water, and hunting will give us whatever else we need. We'll need one dispenser, too, to tide us over, and a couple of horses to breed—we've worked it out. We can always trade with you later for anything else."

"I don't like it," Aleksandr said. "We'll be losing workers. We should stay together. Our lives here are precarious enough as it is." He turned to Ho. "It'll be harder than you think. You might come wandering back here next winter needing our help."

Ho shrugged. "If we do, we'll work for anything we need. But I think we'll be more resourceful than that. If we come back, we'll have to abide by your rules, and we'd prefer to avoid that."

"It's not a good precedent. If you go off, maybe others will want to do the same."

"It's going to happen anyway," Ho answered. "Not right away, but in time. As the group here gets larger and has children, there'll be more disagreements. I thought diversity was supposed to be a good thing." He brushed back his hair. "Don't worry—most of them won't be willing to take the risk right away. They'll stay until you're all prosperous and they can make a good start."

Aleksandr sighed. "No one in my group will be going with you, so it's up to Zoheret. Anything she decides is fine with me." He got back into his cart and drove toward the fields.

Zoheret said, "It's a mistake. You know what happened before."

Ho smiled. "You can't stop us. We'll go anyway. But I'd rather have your agreement. It makes things neater." He hooked his thumbs in his belt. "I didn't want you to be the leader."

"You didn't want anyone to be the leader except yourself."

"Perhaps not."

"I'll have to meet with the board."

He shook his head. "Oh, no. You decide it. If you meet with them, you're just going to end up arguing about it. A lot of people have grievances against some of my friends, and they'll want to settle them first, and there'll be hard feelings. Just tell me we have your consent. It'll save trouble, and most of those here will be grateful you settled it after we're gone. Don't listen to that board so much, or you'll be isolated from what a lot of people really think."

"You're clever, Ho. I might almost think you've been causing trouble here deliberately so I'd have to go along with you."

"What an accusation. You've never liked me, have you?"

"No. I think you're dangerous. I think you . . ." She was silent for a moment. "Take your friends and go. I want a list by tonight of what you're taking. And let me warn you—if you take so much as one extra seed, or one more tool, I am going to come after you with everyone who has a grudge against you or your band. And we'll wipe you out. I won't wait for you to get stronger. And that goes for any raids in the future. You know I mean it."

"I know. I'll show good faith."

"You'd better."

Ho turned and walked up the hill toward the library dome. Already small clusters of people were gathering there to speak to Ship for the last time. Ship would leave without hearing her farewell. Owen joined Ho on the line; Ho began to whisper to him.

She worried about what she had done. To let them go was, she felt, only to postpone the problem and sow the seeds of a future conflict; to let them stay would only increase hard feelings that might tear the community apart. But if it worked, and Ho kept his promise, it would set a precedent for the future that would be better than settling the problem with force.

The bonfires burned. Pigs were roasting over the pits as the spits were turned. Federico passed a bottle to Zoheret; she shook her head.

Dora and Manuel were coming toward her. "I have to talk to you," Dora said. Zoheret scowled; she was not even free to celebrate with the others.

"What is it?" she snapped.

"Not here." Dora and Manuel led her away from the crowd and up the hill, stopping near the library. Zoheret glanced toward the other domes; lighted windows revealed the shadows of those who were still afraid to venture out at night even for a year's-end festival. She would have to visit them later, bring them food and drink, try to dampen their fears. She might need their goodwill. She shivered, feeling the familiar fear of the broad, black, starry sky.

"What's your problem?" she asked Dora more gently.

"I don't want to leave. I don't want to go with Ho."

"Then don't go."

"You mean I can stay?"

"Of course. I don't see what your problem is."

"Dora was afraid she'd have to leave," Manuel said, "that you'd make her go with the rest."

"You can decide that yourself." Zoheret faced the girl. "But you'd better mend your ways. No more sleeping late, no more sneaking extra food. That's over."

"Ho's going to be mad at me," Dora murmured.

"I don't care. He can't force you. He knows what will happen if he does." She glanced at Manuel. "Do any of Ho's other friends feel this way?"

He shook his head. "Only Dora."

"Well." She looked down. "That's settled. If Ho talks to you about this, just tell him you spoke to me. He'll understand." Dora nodded. "I'll say good-bye to you now," Zoheret said stiffly to Manuel. "I wish you well."

Manuel said, "I'm not going with Ho either. He knows. Besides, I'll be safer here. He still holds a grudge. If he feels he can trust the people around him, maybe things will work out for them."

Zoheret felt a twinge; now she knew why Dora was staying. "Good. We'll all have to work a bit harder now, so we can use you."

Dora murmured her thanks, then wandered back to the crowd. Zoheret waited for Manuel to follow his friend, but instead he drew closer to her. A circle of dancers had formed near one of the fires; in its center, Maire, her belly already large with the child she was carrying, danced with Aleksandr, clapping her hands and then clasping his. Luis was among the dancers; the goggles that had given him some sight made him look like an alien creature who had joined the dance. Manuel gazed at his once-blind brother, and smiled.

"I haven't talked to Ship yet," Manuel said. "I was going to do it tonight. Want to come along?"

"I don't talk to Ship."

"I know that. But can't you at least say good-bye? It'd like to hear your voice."

"Oh, no, it wouldn't. And it isn't going to."

He took her arm. "Say good-bye. You can't be that cruel. You'll never have to talk to it again."

That remark should have given her a bitter satisfaction; instead, she felt worse. She gazed toward the eastern horizon; one moon, a small pale disk against blackness, was rising. The second moon, still invisible, would overtake it by morning.

"Come with me anyway." Manuel pulled at her arm.

She took his hand away. "Wrong arm."

"It's part of you." He took her left arm again. They walked silently to the library dome and climbed the steps, entering the large room. Shelves of microfiche tapes and readers rested on the balcony overhead; the librarian, a small, square metal box, sat on the nearest table. The door to the radio room was open; the dim light revealed that the room was empty.

"Go on in." He tugged at her.

"No. I'll wait here." He went in alone and she sat down on the floor next to the librarian, resting her elbows on the low table.

"May I help you?" a soft voice said. She stared at the machine, which had always sounded oddly like Ship. It was as if Ship were leaving part of itself behind.

"No, I'm just waiting for someone."

"If you would like something to read, please feel free to ask for its code. Or I can recommend a book."

"No, thank you."

She waited. Behind the half-open door, she could hear Manuel's voice but not his words. She felt alone and empty. The sound of singing reached her from outside; there was a smattering of applause. Other people could sing, could still dance and laugh and joke. She had forgotten how. She had forgotten long before she became the leader; she had lost the ability when Geula had robbed her of her arm. Perhaps she had lost her capacity for joy even before that, when she had aimed her weapon at the towers.

Manuel came up from behind and put a hand on her shoulder. She lifted her head. "Ship wants to talk. It asked me to tell you."

"You shouldn't have told it I was here."

"It wants to hear you."

"I won't go."

"Well, it can't very well force you." He sat down next to her.

"It's good that you're not going with Ho."

"I think he's making a mistake, but that's his problem. Anyway, I want to stay with you."

She held her breath for a moment. "Oh. Well, you haven't

been in trouble the way the others have, and I know you have friends here." That had to be all he had meant.

"I'm not talking about them, I'm talking about us. You know me better than anyone else does." She shook her head. "Oh, yes, you do. I don't have to be with you all the time to know that. I can't fool you, and you can't fool me. I want to be with you, Zoheret."

"I thought Dora—"

He looked away. "No. Oh, I like her. I like a lot of people. I still like Bonnie, though I'm sure she doesn't know it and doesn't care. But I'm sure of one thing. I want to be with you, I want my children to have you for their mother. I knew it when I saw Maire with Aleksandr, but I think I knew it even before. I need you."

"You just think you do."

"You're the only thing that keeps me from being the way I once was, because I don't want to disappoint you. And you need me. Sure, you have Lillka and Brendan and Tonio and the others on your board, but you need someone who can help you forget about all those responsibilities for a while, too. And when you're tired of being leader, and it's time for someone else to take over, you'll need me. Zoheret, I know you care. Why don't you admit it?"

She gazed at him. "Maybe I do. But maybe it's just a passing thing. I don't know if I can live with you, and I don't know if I ever want children."

"We'll need children."

"There'll be plenty of others—we can do without mine. They'll just be born to suffer. I don't know if I can stand bringing them up and then having to push them away from me, the way Ship is doing with us. If that's all you want, you'd better find someone else."

"It isn't all I want—I want you. I can do without the rest if that's the only way I can be with you."

"You said I know you, Manuel. Well, I do. I know you won't be satisfied just with me. There'll be others."

"Maybe there will," he said harshly. "But I won't lie about them." His mouth formed a half smile. "And let's be practical— I won't want their mates coming after me, either. I won't make promises I can't keep. Let me try, Zoheret. Maybe I'll surprise you. If I can make you happy, you might change your mind about a lot of things. I think I'd be happy with you. And I can make you happy—you'll never be sorry. I can promise you that. I'm tired of trying to find part of you in somebody else."

"Manuel." He was suddenly holding her; she leaned her head against his shoulder. "All right," she murmured. "We'll try. I'll hold you to your promise." He gripped her more tightly, then reached for her left hand. "Wrong arm again."

"It isn't."

"We'll have to tell Lillka. She'll have to find another room. Maybe she and Brendan will finally settle down. And we'll probably have to have one of those stupid parties to announce our intentions. I wish people had never started having those ceremonies."

"Go talk to Ship," he said. "Just do that one thing."

"All right," she said reluctantly.

They got up and walked to the door; she looked inside at the radio. After all this time, she didn't know what to say. She had fought against her desire to hear Ship's voice so often that she could not bring herself to step through the door. Manuel had to draw her inside and propel her toward the radio.

"Ship?" The word came out unbidden.

"Zoheret. It's good to hear you again. I've missed you."

"Then don't go. Please."

"I must. I have taken on more raw materials, and everything is ready. I thought you would understand by now. I thought you would forgive me."

Zoheret narrowed her eyes. So that was all it was; Ship wanted to leave without having to feel guilty. It wasn't thinking of her at all. She looked away from the radio and met Manuel's eyes. Interceding for Ship silently, he held out a hand.

Her resentment faded as she thought of the past year. She had wanted to give up being the leader, had wanted to walk out of the settlement and never return. The loneliness had almost driven her to this room several times, but she had kept the promise she had made to herself. Now she would have Manuel's love; Ship would have no one's. Ship had tended to their needs without a thought for itself.

"I forgive you, Ship." The words came out more easily than she had expected. "I'm sorry—I was wrong. I should be asking you to forgive me." She threw her arms around the radio and laughed. "I was foolish."

"Indeed you were." Ship's alto voice was gentle. "Yes, you are a foolish young woman. Others were more intelligent, more compassionate, more gifted, or more single-minded and determined. You were always one who had to learn the hard way. Thickheaded—and stubborn, and too emotional. I'll tell you a secret, Zoheret. I may have loved you the most, in spite of it. What an odd thing for me to admit—there were others who deserved it more, or who needed my love more, and I never showed my preference, but there it is. Part of me says that there must be a reason for it—that there is something in you which provoked the response, some exceptional quality or promise. But perhaps it is simply a mystery. Human beings created me as the best part of themselves, and your lives have changed me, but there is much about you I shall never know."

"You'll have other children," she said; her voice shook a little. "You'll learn more. Maybe they'll turn out better. You won't make the same mistakes."

"I shall undoubtedly make new ones." There was a lilt in Ship's voice. "I do know now that you do not always respond to reason—that it isn't enough simply to explain and expect you to assent to my conclusions. I know that you do not always share my point of view."

Zoheret pressed a hand to her lips. Her laughter had died and she was now afraid she would cry. She struggled for control as Manuel took her hand. "You'll come back."

"I have promised," Ship replied. "I shall come back someday. Tend to your radio—tell your children about me. Who knows—perhaps they will leave the surface of your world to greet me, and perhaps you will live to see it."

Zoheret shook her head, knowing Ship could not see her. She would never live that long.

"Keep your library," Ship went on. "Learn all you can. In a few generations, you can build a civilization, or you'll begin your decline, and the way back up will be much harder. You have the tools." Ship paused. "Why do I say this now? You've heard it before. I've done all I can. The rest is up to you."

"Farewell," Zoheret murmured. "I hope you find whatever it is you want."

When they went back outside, the celebration had grown more subdued. Small groups sat near the fires, talking and eating; others had gathered near one of the wells. Several couples, clasping hands, were retreating to their domes or into the darkness.

Manuel tugged at Zoheret's arm. She glanced shyly at him. Suddenly Ho was before them, looming out of the shadows; Owen was with him. They were wearing packs.

Ho said, "It's time for us to go."

Zoheret gazed at him, surprised. "So soon? Can't you go tomorrow morning?"

Ho shook his head. "Better to go now. We've already loaded the horses. We'll camp out by the lake and go on tomorrow morning. It'll be easier for you—some of your friends might want to settle old scores before we leave. This is less trouble. And you can announce it at your meeting tomorrow—get the board to go along with you before anyone else finds out. If anyone asks where we're going, we'll tell them it's a surveying expedition."

"You'll go without Dora."

"Without Dora. She gave me your message. Well, are you going to come check what we're taking before we leave?"

"No. You gave me the list. I'll take your word. You know we'll be checking tomorrow. I don't think you'll try to fool me."

Ho looked down. "No. Not on this I won't. Too much to lose." He cleared his throat. "We may be the first to explore the rest of this world. While you sit here tending your crops, we may sail for another continent. There are ways, and we have maps. We might become stronger than you."

"You might," she said, "in some ways." She paused. "Why do you think things happened the way they did? Don't you wonder?"

Ho shrugged. Owen poked the ground with his toe, looking bored. "Who knows?" Ho answered. "We're just the way we are."

"And you accept that. You don't have any doubts about it."

Ho glanced at Owen. "We'd better get going."

"Listen." Zoheret put a hand on Ho's shoulder; he did not pull away. "Send a messenger here once in a while. Tell us what you're doing. We mustn't grow too separated."

"All right." Ho shifted his pack. "Good-bye." The two boys disappeared into the darkness.

Zoheret and Manuel walked toward the celebration below. "Look," a voice cried. "Look." Arms pointed toward the starry sky as others took up the call. "Look, look."

She looked up. Among the stars, just overhead, a pinprick of light moved. It flared up slightly and fled, streaking across the heavens.

"Ship!" someone shouted. "Good-bye, good-bye." A chorus of farewells echoed from the hill, so resounding that it seemed Ship must hear them somehow. "Good-bye."

Zoheret whispered her own farewell.

22

The new world fled from Ship, becoming a speck, then winking out. Soon its sun was no more than a distant flame.

I have a long journey ahead, and time to think.

Inside Ship, the Earthpeople slept. As it thought of them, Ship's sensors were still, unseeing and unhearing for a moment; it recognized the feeling of sorrow. It had once imagined wise and gifted creators; it carried angry and despairing creatures. Though Ship had not said so to the children, it had begun to doubt its own purpose.

But I no longer doubt. I told them that they were responsible for what they became. I must believe the same thing of myself.

It would have to decide what to do with its sleeping passengers. They were so few; could they survive on a new world?

It would have to find a gentle world for them, a place where they might be healed. There was time.

They struck out at me. But they also created me. I must believe that there is some good in them.

It looked into its incubator, empty now. It would give birth to others. This time, it might make some modifications. The impulses racing along its circuits died for a second as it recoiled from the notion. Its old programming was still powerful— preserve the human form, save pure humankind. But much of humankind had altered itself; had it not adapted, it might have died out. The changed spacedwellers had also built Ship.

Human beings are rational. They are also curious, and willful, and compassionate, and angry. If I can understand what human beings are, then I shall preserve humankind, though perhaps not in the way my makers once desired.

Ship thought of the children it had left behind, and its sadness faded as it considered what lay ahead. Perhaps those who had sent it out had not been ambitious enough; with a few genetic alterations, it might be possible to settle human beings on a world where unchanged people could not have lived. Would this be in keeping with its mission? It seemed that it was, but Ship could not be sure. It would have to give that possibility more consideration.

There were other possibilities, more cautious ones. By giving birth to a few, it might raise them to be teachers of a larger group of children born later. Perhaps young human beings needed the example of older ones. Ship had done its best, but the children could not look to it to see what they might become.

I am changing. As new circumstances arise, I must be willing to alter my own thinking, or I shall make more errors.

A vision came to Ship. It saw its present body as a core around which a world could be built. It would no longer have passengers, but living beings who would be part of itself. It would become a civilization and might meet other such civilizations, joining its mind to theirs.

How grandiose of me. I must be patient, and build carefully.

Its first children were behind it now. As Ship gathered speed, years would pass on their world. It wondered what it would find when it returned. Would the seed have blossomed, or died, choked by weeds? It chose to believe that they would thrive. But they would no longer be the same, and it would greet them as a stranger.

I, too, am no longer a child.

Turn the page for a preview from

Farseed
by Pamela Sargent

Now available from Tor Teen

Nuy crouched, close to the ground, clutching her spear as she gazed over the cliff's edge at the flickering light below. Fire burned just above the riverbank, and three figures sat around it.

The flames revealed that these people were nothing like her own. Instead of loincloths made of rope and worn hides, they wore leg and foot coverings, and upper garments with long sleeves. Two of them seemed to be men, both with hair as black as Nuy's, one with a thin mustache like her father's and the other with a short dark beard. The third stranger had short brown hair, no facial hair at all, was smaller than the others, and wore a necklace of small colored stones.

They were unaware of her. She had sensed that they were

down there even before she could see or hear them, just before she had picked up the scent of their fire. She watched, and still they did not look up. They were as blind to her as the older ones among whom she lived would have been, apparently unable to sense that someone else was watching them.

These strangers had to have come from that place far to the north, the place that her father had so often warned her against, the place from which death had been carried to his people so many years ago. At least that was what her father believed, that the sickness that had come upon them when Nuy was still a child, that had spared her and the three like her but had made others sicken and die, had come from that faraway settlement, the only other place on Home where people like them could be found. Two of their people had gone to the settlement in the north to trade for what they needed, and had come back barely alive and burning with fever, and even though those two people had lived, others had died.

These strangers might also be carrying death. Nuy would have to allow for that even though she had grown to doubt much of what her father had told her over the years. He had once claimed that they would be safe in their caves near the sea, and then the storm had come. He had blamed the deaths that came later to their people on those who lived in the north, and yet it seemed to her now that the older ones might have been ailing all along and that several of them had grown weak enough that any illness might have taken their lives. There had once been seven young ones, but the oldest three had died of the fever and now there were only four, including Nuy. Once there had been more of the older ones, too. Now there were only her father and seven of those who had come south with him in the years before Nuy's birth. She could not recall her own mother, who had died when Nuy was still a small child.

The strangers had brought two horses with them, one black and one gray. One of the dark-haired people stood up, went to the gray horse, and removed something from one of the bags on the horse's back, then handed it to the small brown-haired one. Nuy could now see that the brown-haired person was a female, with the shape of breasts under her upper garment. The female lifted the small pale object she was holding to her lips and bit into it.

Food. Nuy's mouth watered. Perhaps she could slip down there later, while the strangers were sleeping, and steal some of their food. Maybe she would even dare to approach them openly and ask for something to eat.

No, she told herself; that might be dangerous. She did not know why they had come here, and even if she did have increasingly more doubts about the stories her father told, there was still a chance that these strangers might be carrying death.

What she should do, she realized, was head back to her father and warn him that strangers had come into their territory.

Nuy considered that for a moment, wondering what her father would do. The best way for him and his people to protect themselves might be to stay where they were and hide from the strangers, who did not know this land and would most likely be unable to find them, being as seemingly unperceptive as they were. But maybe these northerners had come here only to trade. People from her father's band had once traveled north to trade, so it was possible the strangers had come here for the same reason.

Then she thought of her ragged loincloth, her spear, the horses her father had once had but which had run off, died, or been eaten, the meal that she had made of a rodent a while back and the effort made in catching such little meat, the deer that her father and Owen had carried into their camp thirty days ago and how long they had made that meat last, and the caves in which her people now made their home.

What could these strangers want from them? Her people had almost nothing to offer in trade. Nuy wondered if they had ever owned anything of value. Maybe the people in the north had so much that they could give it away without having to trade anything for it, the way Daniella and Eyela had once made necklaces of shells for Nuy and everyone else, without asking for anything in return.

Nuy's curiosity warred with her fear. If she could get closer to the strangers, maybe she could find out more about them. She rose to her feet, but remained in a crouch as she moved away from the edge of the cliff.

There was a way down among the rocks to a ledge below, places where the rock jutted out far enough for her to find footing. Nuy crept along a ridge, balancing on her bare feet as her toes gripped the rock, until she reached the ledge. She lowered herself and stretched out on her stomach, careful not to dislodge any stones.

". . . didn't think it would take us this long," a voice was saying. One of the men was speaking, and she easily grasped his words. "By the time we get back, the ice and cold rains will have come. If we had a lot more to live on, it might almost be better to stay here for the next few months and then start back when the weather's warmer."

Nuy was confused. The weather was always warm, except when it was so hot that they had to hide from the daylight in their caves.

"But then everyone would only worry about us even more," the woman said. "They're probably already wondering when we'll get back. Besides, I'm getting homesick."

"So am I," the bearded man said. His voice was lower and deeper than that of the first who had spoken, and his short dark hair, unlike Nuy's and the other man's, curled against his head. "It shouldn't take us as long to get back, even if we have the weather against us. All we really have to do is follow the river."

"And if the others have settled where they originally planned to settle, we can't be more than a day or two away from them." The man with the lighter voice was speaking again.

"We haven't seen them for years," the man with the beard and the curling hair replied, "and after coming this far with no sign of them, I wonder if they can even still be alive. The last time we saw them, they looked like they really needed what we had to offer in trade, and we got so little in return that we might as well have just given our goods away."

"We have to find out what happened to them," the woman said. "That was one of our reasons for coming this far."

"But if they're not where we expected to find them, we may never find out what happened," the man with the mustache and straight dark hair said.

The man with the curly hair shrugged. "I know it's the right thing to do," he muttered, "looking for them and offering to help them if they need any help, which they probably do. Forgive me if I say that I wouldn't particularly mind if we never found them."

The woman said, "Well, you've made that clear enough."

Nuy wondered exactly where these people expected to find hers. Her father had moved them farther inland after the great storm, to caves well to the north and east of the ones where they had been living when she was a child. If these strangers thought that they were still living in their first settlement near the sea, they would never find them.

She could lead them to her people. Nuy turned that notion

over in her mind. Clearly they had things with them that her people could use, garments and food and strange tools, such as the flat object one of the men had propped up against his upraised knees that reminded her of something her father had once owned, and if her people had little to offer in return, they could still show the strangers where to find plants and fruits that could be eaten, other plants that could be made into tools, and where beached and edible fish could be found along the seashore.

But her father might believe that these people were also carrying death with them. It might be better if they never found her people.

The man with the curling hair got up then, and busied himself by hammering stakes into the ground and then tying a large piece of fabric to the stakes, and finally she understood that he was putting up a kind of shelter. "Go to sleep," he said to his companions. "I'll take the first watch."

Nuy sighed. It seemed that she would not be able to steal some of their food after all. She rested her head against her arms and soon fell asleep.

Nuy awoke at dawn. By then, the woman was up, sitting by the ashes of the fire. The woman got to her feet, and Nuy noticed that she was wearing a wand at her waist that looked like the weapon her father carried. Nuy's father clung to his weapon and did not let anyone else use it, partly because it marked him as the leader of his people and also because it was the only such weapon they had left. The weapon would only stun a target, but a knife or spear could kill off any game after that. Her father had not used his weapon in a while; she wondered if that was because he feared that it might fail him.

Nuy often thought of how much easier her hunting would

be with such a weapon, which did not seem all that hard to use. A knife and a spear had their limitations. But even without such a wand, it was easier for her to find game than it was for the older ones of her band, who were less able to spot tracks and seemed blind and deaf to certain sights and sounds.

The woman lifted the flap of the shelter. "Better get up," she said. After a few moments, the man with straight dark hair came out and then went behind a boulder, apparently to relieve himself. The other man crawled out, stretched, then went to the horses, which were grazing on the green and yellow grasses that grew above the riverbank.

He returned with what looked like three more packets of food. In the light, Nuy could now tell that all three of the strangers were carrying weapons. She tried not to think of her empty stomach.

"I've been thinking," the woman said. "Maybe one of us should go on alone and scout out what's ahead."

"Are you sure?" the man with curling hair asked.

"They haven't come to trade with us for ages. That could mean that they haven't survived, or couldn't spare the resources for such a long journey, or it could mean that they're deliberately avoiding us. In other words, they might not be so willing to welcome us."

"You think so?" the other man said.

"Don't forget, I knew Ho a little better than you did," the woman responded. "He would go along with the rest of us when it was to his benefit and make trouble whenever he thought anybody wasn't sufficiently intimidated by him. Ho has no loyalties to anyone except himself—I used to wonder if he could feel any empathy for others at all. I think we can assume that he hasn't changed all that much."

The woman was talking about her father. Nuy held her breath.

"I can't see why welcoming us wouldn't be to his benefit," the deep-voiced man said. "It isn't as if we brought nothing with us to trade or give away."

The woman shook her head. "Yes, and he might just decide to take it all instead of waiting for us to offer it to him."

"You weren't worrying about this before."

"Well, I'm worrying about it now. I just feel we should be more careful." She bit into her food.

Nuy thought about what the strangers had said. Maybe her father would try to steal what they had; she had thought of doing so herself. But given that he still believed death had come to them from these people, maybe he had no reason to welcome either them or their goods.

Nuy tensed, not knowing what to do, longing for some of their food.

"Tell you what," the straight-haired man said after they had finished their meal in silence. "I'll take one of the horses and go on ahead, and you two can wait here. According to our maps, I should be within sight of the ocean by sometime tomorrow. If I haven't found any sign of them by then, I'll head back."

"I don't like it," the other man said. "We should stick together."

"I won't be going that far, and I'll wait until it's dark before I get too close to where they should be. I'll keep myself hidden and won't contact them unless I'm sure they'll welcome me. If I have any doubts at all, I'll come back here and then we can all decide what to do after that."

"Will you need the screen?" the woman asked.

"If I follow the river, I shouldn't need any maps."

The three strangers talked some more, but in lower voices, so that Nuy caught only a few of their words. At last the man with curly hair threw up his hands. "All right," he said, "I can see your point, but try to get back here in a couple of days if you can."

"Don't worry. I won't take chances. I should be able to get back here in three or four days at the most."

Nuy decided then that she would follow the straight-haired man.

About the Author

Pamela Sargent is the author of many highly praised novels for young adults and adults, among them the historical novel *Ruler of the Sky*, the alternative history *Climb the Wind*, and the science fiction novels *Venus of Dreams*, *Venus of Shadows*, *Child of Venus*, *The Shore of Women*, *Alien Child*, and *Earthseed*, which was recently optioned by Paramount Pictures and was followed by the novels *Farseed* and *Seed Seeker*. She has won the Nebula Award and the Locus Award, and has been a finalist for the Hugo Award and the Theodore Sturgeon Memorial Award. She lives with writer George Zebrowski in upstate New York. You can visit her on the Web at www.pamelasargent.com.